Stuck On You

Stuck On You

Monica Walters

www.urbanbooks.net

Urban Books, LLC
300 Farmingdale Road, NY-Route 109
Farmingdale, NY 11735

ISBN 13: 978-1-64556-549-9

First Mass Market Printing February 2024
First Trade Paperback Printing February 2023
Printed in the United States of America

10 9 8 7 6 5 4 3 2 1

Distributed by Kensington Publishing Corp.
Submit Orders to:
Customer Service
400 Hahn Road
Westminster, MD 21157-4627
Phone: 1-800-733-3000
Fax: 1-800-659-2436

Stuck On You

Monica Walters

Prologue

Lazarus

"I'm tired of living like this, Lazarus! I'm tired of taking care of you. I can do better without you."

"Do you realize what you're saying to me? I sacrificed everything for you! You went to school for ten years, Jamie. I put my dreams on hold for you to accomplish everything that you have. Now that it's my turn, there's a problem? I dropped out of college after my freshman year to take care of us and to assure you made your dreams come true. This is bullshit, and you know it!"

"No, it's not! You are the man of the house, and if I have to take care of you, what are you here for? That salary you make driving a garbage truck is barely enough to pay the utilities, let alone the house note. I'm tired of struggling, and here you want to take a break from working so you can go to school? You have to be out of your mind. I'm done with this. I want a divorce. In the meantime, you need to get out of my house."

My heart was crumbling. My wife of fifteen years, the one I'd sacrificed everything for, was done with me like we never mattered. This shit was painful. What did I do to deserve this? When she graduated from high school, I promised her that I would take care of her. When she said she had dreams, I told her that I would be there to help her. I dropped out of school against my mom's wishes, married her, and put her through school for ten years. She now had a successful practice as a psychologist and had been in business for three years. We'd purchased a new home and everything. She'd upgraded our living, but that wasn't supposed to happen until I was able to attain my finance degree. We had a fucking deal, and she reneged.

Things had been different ever since she lost our baby four years ago. She went into labor at eighteen weeks, and that nearly destroyed us. We never expected to have to bury a child . . . a baby boy. Trying to overcome the heartache took a toll on our marriage. It was like she started detaching from me then.

In true Lazarus fashion, when it came to the woman I loved, I blamed myself for not being sensitive and compassionate enough, although I was hurting as well. No matter what I did to try to make amends and bring us closer, nothing helped.

She stormed out of the room, leaving me here in my sorrow. My marriage was over, but I refused to accept it. I left the room as well, in search of her. When I saw her in the kitchen pouring a drink, I made my way to her.

She turned around when she heard me, but by then, I was pressed against her. "No, Lazarus! This is done!"

I pressed my lips against hers, trying to make her feel what I felt. As she fought, I pulled her waist closer to mine and eased my hands to her ass. The sting her hand left on my face caused me to release her.

"Please, Jamie. Don't do this. Don't do this to us. We can try counseling . . . whatever you want. Just don't leave me, baby. I love you, and I thought I'd shown that for the fifteen years we've been married. Jamie, please. I'm begging you, baby."

I went to my knees and wrapped my arms around her legs as the tears streamed down my cheeks. We had a lot more than we'd had when she was in school. Why couldn't she see the progress we'd made?

She made more money than me, but somehow, she'd forgotten how I was the one to help her get there. Her parents had been robbing Peter to pay Paul when we met. I paid for all her senior stuff when she graduated from high school because they said they didn't have the money. She'd been on my dime since we met.

I was a junior, and she was a sophomore when I saw her outside of the school after football practice. Her ride was terribly late. I offered her a ride home, and the rest was history. She was the most beautiful girl I'd ever seen, and after a year of dating, I knew I wanted her—all five feet, eight inches of her.

I loved everything about her, from her straight, long hair to her light brown skin. Being of mixed heritage, she looked more white than black, but that had nothing to do with her beauty. She clearly took every good gene her parents had to offer and became the beautiful Jamie Hightower. She could have easily become a model if that were the career path she'd chosen.

Now that she had been the breadwinner for the past three years, it was too heavy for her. What about me? What about all the years I had sacrificed? It was like none of that shit mattered now, and I wondered if that was what had happened to her parents. They divorced not long after she graduated. Her mother had landed a good job at NASA and was driving back and forth to Houston. Somewhere along the way, their marriage fizzled, and they divorced. Was that what was happening between us?

She pried me away from her by pulling my hair. She knew that my scalp was the most sensitive part of me. I released her quickly to keep her from inflicting any more pain. The tears fell from my eyes, and that irritated the hell out of me.

She'd often said that I was too sensitive for her. These past four years had been hell. Because I was a man that wasn't afraid to show his emotions, it made me weak in her opinion. Soft.

I couldn't change who I'd always been. I knew that didn't make me soft, because there was nothing soft about hauling trash for a living. Before we had the trucks and garbage cans we had now, I was picking up cans and manually dumping them in the truck. I worked out constantly to get stress off me.

Maybe I did *too* much for her. I literally took care of everything. Monday through Friday, I worked my ass off and, on the weekends, I took care of the house and her. All she had to do was go to school and do well and fuck her husband. That was it.

She was the woman I loved, but I watched her walk away from me. I wiped the tears from my face and went back to the room to pack. The last thing I needed her to do was eventually call the police. While my mind wanted me to pull myself together and say fuck her, my heart wouldn't allow that. My heart wanted her to think this through.

After packing a week's worth of clothes, I walked out of my house to head to my mama's house. That was the only place I knew I could go other than a hotel. Till this day, she wasn't too fond of Jamie. Maybe she had seen this coming.

Love was a battlefield and had blinded me for over fifteen years. Jamie had used me, and that shit was threatening to destroy me from the inside out.

Chapter 1

Lazarus

A year and a half later . . .

"If you don't get your ass up! I'm sick of you just going to work and coming home to wallow in depression. It has been almost two years. It's time for you to come forth!"

I hated that I'd even given my mama a key to my apartment. She just barged in whenever she got good and got-damn ready. I rolled my eyes at her. If I did have something going on, she would have walked in on it.

"You have *got* to start knocking. One day, I'm gon' shock yo' drawz. You gon' bust in here and a woman is gonna be in here having the time of her life."

She rolled her eyes. "Nigga, you must have forgotten who you talking to. I'm yo' mama. I been knowing you yo' entire life. If you had a woman or was getting some pussy, I would be the first one to notice."

I slowly shook my head. This woman stayed in my damn business, but I was glad for it. It was her that kept me from falling into an even deeper depression than what I'd fallen into. For the past year and a half, I'd been working nonstop, saving money. I hated living in these raggedy-ass apartments. There was always some shit going on. Sirens blared all time of the night, but they were affordable. If I had a woman or kids to protect, I wouldn't dare live in this hellhole.

I stood from my bed and stretched. I'd just gotten off from my job as a bouncer six hours ago. Only my mama visited at the ass crack of dawn. It was only nine in the morning, and I hadn't gotten home until almost four, because my coworkers wanted to talk and had held me up. By the time I got cleaned up and had eaten, it was nearly five thirty.

Since it was the weekend, I didn't have to worry about getting up to go to work at my full-time job. I was still driving the garbage truck. I worked at least seventeen hours on Fridays between the two, and I usually slept most of the day on Saturday, until it was time to go back to work Saturday night at the club.

Life had been tough after the demise of my marriage. I was depressed for months and was still somewhat depressed. When I first left and went to my mother's house, I stayed for a week. When I went back to talk to Jamie to see if she had calmed down, she'd already packed the rest of my things and put them in the garage. Rage filled me, and had she been home, I probably would have gone to jail for choking the shit out of her ass. She didn't realize I was only soft-ass Lazarus around her. She was the only one that saw that side of me. I would have done anything for her. I thought I'd proven that when I *did* everything for her.

"You working tonight?"

"Yeah."

"Monday, I need you to get registered for school."

I frowned at her. "Mama, you know I can't afford to go to school right now. I'll probably never be able to afford it at the rate I'm going. I gave up on that when Jamie put me out."

"Boy, what did I say when I first came in this hellhole? I named you Lazarus for a reason. Now, I need you to come forth! You've been dead for far too long. Pack up this place, and you're moving in with me. I don't know why you moved in this shit anyway. You don't need privacy because you don't do shit. Come home and eliminate these unnecessary bills and get enrolled in school. Quit that night job and see if you can rearrange your schedule to go to school."

I huffed loudly. There was no way I was quitting my night job. I didn't know how she expected me to be able to pay for school with a limited amount of money coming in.

Before I could respond to her, she continued. "I don't want to hear any excuses. I just wanna see action. Do what you have to do. If you don't want to quit the other job, that's on you. But you *will* enroll in school and quit fucking pining over that bitch that don't give a shit about you."

I slid my hand down my face as I walked away from her to go to the bathroom. Jamie had been my everything since I was sixteen years old. When we divorced, we had nearly nineteen years of history. How could I let all that go in a year's time? I was trying to, because I knew the shit wasn't healthy, but it was hard as hell. Old habits die hard. For over half my life, I had been looking out for and taking care of this beautiful woman who was the love of my life. I just couldn't believe that it was all a lie. She had to have loved me at some point. I refused to believe that the whole nineteen years had been acts of greed, opportunity, and lies.

While in the bathroom, I tried to clear my head of those thoughts so I could deal with my mama and her foolery when I came out. I already knew she would be on me moving in, then would have the nerve to tell me to move on to another woman.

I was *not* moving in with Natalie Mitchell. What woman at my age would want a man who lived with his mother? I wasn't sure how I would feel about a woman that would overlook something like that. Although I was far from being a bum, if I lived with my mother, I would definitely feel like one, no matter how temporary that arrangement would be.

"Hurry up so I can do something with your head, boy! You need to cut that shit."

I rolled my eyes as I listened to her move around the apartment, probably straightening up for me.

"Thirty-six years old and can't let go," she mumbled.

Let go of what? Growing my hair out made it seem like I was holding on to something? Old people were weird as hell sometimes with their theories and judgments. I supposed she thought I was trying to hold onto my youth by needing her to braid my hair.

I naturally looked young anyway. People always thought I was still in my twenties. Whenever I told them I was thirty-six, they'd nearly swallow their tongues. But I liked my hair, and most times, it looked nice. Even when it didn't look nice to my standards, I still received compliments on it at the club. I even had a couple of women gather the audacity to run their fingers through it. I quickly put them in their places, though.

There were two things I needed to let go of: my love and respect for Jamie. She was the only person besides my mom that had run her fingers through my hair. She loved my hair as much as I did—unless that shit was an act.

Staring at myself in the mirror, I took a deep breath and whispered, "Get it together, Laz."

After handling my hygiene, I walked out to see my mama had retreated to the front room. When I peeked around the corner, I saw her sitting on the couch with her legs spread and the comb in her hand, watching TV. I smiled at how she always had my back.

She was never in my business when I was married, but she had always told me to be careful with Jamie. It was like she could see right through her ass, but I didn't listen. I was in love. She hadn't thrown it in my face maliciously, and I appreciated her for that.

I walked in the den, and she smiled at me and sat back on the couch so I could sit on the floor in front of her. She spent time detangling my hair then massaging and greasing my scalp before beginning to braid. The massages were always my favorite. I tended to hold tension there, which often gave me headaches.

She didn't try to talk me to death when I sat. She turned off the TV and hummed as she made my hair look more presentable. It was soothing to my soul, and I nearly fell asleep listening to her.

It had always been just me and her. I had no siblings, and my dad was killed by the police when I was young. Supposedly, it was a case of mistaken identity. They settled with my mama for five hundred grand. She shouldn't have accepted that, but she was young and had no one close that she trusted to advise her. She took the settlement, and we moved to Beaumont. She refused to live in Birmingham any longer after that.

I was only six years old at the time, so I barely remembered anything about Birmingham. However, that was where her family still was. She refused to go back to visit until my grandmother passed a few years ago. Thankfully, my grandmother had visited us here, though, so there was no guilt associated with Granny's death.

As she braided my hair, I looked around at my tattered couches and sparsely furnished apartment. I didn't own a table because I felt it wasn't necessary for just me. When Jamie divorced me, I was left with all the bills I had incurred while we were married. I had a few loans I was paying on, and thankfully, the biggest one was almost done.

When Jamie started working, I thought she would have helped me pay them off. It wasn't like I was bad with managing money. I was just running short from time to time when it was time to pay tuition. I didn't want her to be burdened with student loans, but school wasn't cheap. This country was ass backwards, charging all that money. People were penalized for wanting to better themselves. This country was just fine with its citizens being crippled with debt, especially those of us stuck in the middle that lived paycheck to paycheck but made too much money to qualify for any type of assistance. It wasn't that I was looking for a handout, but shit, it definitely would have made things easier while Jamie was in school.

The grease-stained walls in the kitchen and the dirty walls throughout the rest of the place were disgusting. My efforts to clean them were in vain because the shit wouldn't come off. While I wanted to just paint it, I knew I wouldn't be reimbursed for the shit. Until I couldn't take the look of them anymore, I would just deal with it. I was the only person that saw the inside of this apartment anyway, and the only other person that saw it didn't give a damn.

"You have to be able to find somewhere else to live that's cleaner, Lazarus. This shit makes my skin crawl."

Well, I *thought* she didn't give a damn. I was clearly wrong about that.

"Eventually, Ma."

"Yeah, 'cause I know you ain't gon' move in with me. Stubborn ass."

She went back to humming, and I was grateful. I just needed peace and quiet since I was only working with three and a half hours of sleep.

There wasn't much I needed to do today other than speaking with my therapist. Thankfully, my health insurance through my job was covering the costs I incurred, because there was no way I would have been able to afford it.

My sessions were only once a month now, and they'd helped me tremendously. There were things that I didn't want to share with my mama that I was able to articulate to the counselor. She helped me to see the worth within me. I'd allowed Jamie to rob me of that. I felt like I wasn't worthy of anyone's time, love, or affection, and I was fighting a losing battle within myself. I always knew I had the looks to get a woman, but I felt like my personality was what drove Jamie away. My thinking was so screwed up. It took me months to crawl out of that mental space. And crawled, I did. *Slowly*.

After about thirty minutes or so, Mama tapped my shoulder to let me know she was done. I went to the mirror to see the four braids she had put my hair in, and it looked fresh as always. Going to her, I kissed her cheek and hugged her as she smiled.

"I just have to get my beard groomed and I'll be looking fresh, Ma."

She chuckled. "Yeah. You look nice, son. I need your mental to be as put together as your physical, though. I know yo' ass ain't gon' move in with me, but please consider going to school. It's time to stop deferring your dreams. Even if you only take two classes, that's progress. Just start, baby."

I gave her a slight smile and nodded. "Okay. I'm going to look into it."

She smiled again. "Okay. Now let's go get breakfast. My treat."

"Yo' treat? Where we going?"

"Toasted Yolk."

"Oh, you fancy, huh? Let's go get it then. I'll drive. Let me put on something more presentable first, though."

"Absolutely. You ain't going nowhere with me looking like a bum."

I chuckled as I went back to my room to change into some jeans. Even with the lack of sleep, I felt good today. Maybe I would paint those walls after all.

Chapter 2

Kiana

I stretched my arms over my head, wishing that I could just sleep all day long. However, if I missed church, I would never hear the end of it. Deacon Otis Jordan and Missionary Lisa Jordan didn't play that foolishness. Even though I was twenty-four years old, I still lived "under their roof" as they would say, so I had to abide by their rules. One of their rules was that if I lived here, I had to go to church. That was fine by me. I usually didn't mind going to church. I enjoyed the sermons my pastor preached as well as the songs the choir sang. It was just days like today, when I felt extremely drained, that I didn't want to go.

I had finals last week, and yesterday, I'd volunteered at the clinic the church put on, administering free tests for diabetes and conducting seminars on overall health and prevention of illnesses that plagued the Black community, such as high blood pressure. Since I had extensive knowledge of medical diagnoses and medicines, I knew I could be an asset to the clinic. I was one year away from graduating and becoming a pharmacist, so I definitely qualified. I was surprised by how many people didn't have health insurance and who couldn't afford to go to the doctor. It was eye opening.

Growing up in a two-parent household that was financially stable created a smoke screen as to how life really was for a lot of people. Most people were living paycheck to paycheck and doing the best they could to survive. Healthcare was expensive. Having insurance was expensive. I never had to worry about either because I was on my dad's insurance. I had a person tell me that it would cost them nearly fifteen hundred dollars a month to insure their family, and after that, they would still have to meet deductibles and pay copays. What was this country coming to when people couldn't afford the necessities? I didn't know what it meant not to have a yearly checkup. My sister and I didn't want for anything and while I was grateful for that, it certainly blinded us to the issues many hardworking people faced.

After going to the bathroom, I turned the shower on to prepare to get ready for church service. It started in two hours, so I knew I needed to get going. I had a horrible habit of being late. I stood in the mirror forever, simply trying to decide on eyeshadow color. I was somewhat of a fashionista. My outfit, makeup, and hair had to be as close to perfect as possible before I could leave the house.

It was my mama's fault. She'd created this monster. When I was little, kids used to tease me, calling me fat. She used to make me stand in the mirror and stare at myself, then tell myself just how beautiful I was. I would have to give myself compliments every day before I left the house. By the time I was a teenager, I was in full bloom. No one could tell me anything about how I looked. This five-foot-seven-inch, two-hundred-plus frame didn't owe anyone a thing. I was happy in my size sixteens and some eighteens. God had made me perfectly, and I was sure to act like it.

I wasn't stuck up or anything, but I didn't tolerate insults from anyone. If the person handing those out was at church, I would find a creative way to be nice-nasty. However, if they weren't at church, they got a version of Kiana my parents had never met. The sheltering they had done didn't shield me from a damn thing concerning that. Although I couldn't go to a lot of places, plenty of my friends reported back. Not to mention, there was TV and the internet. I was abreast of the times and latest trends.

Once I started college at Lamar University, it was like the world was at my feet and mine for the taking. My parents loosened the reins some and allowed me to come and go as I pleased just as long as I was home at a decent hour and did well in school. That I did. I was getting my master's in chemistry along with my PharmD degree.

After showering and standing in the mirror, fixing my hair and makeup for at least an hour, I got dressed and headed to church. The journey wasn't far. We only lived five minutes from church. Antioch Baptist Church was the place to be on Sunday morning, whether attending the early service at eight a.m. or the ten-a.m. service. The spirit was always high, and the word was always preached. I loved my church. I loved Pastor John Adolph.

What I didn't like was my parents trying to hook me up with their friends' son, Braylon. He was twenty-five and fine as hell; however, there were no sparks. We grew up as friends and knew one another well. My parents thought because their friends were God-fearing and loving Christians, their son was too. He was a ho. One time, that nigga had sex at church. Like . . . he had no fear that God would strike him dead with his dick out.

When I got to church, Braylon was just getting there too. I slowly shook my head as I rolled my eyes. Despite my annoyance with him, he was still interested in me . . . well, interested in my honey pot. That nigga had the nerve to tell me that he heard big girls had juicy pussies and that he would give his right lung to fall up off in mine. *Bold ass*.

I got heart palpitations at his words. It bothered me for weeks because my coochie had the audacity to be turned on. I didn't lose my virginity until I was twenty years old, only four years ago, and I had only been with two men. However, the way she cut flips whenever he said something nasty to me irked the hell out of me.

I got out of the car and hurriedly made my way to the entrance, hoping he didn't see me. I was thoroughly disappointed when he appeared next to me, sliding his hand in mine.

"What's up, beautiful? You look good enough to eat, girl."

I rolled my eyes and removed my hand from his. "Braylon, do you ever behave like a normal human being?"

He gave me a smirk as he opened the door for us to enter the sanctuary. "I am normal. I'm just outspoken. I promise you, every man 'round this place is thinking the same thing when they look at you."

He licked his lips as I rolled my eyes once again and walked off to go to my seat. I sat in the same spot every Sunday, next to my sister. She was only a couple of years younger than me, and people often thought we were twins. We didn't agree with that comparison. I was a shade darker than her and to us, I looked like my father, and she looked like our mother. Her cheekbones were higher, her eyes were smaller and slanted like she was Japanese, and her smile was bigger.

She was also my best friend. We talked about everything. She seemed to be a lot more experienced with men than me, but she was extremely discreet. Of course, she had to be discreet because of our parents. If they found out we were no longer virgins, there would be chaos in the house for a while. My mom took the time to explain exactly what sex was and what God intended. She encouraged us to save our goodies for the man that we married. Needless to say, we didn't follow her advice.

I plopped next to Kinisha, and she glanced over at me with a smile on her face. She'd been here since the first service. She had obligations to the graduation ministry to fulfill. However, she was more of a morning person than I was. Most of my classes in school didn't start until ten or later when I could help it. My parents took care of us financially, so I never had to worry about finding a job. I was just sure to volunteer whenever I could at different clinics and at church.

"That clinic ate you up yesterday, huh?"

"Girl, you have no idea. It was busy the entire time. That's okay, though. I know Rev. Adolph has a word for me, because it took everything in me to get here this morning. When I press my way is when I usually hear something that I needed to hear. But I was two seconds from just letting Mama and Daddy fuss."

She chuckled as the praise team and musicians got in position, then nudged me. "Your boy is looking at you."

I slowly shook my head and stared up at the ceiling. "Lord, my prayers must not be reaching your ears. Braylon is a nasty thorn in my flesh. Get thee behind me, Satan," I mumbled right before the music started.

Kinisha laughed then stood to join in praising God. I remained seated as I tried not to let sleep overtake me. Instead of allowing me to fall victim to the sleep demon, Kinisha pulled me from my seat to stand next to her. I took a deep breath and began clapping and singing along with everyone else.

I glanced over at my mama sitting with the deaconesses and my dad on the front row with the deacons. I smiled at her as she winked at me. They were so respected here. I respected them too. They'd always done what was right by me and Kinisha and raised us to the best of their abilities. They weren't afraid or too prideful to apologize when they were wrong, and that was what I loved most about them.

As the Holy Spirit began moving throughout the choir, then the parishioners, I felt like I was being watched. Sure enough, Braylon's eyes were glued to me. It was like my body was telling him it needed him or something. She was telling him stuff that she didn't discuss with me first, and it was unnerving. He was so damn fine, but he was no good for me. I didn't need that spawn of Satan in my system, throwing off my energy.

I looked away and tried to focus on feeling the spirit like everyone else, but Lucifer was tap dancing on all my nerves. He had me turned on, feeling sexy, and thinking about getting an orgasm during the time I should have been thinking about how the Lord died for my sins.

Jesus, keep me near the cross!

By the time Rev. Adolph got up to preach, the Lord had answered my prayers and had removed Braylon from my line of view. He probably had found something or someone else to dive into. He was just a nasty person and had no respect for the

Lord's house. I liked getting nasty, but there was a time and a place for everything. This was neither.

The sermon really touched me. The pastor talked about how much God loved us and how Zephania was the only place in the Bible where God said he would show His love through song. When he began talking about love songs and how none of us were so holy that we hadn't entertained them or used them to be the background to our sexual entertainment, I nearly fell out. His words . . . *Nobody in here was conceived to "Amazing Grace."* The church erupted.

After leaving and heading to Longhorn Steakhouse with my family, I received a text message from my advisor. I didn't know why she was texting me on a Sunday, but when I stopped at the traffic light, I looked to see what she had to say.

Hey, Kiana. Whenever you have time, could you please call me? This is regarding you tutoring. We wanted to see if you could be a full-time tutor from here on out, until you graduate. Thanks.

Hmm. That was interesting. I was only tutoring part-time because there were no full-time positions available. I wondered who could have possibly quit or graduated. I didn't know all the tutors because I kept to myself, but I knew their faces. I placed the call as I drove, and she answered on the first ring.

"Hey, Kiana! I didn't expect a call so quickly."

"Well, I had a little time. I'm on my way to meet my family for lunch. I would love to accept the position, Professor Carol. Who left?"

"Thank God! I feel like you're one of the smartest people we have. Lance graduated yesterday. The first session will start in two weeks since summer school starts the week before. With you being full-time, I think it will increase the number of students who take advantage of our services. Your students rave about how good you are with helping them understand their material."

"Okay. That's awesome. We can discuss the hours and pay later, but I am willing to go to full-time. I love working with students, helping them gain the insight they need to learn the material."

"You ever think about being a professor when you graduate? I think you would make a great one," she said.

"No, I haven't, but it's definitely something to consider. I've only been thinking about being a pharmacist. I just love helping people."

"Absolutely. Well, I'll let you go. Enjoy your lunch, and we'll talk later."

I thanked her for the opportunity, then ended the call. Tutoring was really something I had a love for, so I was grateful that God had blessed me with this opportunity. Being a professor had never crossed my mind, but I was actually thinking about it now. I could even do both, be a pharmacist and a professor. As I turned into the parking lot of the restaurant, my mind was already flowing with thoughts of how I would arrange my schedule for the fall semester to accommodate more students.

Chapter 3

Lazarus

After unbraiding my hair, I looked in the mirror to see how I cleaned up. I was about to head to my second job, and I always did my best to look fly, or at least like I belonged there. It was a hip hop club, so most of the club's attendees were in their twenties and early thirties. My short-sleeved black tee was tucked into my black slacks, and I put on my black shoes and black blazer to complete my fit. I fluffed my hair a bit, then made sure my diamond studs were secure and headed out of the door.

When I got to the club, the line was already wrapped around the building. We had a couple of VIP parties going on that night, and I was more than sure that everybody and their mamas would be trying to gain access to them. People were weird. I never cared about stuff like that. Being seen wasn't a priority of mine. I couldn't care less if I was popular or not. I'd go to the bar, get a drink, enjoy the music, and carry my ass home just as satisfied. If I met some cool people while I was there, then that was a bonus. I was the type that shied away from the limelight, instead of diving in it.

When I got to the entrance, my hair was a disheveled mess thanks to the breeze, but that was what I found the women really liked. As I slapped my coworker's hand, I could see the eyes on us.

"What's up, nigga? It's gon' be packed tonight. Here's your VIP guest list. These people don't have to pay a cover charge."

"A'ight, my nigga," I responded.

Aaron and I worked together most weekends at the door. It was rare that I was placed anywhere else. Being at the entrance was the most entertaining anyway. I got to see everyone going inside the club. It was where most of the women flirted so they didn't have to pay, although there had only been a couple that got by me without paying for the past year that I'd been working here.

As I glanced at the line, I met a couple of pairs of eyes that could possibly come through tonight without paying. While I knew I probably wasn't ready for a relationship with anybody, there was no harm in flirting. Taking a look at the list, I noticed there were only about forty names on it that were exempt from the cover charge. Hopefully, the eyes that caught my attention were on the list.

As I looked over the list again, Aaron yelled for VIP to come to my line and have their IDs ready so I could check them off. The shitstorm was about to start. I already knew there would be people in my line that knew good and got-damn well their names weren't on the list, especially women. They tried to use their bodies to get inside, and for some bouncers, that shit worked. Not me. VIP was strictly for the names on the list. The regulars knew not to fuck with me.

As they crowded in front of me, I took a deep breath, already ready to go back home. I stared at the first woman in the line for a second, then said, "ID please."

She smiled slightly as she handed it over. Her name was on the list, so I checked it off and gave her the ID back, then allowed her to walk past the velvet rope. Some of these women I had to look at twice, because they looked totally different on their driver's licenses. Most of them didn't have on makeup in their pictures.

By the time I got to about midway through the line, my eyes met with a beautiful woman's big, brown eyes. Her mocha-colored skin was glowing, and her thick lips were glossed perfectly. The way her curly braids framed her face only made her that much more irresistible. She smiled as she handed me her ID. I took it from her as I secretly scanned her body while looking at the list.

The pink dress she wore stopped about mid-thigh and clung to her voluptuous curves. Her thick legs were making me feel things I hadn't felt in a while, and I knew I needed to hurry and get her out of my face so I could do my job. The problem was that I couldn't find her name on the list.

I looked up at her, and she smiled again, not in a flirtatious way, but simply being friendly.

"I'm sorry, Ms. Jordan, but your name isn't on the list."

The smile fell from her lips. "I can't believe this. She invited me to this bachelorette party knowing I couldn't care less about being in a club, and she didn't put my name on the list? If I have to stand in that other line, I'm going back home. She can go to hell."

I smiled slightly. I couldn't let her leave. I wanted to be able to gaze into those beautiful brown eyes a little longer. "Don't leave yet. Let me make sure my boy gave me a current list. Okay? I don't think you tryna pull nothing on me."

She frowned slightly. "I would much rather be in my bed, watching a movie and eating popcorn."

I chuckled, then called Aaron over. Upon further inspection, he realized he had given me the wrong list. When he said so, I watched Ms. Jordan roll her eyes.

"I was hoping I had an excuse to go home," she mumbled.

I chuckled again as he left to get me the updated list. While we waited, I allowed a couple of ladies in. She wasn't the club-going type, and she still looked fairly young. She probably *was* still fairly young. I glanced at her driver's license again and made out that she was twenty-four. Shit, she was still a damned baby. Her body wasn't a baby, though.

When the next woman came up, she immediately said, "Can I touch your hair?"

"Naw, but you can hand me your ID."

I could see Ms. Jordan frown slightly in my peripheral vision. Her first name was Kiana, but I wasn't totally sure that I would pronounce it right, so I stuck with calling her Ms. Jordan. Besides, I needed to remain professional, despite the given atmosphere.

The woman in front of me rolled her eyes and walked over to where Ms. Jordan was to wait. Aaron came back with the right list, so I called Ms. Jordan back over.

"Women are bold as hell. They ask to touch your hair?" she asked.

"All the time," I said as I searched for her name.

When I found it, I looked up at her and smiled slightly. "You're on this list . . . Kiana?" I asked, taking a shot at pronouncing her name.

She smiled big, and I knew she had to be an angel. "Yes. That's right."

"A'ight. Enjoy your night," I said as I handed her ID back to her and stared into her mesmerizing eyes.

"Thank you, sir. Try to enjoy your night as well."

I wanted to tell her my name so bad, but since she didn't ask, I didn't volunteer it. I pulled back the rope and watched her walk her thick, fine ass through it.

Jamie was skinny for most of our marriage. She didn't start to gain weight until the pregnancy. I thought that it looked so good on her, but she hated it. When she lost the baby, the first place she headed to was a gym to work it off. However, Kiana didn't seem to be bothered by the extra weight. I was the only one bothered—in a good way, though. The way her dress hung off her shoulders had me wanting to lick them to see if she tasted as good as she looked.

I needed to go to the bathroom and adjust my dick. For the first time since Jamie and I had divorced, he was fiending for a taste of a particular woman. Usually, he just got hard and I would jack off, but having inspiration made that shit so different.

I couldn't get through the line fast enough so I could go inside and see exactly where she'd gone and watch her.

As I searched the upper level with my eyes, Aaron asked, "Yo, you good? You seem a little distracted."

"Yeah. I'm good."

After I realized I wasn't going to find her, I decided to do my job before I got fired. Being distracted was a huge no-no. If they felt like you couldn't effectively do your job, you were dismissed without warning. Lord knows I couldn't afford that, especially since I'd registered for school. I was able to rearrange my schedule with the city. Surprisingly, they'd given me a split-shift where I could work fourteen hours a day for three days a week. Tuesdays and Thursdays would be my days to go to class, and I'd work at the club on Thursday and Saturday nights. I supposed since we were shorthanded at the city, they were okay with me working my ass off on those days. Those were the busiest days anyway.

I'd registered to take chemistry and statistics. I'd only completed one science course years ago. I used to be fairly decent with science in high school. I could only hope that nothing had changed. I was scared to death about my new endeavor because I hadn't been in school in seventeen years. However, the most important part was that I was doing it anyway. As my mother had said, it was time for me to come forth. When Jesus raised Lazarus from the dead, those were the words he used: *Lazarus, come forth!* I'd been dead for a long time, stagnant in my potential and my purpose. While I didn't know exactly what my purpose was, I knew I wouldn't find it by doing nothing. Plus, I was tired of being stagnant. I was destined for more, and it was fine time that I found out what exactly that was.

The night was uneventful, just a normal night at the club, thankfully. Everyone seemed to be having a great time and getting along with those they came in contact with. It caused my mind to roam with thoughts about the direction my life was going in. I was here, in a club, doing meaningless shit to get a bag. Why couldn't I take a summer class? I could take something relatively easy like an English or algebra class. Math was my strong suit. It came easy to me, and I knew once I was back in the saddle, all of it would come back to memory under the instruction of the professor.

My mind was so focused on that shit that I didn't see Kiana approaching me until she was nearly in my face. I slid my hand over my face, trying to convince myself that I needed this job, so I needed to start doing it before I got sent home.

She smiled when she was in front of me. "I'm sorry. I didn't get your name," she said as her eyebrows lifted slightly, I supposed in hopes that I would give it to her.

I nodded and gave her a slight smile. "Lazarus, but everyone calls me Laz."

She frowned and leaned closer. "Did you say Lazarus?"

"Yeah. My mama was tripping."

Her frown lifted, and she smiled. "I thought the music had my ears tripping. I like it. It's very different. Besides reading it in the Bible, I've never met anyone with that name. Are you familiar with Lazarus?"

"Yes, ma'am. I am. I've known since I was a kid. My mama had to explain that with a name like that."

She chuckled, and it was a beautiful sound, just as beautiful as she was. I quickly looked away from her and scanned the club to make sure things were still okay. "I'm sorry, Lazarus. I'm stopping you from doing your job. I'm about to leave, and you were nice to me, so I wanted to get your name."

"You weren't here long."

"No. I showed my face, and now I'm going home. This isn't my scene. My sister enjoys this crowd. I'm not a club-goer."

"I get that. Neither am I. This is a job for me."

She placed her hand on my arm as she smiled. "It was really nice meeting you."

Everything in me wanted to ask her for her number, but I convinced myself that I wasn't good enough for her. She seemed to be a church girl who had her shit together, someone the opposite of me. I was trying to get my shit together, and I was far from being a religious person. Plus, she was twelve years younger than me. I needed to get my head out of the clouds.

I nodded and gave her a smile. "It was nice meeting you too, Kiana."

She smiled big again, then left me at my post and headed out of the club.

The night couldn't be over fast enough now. She had been my whole reason for enduring the night. I hadn't been expecting to see her until it was close to quitting time. I should have known better. I supposed I would have to find other motivation.

She had looked out of place here anyway, despite her attire. She knew how to dress the part, but her innocence came shining through the moment she opened her mouth. No one had caught my attention the way she had since Jamie left me, and that alone caught me off guard. However, that fact alone spoke volumes. It told me that she was special, but I let her walk out of the door without a promise of seeing her again.

It was like Kiana provided the motivation I needed to get my shit together quicker than I intended. I would just have to trust that everything would work itself out. I'd been idle long enough. Whenever the second summer session started, so would I. I could take an evening class and just work at the club on Friday and Saturday nights. It was time to stop making excuses and just do the shit. The man I once was did whatever he had to do to make shit work. If I could do that for Jamie, then surely, I could do that for myself.

It was all the shit my therapist and my mama were trying to make me see, and being around this beautiful woman had somehow pulled it out of me. Another opportunity like this couldn't pass me by simply because I felt inadequate. Jamie was moving on with her life, according to my mama. She had started dating one of the local politicians almost immediately after our divorce, and all our history and love seemed to be a thing of the past. It was time that I made it a thing of the past as well.

Chapter 4

Kiana

I was so tired, and I didn't have a clue why. I'd made it through the first summer session with a small group of people to tutor. When others realized I had more available time, they wanted to switch tutors. I refused to allow that, though. They would have to wait until the second summer session or the fall.

The second summer session was starting tomorrow, and I was beyond ready to get it over and done with. Summer sessions were always more tedious. They crammed information and instruction that normally took three months into six weeks. So, tutoring sessions were longer. More information had to be crammed into one session as well in order to keep up with what the professor was teaching.

However, today was slow. People were taking finals. If anything, they were coming in to register for time slots for next semester. They were also taking pictures for ID cards in the far corner. It was hard to believe this was a library, because the first floor was always bustling with activity. It was relatively quiet, but people were moving quite a bit and could distract others. That was why I always tutored my students on the second floor. Quite a few other tutors ventured to other floors as well.

As I packed up my things to head out for the day, someone caught my attention. It was like a ball of hair in my peripheral vision that caused me to look up. When I did, I was stuck.

Lazarus. I'd met him at the hip hop club a little over a month ago. Although I had only been there for a couple of hours, I could never forget him. He was the best part of being forced to be there. Had he not been working, I would have spent the entire time I was there talking to him. He was so friendly and didn't seem to really fit in with the crowd either. He was gorgeous. The finest man I'd seen in years. His hair was his glory. His mama should have named him Samson.

I watched him rush to the area where they were taking pictures for the student IDs. It was nearly five o'clock, and they were going to be closing soon. I nervously tugged at my fitted T-shirt as I watched him.

Why are you watching, Kiana? Just go over there. When my mind spoke, I typically listened, but this time, my nerves were on edge, just like they had been in the club. I didn't want to seem like I was throwing myself at him or begging for his attention. He was fine as hell, but just because he was friendly with me in the club didn't mean he wanted to get to know me.

I was finally able to pull my gaze away from him to continue packing my things. After grabbing my satchel and purse, I was about to head to my car. However, the moment I looked up, our eyes met. He smiled, and I couldn't help but smile in return. He was still handling his business, and I took his smile as an invitation to be in his space.

My body shivered as I made my way to him. *Lord, he is definitely Your creation.* His hair was tousled but even sexier than I remembered.

Before I could utter a word, he said, "Hey, Kiana."

He remembered my name. *Damn.* "Hey, Lazarus. How have you been?"

"I've been good. What about you? You attend here?"

"Yes. I'm a graduate student. I have one more year. You just getting started, or are you taking a new pic?"

"I guess you can say that I just started. It's been years since I was here. I dropped out after my first year."

"Well, you're a returning student. Welcome back!"

He smiled again, and my insides felt like they were melting and leaking down my legs. He bit his bottom lip as he stared at me, then said, "Thank you."

His lips. They were so thick and juicy looking. God had to be rewarding me for being faithful and not folding to Braylon's ass. Had to be. I'd been resisting temptation for a long time because I wanted something with substance. If Lazarus wasn't the man for the job, then the Lord was being cruel to me to even allow Satan to tempt me this way. As gorgeous as Lazarus was, he had every right to be arrogant. *God bless it.*

After he took his picture, he grabbed some papers from the desk and made his way to me. "So, you about to head home, or to work?"

"I was about to head home. I've been in this library all day doing absolutely nothing."

He chuckled as we made our way outside. "Why are you here then?"

"I tutor people. Being that it's the last day of the semester, no one needs a session."

"Oh, okay. What do you tutor?"

"Chemistry mainly. Sometimes I help with physics, algebra, and statistics."

"That's what's up. I may need your help in the fall. I'm taking a public speaking class this summer, and I'm already establishing a heavier prayer life."

I giggled as he held the door open for me. "I take it you don't like speaking in front of people."

"Absolutely not. I'm extremely reserved, and I do just fine in the background. One on one conversation doesn't bother me, but speaking in front of people makes me nervous."

I didn't have a clue why he felt that way. I could stare at him all day and would applaud him for reciting the alphabet. He was just that fine. "I'm sure you will do well, Lazarus. What's your major?"

"Finance. I've always been great with numbers. Math was my thing in high school, so I decided to pursue that. Maybe I could end up working at one of those fancy investment firms."

"Well, if you want it, have faith that you'll attain it. Just work hard."

He nodded repeatedly, then stopped walking. I stopped as well as I adjusted my satchel on my shoulder.

"Thanks, Kiana. Let me carry that for you," he said, taking it from my shoulder.

"Thank you. If you don't mind me asking, how long have you been out of school?"

"I haven't been here in seventeen years."

I frowned hard. *Seventeen years?* He chuckled as I did the math in my head.

"You don't look any older than twenty-eight or so."

"I'm thirty-six."

My eyebrows hiked up, nearly flying right off my face. "There's no way. Thirty-six? Impossible."

He chuckled, but I was baffled. Lazarus looked closer to my age. I was lusting over a man that was twelve years older than me. How in the hell? He was out here at Lamar seventeen years ago, and I was still in elementary school . . . first grade to be exact! Although we were both grown now, I was tripping. He was out of my age range. I would have to settle for just being his friend.

He seemed to be feeling me, though. I knew he knew my age because he'd practically analyzed my license at the club that night. Maybe it didn't matter to him. Or maybe I was reading him all wrong. He could have just been looking for a friend, and we seemed to click effortlessly.

"What are you thinking about, Kiana?"

I cleared my throat and stared up at him. "Nothing. So, what's your last name?"

"Mitchell. Lazarus Mitchell."

"Do you have a middle name?"

"Naw. My mama said with a name like Lazarus, I didn't need a middle name. That name was statement enough."

"She was right," I responded with a chuckle.

"So, what's your field of study?"

"I wanted to be a pharmacist, but lately, I've been seriously contemplating being a professor. I absolutely love teaching and tutoring. I thought about doing both, but I feel like I would be cheating myself if I did. I wouldn't be able to be totally dedicated to either profession. Helping people is my heart, so I'm leaning more toward being a professor. I feel like I'll reach more people that way."

"You're pretty mature for a twenty-four-year-old. I suppose working in the club, I see all the typical people in that age group, and I miss out on the exceptional ones."

His gaze penetrated mine, and I realized I was no longer walking. I watched his hair blowing in the breeze and decided to change the subject. He'd just proven that he was well aware of my age.

"I see why they want to touch your hair. It's beautiful."

He chuckled. "Thank you. You can touch it if you want to, Kiana."

My eyes lowered to meet his, and I felt like he was undressing me slowly, taking off one article of clothing at a time as his eyes roamed my body. I lifted my hand then hesitated as he stepped closer to me, closing in the space between us. I didn't just want to touch his hair. I wanted to kiss his juicy lips too.

After swallowing hard and building up the nerve to continue, I brought my hand to his head and slowly threaded my fingers through it. His hair was so soft.

"Do you braid it? It looks crinkly."

"Yeah. Well, my mom does it for me. She hates when I take it loose. She thinks I'm trying to be young."

"Does she think thirty-six is old?"

"Do you?"

I looked away from him because his eyes were grabbing ahold of me in ways that I couldn't allow. "No. Not at all. I think I get along better with people in their thirties. I think my soul is older than my body. The opposite of Robin Williams in *Jack*."

"Man, I haven't seen that movie in years." Lazarus reached out to me and grabbed my hand. "Since we've stopped walking, I'm going to assume that this is your car."

"Umm . . . no. It's a little further down."

He licked his lips, and I was again stuck, like I'd walked in wet cement. He pulled me in the direction of my car, and I looked away from him and cleared my throat.

Changing the subject, he asked, "What's your middle and last names? I forgot."

"Solé Jordan."

"That's right. You have a beautiful name, Kiana Solé Jordan."

I had to be blushing. My cheeks were hot as hell. The way my name rolled off his tongue had my lady parts tingling. My nipples had hardened, and as reserved as I was, if he wanted to make love to me right now, I would have let him.

I brought my hand to his hair again and watched a slow smile appear on his face. Quickly pulling my hand back, I looked away from him and walked a little farther to my car.

"I'm sorry, Lazarus. Your hair is just, it's beautiful. I see why women want to touch it."

His beard was just as sexy. I was happy that beard season was flying high. I thought they were so sexy, especially on the right man. *On Lazarus*.

He stepped closer and handed me my satchel as I unlocked my car. He opened the back door, and I placed it in the back seat.

"So, I guess I'll umm . . . see you around," he said.

I believed he'd caught my vibe about his age. Although it was a shock and what I considered out of my age range, I would have still given him my number had he asked for it.

I swallowed hard, slightly disappointed, and said, "Yeah . . . umm . . . I'll see you around. Thank you for walking me to my car. I enjoyed your conversation."

He smiled and took a few steps back, then turned and walked away. I found myself just staring at his back to see if he would look back at me. He didn't.

I got in my car feeling weird as hell for wanting more time with a man I didn't really know. There was something intense about him. Something serious. It was like he'd been through some things in life that made him wiser and more intentional.

Whatever it was, it made him that much more attractive.

After starting my car, I took a deep breath and exhaled slowly. I could have asked him for his number. There was no law against that. I allowed my shoulders to slump slightly. I was an old soul, and I had never made the first move when it came to a man, whether I knew they were interested or not. Lazarus was interested; that was apparent.

At least I knew where to find him. He was enrolling in school after a seventeen-year hiatus. I wondered what made him come back. Something had to make him want to come back after being away that long. I should have asked him.

Maybe that would be something I could ask him whenever we saw one another again. The building for the public speaking classes wasn't far from the library. Maybe we would park in the same parking lot. Then again, I didn't even ask what time his classes were. They couldn't be that early if he worked at a club. He probably slept in most days.

If I were more like Kinisha, I would know all the answers to my questions. Ugh!

When I got home, my dad was in the driveway washing his car. That was something he seemed to enjoy doing. He handwashed all our cars.

After parking and getting out of my car, I said, "Hey, Daddy. Mine next?"

He chuckled. "Not today, baby. Maybe tomorrow. They thought I went to work today to actually work."

My dad worked at Union Pacific Railroad. He was gone a lot when we were young, but it had paid off. He was normally sitting at a desk pushing a pen most days, planning training classes and safety meetings. Sometimes he conducted them as well.

"What did you have to do?" I asked.

"I was planning meetings for the next few months. There was a derailment, and my truck got filthy driving through the yard and fields. It was a mess today, baby."

I kissed his cheek when he came up from wiping his rims. "I guess I'll let you make it today then."

He chuckled as I headed inside to see my mama and Kinisha in the kitchen. My mom worked for the Social Security Administration office. She helped people obtain benefits. I wasn't sure exactly what her job title was even called, other than a clerk. She made a decent living. She'd been there for at least fifteen years and seemed to enjoy it. She was rarely in a bad mood about her job. She was rarely in a bad mood ever and was extremely pleasant to be around most times.

"Hey, Kiana. How was your day, baby?"

"Hey, y'all. It was boring, but it was necessary that I be there to assist people getting situated for the next summer session."

My mind immediately went back to Lazarus. *Why didn't I get his number?* I wanted to cry. My mind wouldn't allow me to stop thinking about him. He was just that intriguing.

"So, who has you grinning like that?" Kinisha asked.

I rolled my eyes at her because my mama rarely wanted to hear these types of conversations. She and my dad were hell bent on me being with Braylon's no-good ass. I didn't want to expose him, but if they became unbearable about it, I would. I would never be with a man-whore like him. The only thing he was good for was a romp in the sheets, and technically, I didn't know if he was good for that either, since I'd never had him.

"Well? Is it Braylon?"

I rolled my eyes even harder at my mom's question. I shook my head and said, "No. A man I met in the library. I first met him at the club that Jarielle's bachelorette party was at. He was a bouncer there. My name wasn't on her list, and he was helpful in finding out why and allowing me access to the party. So, when I saw him in the library, we were familiar. He walked me to my car, and we talked a little bit."

"Apparently, he's fine if he has you grinning like that. He's not even here and your mind is gone!" Kinisha added.

I released a sigh as she laughed.

My mama wasn't as amused. "So, Braylon doesn't have a chance at all, does he?" my mama asked.

"No, Mama. Sorry, but Braylon isn't a prospect."

She poked her lip out, but fell in with Kinisha, firing off questions about him.

"Hold on, y'all," I said. "I don't know much about him. I just know his name and his major. He's just coming back to school after taking a break for whatever reason. We didn't get into all that personal stuff."

"Well, what's his name? What does he look like?"

I chose to describe his six-foot frame first and how smooth his milk chocolate skin was. Then I went to his mane. I swore that man was the king of the jungle. His name should have been Mufasa. To hell with Simba. His voice was somewhat soft, with a medium timbre. It was sexy.

My mama and Kinisha were hanging on to my every word, practically drooling over this man that they'd never even seen.

"Y'all are in a haze just off my description of him, so imagine how I feel."

"You didn't say what his name was. What's his name?" Kinisha asked.

"Lazarus Mitchell."

She scrunched her face up immediately and frowned while my mama lifted her eyebrows. "Lazarus? What kind of name is that, sis? Tell me he goes by something else."

"He goes by Laz, but I haven't called him that. I've only called him Lazarus. I like it, and he doesn't seem to have a problem with it."

"So, when are y'all going to go out?"

"We don't even have each other's number, Kinisha. Gosh! He walked me to my car and carried my bag. He even let me touch his hair, but he didn't ask for my number. I didn't ask for his either."

"Are you sure the attraction was mutual?" my mama asked.

"At the club, there were plenty of women trying to touch his hair, and he refused to let anyone do so. When he saw me looking at his hair, admiring it, he told me that I could touch it. I can tell by the way he looks at me that he's just as attracted to me as I am to him."

"Hmm. Well, he'll be at school. Maybe he's a slow mover," my mama said as she went back to her red beans and fried chicken.

Kinisha gave me the side-eye, so I tilted my head in the direction of my bedroom. I walked away to go put my things away, and she was on me like white on rice.

"What else? What kept him from asking for your number, Ki?"

I took a deep breath and turned to her. "When he told me his age, I had an uncomfortable moment."

She frowned. "He's younger or older?"

"Older."

"Over thirty?"

"Yes."

"Daaaaaamn," she said in a low voice. "How old is he?"

"Thirty-six. He looks my age, Nisha. The man is so damn fine."

"I don't know. He's kinda up there. What could y'all possibly have in common? He's twelve years older than you."

"I know, but you weren't standing in front of him. His eyes caressed every part of me, girl. I felt like I was gonna melt everywhere. How do I walk away from that? I think he sensed my discomfort because he seemed to hesitate a bit before he left me to head to his car."

"So, what are you gonna do?"

"Just be nice and somewhat flirty so he knows I'm still interested. It won't hurt to find out what he's about. I can't go on without at least knowing if we're compatible."

"And if y'all are, how you gon' break that to Mama and Daddy?"

"I'll worry about that bridge when and if I get to it. If he's worthy enough for me to bring him here, then there will be nothing they will be able to tell me to sway me from him."

Chapter 5

Lazarus

I hurried out of the shower and got ready so I wouldn't be late on the first day of class. My public speaking class was Monday through Thursday at five in the evening. I was pushing it since I didn't get off until four most days. Sometimes it was a little later. I would speak to my professor tonight and let him know just in case I was ever late. After grabbing my keys, phone, and bag, I made my way out the door.

I couldn't believe that I was actually doing this, going back to school. I felt an extreme amount of pride. I was finally doing something for me, something I'd been deferring for years. Seeing my mother's pride made me feel amazing as well. She'd been waiting for me to start putting myself first. Jamie had done a number on me. I was so used to putting her needs before my own that I didn't know how to properly love myself anymore.

It was past time that I learned, that I remembered who I used to be before I met Jamie.

Although I was still a teenager then, I was an only child, and my mama tended to spoil me a bit, so it had been easy to only look out for myself. Losing my dad was hard on both of us, and she did her best to try to soften the blow for me. I appreciated her for that. I didn't remember much about him, but she made sure to keep his memory alive.

I looked a lot like him. Sometimes, I believed that was why my mama wanted me to cut my hair. He didn't have long hair. He kept it in a tapered fade. If I wore my hair the same way, then we would almost be identical. She would feel like he was still here by looking at me. I couldn't do that, though. I had to be who I was.

As I made my way to the school, my mama called. She was just as excited as I was. It was only four forty, but I needed to be there early just in case I couldn't find a parking spot. I was only a couple of minutes away.

I answered my phone through the Bluetooth. "Hey, Ma."

"Hey, college student. How are you feeling?"

"A little nervous but excited. I haven't been in a classroom in seventeen years, but I'm ready to start this new journey. I'm not letting anything get in the way of it anymore, even if I have to take you up on your offer and move in with you. I'm tired of being mediocre and walking around here with all this unused potential. I was destined for more, and it's time I started acting like it."

"Hell yeah! Now you talking like you belong to Natalie Mitchell. I got my Lazarus back. Jesus done spoke life into you, boy! I'm ready for all you will accomplish. Have a great first day. Call me as soon as you leave."

I slowly shook my head as I chuckled. "A'ight, Ma. I'm parking now. Talk to you later."

I ended the call and killed my engine, then hurriedly grabbed my things and made my way to the building. As I passed the library, I thought about Kiana. I wanted to ask for her number so bad yesterday, but I could see she was uncomfortable with my age. That discomfort only seemed to last for a minute or so, but it was there. I didn't want to put myself in a position to be used or hurt. While I didn't feel like it was in Kiana's personality to do something like that, I clearly wasn't a great judge of character. Jamie had me looking like an entire fool for years, and I didn't see it.

Just as I was entering the building, I heard my name being called. I immediately knew that it was Kiana. I would be able to hear her voice at a sold-out concert. That was just how in tune I was concerning her.

I turned to see her jogging toward me in her heels. I released the door and checked the time to see I still had nearly fifteen minutes. When we got closer, she said, "Hey!"

"Hey. How was your day?"

"It was good. You excited?"

I nodded, then decided to take a chance and reach out to her for a hug. I lifted my arm, and she came right to me without hesitation and gave me a one-armed hug. She cleared her throat as she pulled away from me.

"You had a busy day?" I asked.

"Yeah. I'm not a morning person. I'm sure you can relate since you work at the club."

"Naw. I get up at five every morning. The club is my weekend gig. I work for the city."

"Oh," she said as her eyebrows lifted. "I'm sorry for assuming."

"It's cool. My salary from the club is paying for school. I've been saving for a year or so. You heading home?"

"Yes. After you complete your fall semester, maybe I can help you apply for scholarships and grants, so you won't have to come out of pocket so much."

"Sounds like a plan. I'm all for saving money." I checked the time again, and said, "I guess I better get in there."

"Sorry. I didn't mean to hold you up. I just wanted to speak."

"No problem. See you tomorrow?"

"I hope so."

Hmm. She was being more forward it seemed. I gave her a slight smile and made my way inside. I didn't want to proceed just yet. I wanted to get to know her a little better. I didn't know how I would do that without asking for her number, though.

I turned around to look back at her through the glass door to find her still standing there. I stopped walking and went back to her. When I opened the door, she stepped inside.

"Did you forget to say something?" she asked as if she were clueless as to why I came back.

"Why were you still standing there?" I asked.

She lowered her head, and I saw a slight smile on her face. Her cheeks had turned slightly red as well. She was blushing hard if I could see that through her dark chocolate skin tone.

"I umm . . . I watched you walk away last time. I don't know. Just to see if you would look back after you walked away."

"So, what does it mean if I look back?"

"That I made an impression."

"Kiana, I was impressed at the club. I want to call you sometimes, but I could see yesterday that you were somewhat uncomfortable with my age."

"I think I was more shocked than anything else. You don't look your age. I would love for you to have my number, Lazarus."

I smiled slightly, then pulled my phone from my pocket, unlocked it, and gave it to her to save her number in it. When she was done, she stared up at me and handed it back.

"I probably won't call tonight. I haven't eaten dinner yet, and I have a li'l bit to do before I go to bed. Do you have a break during the day?" I asked.

"Yes. Around one. That's when I take a lunch break."

"Okay. I'll call you then. Bear wit' me. It's been a while since I've approached or tried to get to know a woman."

"What's a while?"

"Almost twenty years. But listen, we'll talk about that later," I said as her mouth fell open.

"O-okay. Talk to you soon."

I gave her hand a squeeze then headed to class. After I heard the door closed, I made it a point to turn and look back. She was still standing there. She waved, and I did the same, then made my way to class.

When I sat, I only had five minutes to spare. I walked in and realized that I was wrong in my assumption that the professor would be a man. The professor was at the desk, getting papers out of her satchel, which surprised me a little. I thought everything would be done online these days. Maybe she just wanted to be thorough.

She began handing the papers out. She looked somewhat familiar, but I didn't dwell on it.

When she got to me, she studied my face for a minute. "Laz Mitchell?"

My eyebrows lifted. She knew my whole name. "Yes?"

"I'm Trinitee Walker. We went to school together."

"Yeah! That's right. I thought you looked familiar, but I couldn't place you."

"We'll talk after class."

I nodded. She had lost a lot of weight. She had to be at least four hundred pounds in school, no exaggeration. She was kind of quiet, and I believed it was because she was self-conscious about her weight. She was never at any games or dances. I only saw her at school, and she was usually alone.

She started class, and I was extremely excited, despite my reservations about speaking in front of people. I glanced around the classroom and could see I had the attention of a couple of li'l girls. This happened everywhere I went, especially when my hair was a mess like it was now.

I wanted to wash it, but I knew I wouldn't have time. That was on my to-do list when I got home.

As Professor Walker went through what she expected out of us and what we would have to do for this class, my mind wondered off to Kiana. Maybe I would call her before I fell asleep, because if I called her on my way home, Natalie Mitchell would have an entire fit. I slid my hand down my face and tuned back in to what the professor was saying. I couldn't allow my mind to drift on the first day.

The class was supposed to last for an hour and a half, but she dismissed us early. She said since it was the first day, there was no sense in us just hopping right into it after all the instruction. We'd only been in for forty minutes. I wasn't upset one bit. That meant I could get more things done before it got too late. I could probably even get Mama to come braid my hair.

As I was putting my iPad in my bag, Professor Walker called me to her desk. I smiled and made my way to the front.

"I almost didn't recognize you. I like the hair."

"Thank you. I didn't recognize you either."

"Yeah. I had weight loss surgery about five years ago. I had gotten even bigger, and it was extremely hard to exercise. I knew I had to do something before my family would have had to bury me. I worked hard after the surgery. I lost nearly four hundred pounds. I was five hundred twenty pounds when I had the surgery."

"Wow. That's great. I'm sure you feel a lot better."

"I do. So, are you still with Jamie?"

"Naw. We divorced a couple of years ago. I'm just trying to start over."

"I'm sorry to hear that. Well, whatever help you need, just let me know. I don't mind helping my students who are making an effort. It's good to see you, Laz."

"Good to see you too."

I left her class feeling happy about the start of the summer session. I was glad to know I would have this class under my belt with fewer students that I would have to speak in front of, not to mention help straight from the professor if I needed it. Hopefully, she would have mercy on me if I needed it as well.

As soon as I got in the car, I called my mama.

She didn't bother saying hello. "You done already?"

"Yeah. She let us go early. The real work will start tomorrow. The professor is my classmate."

"Oh, well, that's good. You sound excited, so I take it that things went well."

"They did. You mind coming over to braid my hair?"

"No, I don't mind. I'll bring you some food too. I cooked baked chicken, green beans, mac and cheese, rice, and baked beans today."

"What made you cook all that?"

"To celebrate your new beginning. I'm proud of you, baby."

"Thanks, Ma. See you in a little bit."

"Okay."

I ended the call, and when I got to the light, I typed Kiana's name in my contacts. Since she wasn't expecting a call from me tonight, I sent her a text.

Hey. This is Lazarus. We got out of class early. Can I call you?

I was in a great mood, and if I could talk to her for a little while, that would put the icing on the cake. She'd soon realize just how privileged she was. No one called me Lazarus but my mother—well, and Jamie, but I once loved her. Everyone else called me Laz. Secondly, no one touched my hair but my mother either. I didn't know her, but I was already letting her get away with more than anyone else got away with.

As I accelerated through the light, my phone began ringing. It was Kiana.

"Hello?"

"Hi. Getting out early is always a blessing." She giggled, and I chuckled along with her.

"Hell yeah. But since it's my first day, I wouldn't have minded staying the whole time, because that was what I expected. But it gave me a little more time to where I could call you now instead of tomorrow."

"I'm happy about that. So, how was class? Do you think you'll like it?"

"It's okay. The professor was my classmate, so hopefully that'll earn me some leniency."

"I hear you on that."

"I uhh . . . kind of left you hanging earlier, and I wanted to explain. I got married at nineteen to my high school sweetheart. We divorced about two years ago. That's why I'm rusty on the dating scene. I haven't asked a woman for her phone number since I was sixteen years old."

"Wow. I'm sorry you went through that. Did you separate amicably?"

I took a deep breath, not wanting to have this conversation, but I felt extremely comfortable sharing it with her. "Not really. There was some resistance on my end, but there wasn't anything I could do to salvage what we had. By the time I was handed the divorce papers, I signed it and was done. Plenty of hard feelings."

"I'm sorry."

"You don't have to keep apologizing. We wouldn't be on the phone had that not happened. I wouldn't have been working at the club, and we would have never met. I went through that for a reason. Hopefully, I'll find out soon just what that reason is. I have a clue, though."

"What do you think it is?"

"I lost myself. I'm starting to find him again. I was living to please her and had forgotten about me. I'm taking care of Laz now."

"That's good. When you love someone, it's so easy to lose yourself. Although I'm only twenty-four, I know how that feels. Love can make you blind, deaf, and dumb. I've been single for a couple of years because of that."

"Seems like we have a lot in common, Ms. Jordan."

"It seems so. You're easy to talk to."

"So are you."

I turned into the parking lot of the apartment complex and made my way to my parking area to wait for my mama. I didn't like her walking out there by herself, especially when it was getting dark. These niggas out here were crazy as hell. If one of them even thought about fucking with my mama, I would be in jail. I would move earth for that woman.

"So, what made you want to come back to school?" Kiana asked, breaking the silence.

"I dropped out to take care of my ex-wife and put her through school. My turn never came around. I *needed* to do this for me. It was something I always wanted, and it was always understood that once she finished and got established, I would pursue my career dreams.

"I make decent money driving a garbage truck, but I don't wanna do that shit for the rest of my life. I want to wear a suit to work and smell like I did when I left home by the time I get off. Now when I get off, I smell like hot *garbage*," I said, pronouncing it in a French accent.

She laughed loudly, and it caused me to chuckle. I relaxed in my seat as she said, "Well, you smelled really good tonight when you hugged me."

"Thanks. I practically flew home to shower before I got there. I don't think the class would have appreciated me coming straight from work."

"Probably not. So, what are you about to do?"

"Go in and wash my hair so my mama can braid it for me."

"I bet it's extremely long when it's wet."

"Yeah. I be looking like a black Jesus when it's wet."

"I bet it's sexy," she said in a soft voice.

I licked my lips as I rested my head on the headrest. She was making my dick hard. He was already halfway there just from hearing her voice.

Choosing to change the subject, I asked, "So, do you live on campus or in an apartment?"

"I still live with my parents. I'm from Beaumont. I'm going to assume you're from Beaumont too?"

"You can say that. We've been here since I was young. I was born in Birmingham."

We once again fell into a comfortable silence. As I sat there listening to her breathe, I asked, "Can I take you to dinner Sunday evening?"

"I would like that. What time and where?"

"Around six, if that's okay. You can pick the place."

"Can we go to Cheddar's?"

"Sure. Can I pick you up? I mean . . . how would your parents react to you dating an older man?"

"I don't know. They don't have to know right now, though. We're getting to know one another. You may not like me much after you get to know me."

"Why wouldn't I?"

"I don't know. I'm just saying."

"I get it. What happens if things progress and they not cool wit' it?"

"If I really like you, there would be nothing they can say to stop me from seeing you, being with you."

"Okay."

I asked the question because I wasn't trying to set myself up for failure. Kiana was a beautiful woman, and the last thing I wanted to do was get caught up and then have her leave me like Jamie did. How much did her parents' opinions weigh?

Maybe I was asking questions too soon. However, I knew if nothing changed, it would be easy for me to become attached. I was a quick mover usually, so unless she took us slow, I would be all in within a matter of weeks.

There was a knock on my glass, scaring the shit out of me. My mama was standing there with her hand on her hip.

"Kiana, I have to go. If I have time, is it okay if I call you later?"

"Yes. Please do. I know I've been quiet, but I don't want to ask too many questions and have you ghosting me afterward."

I chuckled. "You can ask me whatever you wanna ask when I call back. Okay?"

"Okay. Talk to you later. Send me a pic of your hair braided."

"A'ight."

I ended the call and got out the car to see my mama frowning at me. "Hey, Ma. What's wrong with you?"

"Who were you talking to? It had better not be that bitch."

"It wasn't Jamie. Cool out."

She released a tense breath like she had begun gearing up for war. "Come on so we can get inside. Just my luck, I'll catch a stray bullet standing out here."

I rolled my eyes and grabbed her hand. She was so overdramatic. When we got to the door, I unlocked it and allowed her to go in first.

As soon as I closed the door, she went in on me. "So, who were you talking to?"

"A woman I met."

"Uhh, can you be any vaguer than that?" She rolled her eyes then set the plate of food she was carrying on the countertop. "Who is she? Did you meet her at school? Details, son. Aren't you taking public speaking? Practice with me."

I chuckled and slowly shook my head. "Her name is Kiana Jordan. I met her at the club. She was there for a bachelorette party. I ran into her again at school in the library."

"She not one of those ratchet hoes that be at the club, is she?"

"Not at all. She doesn't frequent the club, and she said as much. She'd rather be at home watching TV than at the club. She's nice. She gave me her number today, but only after I asked for it."

"Okay. Okay. I see. . . . Hol'on." She frowned then tilted her head to the side. "What was she doing at the school? How old is she?"

I exhaled and rubbed my hand down my face.

"Oh, shit! Lazarus! Is she older than twenty-one?"

"She's twenty-four."

"What the fuck? Boy, go wash your hair. What the hell you gon' do wit' a twenty-four-year-old? You know what? Don't answer that."

I rolled my eyes. "Chill out, Ma. You getting worked up over nothing. We're just getting to know one another. We're going to dinner, and I doubt anything will happen after that. She's a good girl, and she still lives with her parents."

"Whatever. Go wash your hair so I can braid yo' shit and go home."

I exhaled and slowly shook my head. I could only imagine what Kiana's parents would say if Natalie was in here tripping. She was acting like I said I was going to marry her.

While I didn't know much about Kiana, I felt like she was definitely wifey material. I could feel it. Whether she was for me or not had yet to be determined.

Chapter 6

Lazarus

I'd taken my cornrows out because I knew she liked my hair wild and uncontained. I just hoped that her parents wouldn't ask too many questions when I went to pick her up. Although I was dressed in all black like I was going to the club, I knew I looked nice. My diamond studs were shining, my skin was moisturized, and my beard and hair line were razor sharp. I grabbed my wallet and slid it in my pocket, put on my watch, and grabbed my phone and keys. Before leaving, I went to the fridge and grabbed the bouquet of flowers I'd purchased earlier.

Kiana had sent me their address earlier that day after they left church. I was rarely at church because I worked Saturday nights at the club. I was drained by then because of the long day on Fridays. I used Sunday as a day to rest and recoup. Maybe one day I would make the sacrifice and go with her if she ever invited me.

The past couple of days, we'd talked on the phone, but not about anything too personal. Friday, we only talked for a few minutes because I only had a two-hour break between jobs.

School had been taking some of my time as well. I had a speech coming up about the disparities faced by Black people. We had a choice of who we would represent. There were Asian people, Hispanics, LGBTQ community, disabled, and the list went on and on. I chose Black people for obvious reasons. Being that I was the only Black man in the class, there was no one who could talk about it better than I could. There were two black women in the class, but one seemed extra chummy with the white girls in there, and the other seemed extremely nonchalant like nothing phased her. I didn't know what to really think of her. We'd made eye contact a couple of times, but there was nothing indicating what she was feeling. She didn't smile or anything.

I was actually looking forward to doing the speech. There were only about twenty people in this class, including myself and the professor, so I would be able to handle speaking in front of them. When I told Professor Walker of how nervous I would probably get, she told me to focus right above everyone's heads. It would look like I was looking at them without me actually looking at them. I practiced on my mom when she was fussing about me going on this date with Kiana, and I found that Professor Walker was right. It would work perfectly.

My mother thought that Kiana was probably immature and not on my level. She said she wouldn't know how to handle a relationship with an older man, but I was ready to find out for myself. She was so attractive, inside and out. She seemed mature for her age. Our conversations were never pointless. We talked a little about ourselves, families, and what we wanted for our futures. Thursday, she'd taken a selfie of us, and I thought we looked good together. We practically looked the same age. She looked a little older than twenty-four. If I'd had to guess, I would have said she was twenty-seven. Since I looked younger than my age, we worked out perfectly.

After getting in my car, I took a deep breath and said a short prayer that things would go smoothly at her parents' house. I had no doubts that the date would be great as long as this short introduction didn't throw off our energy.

As I made my way there, I could feel the nerves starting to bounce off one another throughout my body. This shit was so damn new to me. I'd met Jamie's parents when I was sixteen, but they weren't as involved in what she was doing. They were having their own issues, financial and emotional.

My palms were starting to get moist. This shit was ridiculous. I was thirty-six years old and was nervous like a teenager. If they didn't like me, then they just didn't like me. Why should I give a damn? *Because I really like Kiana.*

I brought the temp down on my air conditioner and continued to Yasmine Dior Street off Washington Boulevard. It was a fairly new neighborhood, about ten years old, if that. The houses in that area were really nice as well.

I took the fifteen-minute drive there, and the moment I parked on side the street, I could see movement inside the house. I grabbed the flowers from the passenger seat and said to myself, "Here goes nothing."

When I emerged from the car, the breeze took my hair and did with it as it pleased. I didn't dare fix it. I wasn't a female. It would just fall however it fell.

I rang the doorbell and almost immediately, a young lady who resembled Kiana opened the door. She smiled big and said, "Hi. You must be Lazarus. Come on in. I'm Kinisha, Kiana's sister."

I nodded as I walked through the door. "Nice to meet you, Kinisha."

She stared up at me like she was in love. Before she could say another word, a woman came from the kitchen. I assumed she was Kiana's mother.

Making my assumption correct, she said, "Hello. I'm Kiana's mother, Lisa." She turned toward the kitchen, where a man was exiting and approaching us. "And that's her father, Otis."

I nodded and shook her outstretched hand. "Nice to meet you both. I'm Lazarus. Most people call me Laz." I shook her dad's hand when he got to us and nodded. "You have a beautiful home," I added as I took in my surroundings. Everything was in its proper place and looked fairly new, a far cry from my tattered furniture and grease-stained walls.

"Have a seat, Laz. I'll go get Ki," Kinisha said.

I nodded, then sat on the couch with her flowers as her parents sat across from me. Her mother's countenance was pleasant, but I could see that her dad was in protective mode, just as I would be if I had a daughter.

"So, Laz, do you have any children?"

"No, ma'am."

She nodded and smiled as her husband stared at me. "What do you do for a living?"

I was starting to feel uncomfortable already. They seemed a little uppity. "I work for the city driving the garbage truck, and I also work at the hip hop club downtown. But I started school to major in finance."

"I can respect a hardworking man. Nothing wrong with that," he said.

That shit helped release a lot of my tension. Just as he was about to ask another question, Kiana came down the stairs in a beautiful white dress that flared out at her waist and stopped at her knees. It was sleeveless and showed a little cleavage. Her hair was in a braided ponytail with more hair added into it that stopped at her waist. Her makeup was light, and her smile was bright.

I stood from my seat with the flowers in hand as she approached me. "You look beautiful."

"Thank you. You look handsome. I see you've met everyone. Sorry to keep you waiting."

"It's no problem at all."

I handed her the flowers, and her smile widened. "I love this arrangement. Sunflowers are my favorite."

"I figured I'd get a mix since I didn't know what you liked. Now I know."

She smiled again, then said, "Let me put these in water. Then we can go."

I nodded, then sat back on the couch.

"Laz, what do you plan to do with your degree?" her dad asked immediately after I sat.

"I'd like to work at an investment firm, helping people to properly invest their money to see the biggest return possible."

"Sounds like a plan. I wish you the best with that. If you'll excuse me, I have to get back to my shows. I catch up on Sunday evenings."

"Yes, sir," I said as I stood and shook his hand.

Right after, Kiana emerged from the kitchen with a smile. "You ready?"

"Yeah. Nice meeting you all again," I said as we headed to the door.

No one asked how old I was, and I was grateful for that. I knew she hadn't told them simply based on what she'd said the other day.

I placed my hand at the small of her back as I escorted her to my car. After I opened the door for her, she gave me a bright smile and said, "Thank you, Lazarus."

I only smiled back at her and closed the door. She was so damn beautiful. I was mesmerized. Staring at her big, beautiful legs wasn't making matters any better.

When I got in, I started the engine and took off toward Cheddar's. We were only about five minutes away. "So, how was your day?"

"It was good. Church was good as always. I would love if you could come with me one Sunday."

I smiled slightly. "Yeah. Sure."

"So, did they ask too many questions?"

"Naw. They were cool. Just if I had any kids and what I did for a living. Nothing too personal. Did you change your mind and tell them my age?"

"No. I'm quite sure they would have had more questions had I done so."

I slid my hand over to hers and held it. Despite how I'd felt earlier, there wasn't a nervous bone in my body—until we pulled up at Cheddar's. Jamie was standing outside like she was waiting for someone. My heart rate picked up. I hadn't seen her since she put me out of our house.

After backing into a parking spot, I just sat there.

Kiana squeezed my hand slightly. "Everything okay?"

"Yeah. Sorry."

Before I could get out, she held my hand tighter. "Tell me. Don't let me be blindsided by anything."

I ran my hand down my face. "I'm sorry. That's my ex-wife standing there. I haven't seen her since she kicked me out of our house almost two years ago."

A sympathetic expression graced her face, and she released my hand. When I got out, I could see her expression harden a bit. I supposed she was putting up her guard just in case things didn't go well.

As I walked around the car, I noticed that Jamie had noticed me. She shouldn't feel one way or the other since she was the one that put me out. She'd switched cell phone providers years back, so I had to get a new phone when she had mine turned off. By the time I was able to get a new phone, she'd changed her number.

After helping Kiana out, I grabbed her hand, but she pulled it from mine and looped her arm around mine. It was like she was staking claim to me. I found it amusing, but I understood it. Being that I hadn't seen Jamie in so long, she didn't know what type of bullshit she was about to walk into, but she was also letting Jamie know that there would be no dipping back of any kind.

When we got close, Jamie was staring right at us, but I refused to be the first to speak. If she didn't say anything, I would walk right by her like she was a damn stranger. I could feel the anger embodying me, and I hated that shit. This was supposed to be a wonderful night, light and free, enjoying time with Kiana.

Just as I was about to walk past her, she spoke.

"Hello, Lazarus."

I gave her a head nod like she was my groupie and kept it moving. I could feel her watching me though, *hard*.

After going inside and getting on the waiting list, we ventured back outside under the awning to a table. Once we sat, I grabbed Kiana's hand.

"I'm sorry if this moment seems a little awkward, but now that I've seen her, I realize that she means nothing to me anymore. I have to admit that I was nervous how I would react if I ever saw her again. You have nothing to worry about. You're the woman I'm here with that I'm trying to get to know."

She placed her other hand on mine and gently rubbed it. "Thank you for that. I felt a little defensive for a moment. I was hoping she wouldn't say much to you. Although I'm young, I'm not one for drama. She left you, so she should keep that same energy," she said as she glanced over at Jamie.

She was still watching us. I could see her in my peripheral stealing glances our way. There was no reason she should have been concerned with anything that I had going on.

I lifted Kiana's hand and kissed it. She closed her eyes for a brief moment. It was the first time my lips had touched any part of her, but it seemed so natural in that moment.

"Your lips are as soft as they look."

I stared at her as I responded. "I've learned to take care of myself, so if any part of me is looking raggedy, please fix me up or tell me what I need to turn my focus to. I won't be offended."

She chuckled as she moved closer to me and slid her fingers through my beard, then touched my hair. "You are such a gorgeous man. She was a fool to push you away. A big-ass fool. But I'm grateful that she did. It gives me the opportunity to appreciate you the way you should be appreciated."

"There hasn't been a time that I've wanted to kiss you more. Am I allowed to feel your beautiful lips, Kiana?"

She swallowed hard, then gave me a tight-lipped smile as she nodded. I leaned into her and allowed my lips to simply graze hers, trying not to smear her lipstick. When I pulled away, her eyes were still closed, but a beautiful smile graced her face.

"When we leave, I want a proper one, Mr. Mitchell." She said all that with her eyes closed.

As she opened them, I chuckled quietly, and said, "Gladly."

I scooted back in my chair, and she did the same, but our hands stayed joined. We were comfortable in our silence. I could only think about the kiss I would get later from her soft lips. Her bottom lip was thick, and I couldn't wait to suck on it. When our little remote went off, I stood and helped her from her seat.

"I'm surprised they're this crowded on a Sunday evening."

"Me too. Maybe there's some sort of special occasion going on inside."

As we went inside, I noticed Jamie was still standing in the same spot. I assumed she was waiting for someone, because if she were waiting for a table, she should have been seated before us. I paid her no attention, though, and followed the fine-ass woman I was with into the restaurant.

We were led to our table, and I noticed why it was so crowded. There looked to be a group of people in the middle area, celebrating something. They were taking up half of the restaurant.

Once we were seated, before I could say a word to Kiana, Jamie appeared at our table. "I'm sorry to interrupt your . . . date. Lazarus, can I speak to you?"

I frowned hard. She had no right to approach us. "Naw. You about two years too late. Now, please don't interrupt our time again, or I'll have someone escort you away from our table."

She looked shocked that I was so harsh, but fuck her. I had never been that rough with her, but she was my woman, so I had no reason to be back then. Today was a different story. She was my past, and I had who could possibly be my future sitting across from me.

I grabbed Kiana's hand as Jamie stood there with her mouth partially open. I refused to give her any more of my attention, not when there was a beautiful sunflower sitting across from me. She cleared her throat and walked away as Kiana stared at me like she had fallen in love.

The waitress appeared and took our drink orders. Once she left, I said, "I apologize."

"No apology needed. You handled that well. She really looks familiar."

"My mom said she has commercials on TV. She's a psychologist."

Her eyebrows shot up. "What's her last name?"

I frowned and rolled my eyes. "Should be Mitchell, but she's probably going by her maiden name, Hightower."

She lowered her gaze. "No, that's not it. I thought she was my mom's psychologist. My mom got into a wreck a few years back and had to see one to cope with the trauma of it. I thought that was her. I guess not."

Choosing to change the subject, I asked, "So, what church do you go to?"

"Antioch. It's off Highway 69."

"Oh yeah. I've visited before. My mama's friend's husband passed away, and his funeral was there. I've also been to a couple of weddings and a christening there."

"Oh, okay. I love my church."

"The pastor can preach. That's for sure."

"Yes. I enjoy him."

"If it's cool wit'chu, maybe I can go with you next Sunday."

"Sounds like a plan. I'll be happy to have you next to me."

I smiled at her as the waitress came back with our drinks and took our order. I was beyond happy that we'd gone out, despite the hiccup with Jamie. This woman was the real deal, and I planned to show her I was the real deal too.

Chapter 7

Kiana

If that woman had come to our table again, I would have intervened. Lazarus wouldn't have had a chance to say a word because I would have let her have it. According to what he'd told me, she divorced him, put him out of their house and everything because he wanted to go back to school after putting her through school. He said she'd told him he wasn't making enough money, but apparently it was enough to put her through school. I bet her ass wasn't complaining then. She sounded like a user and a master manipulator. That was probably why she was a psychologist. She knew how to get into people's minds and have them doing exactly what she wanted them to do.

I was happy that she had forced Lazarus out of her life. He was probably an even better man because of her. However, I knew he had to love her for him to endure everything he had. It sounded as if she was only there to offer him sexual benefits because I didn't feel as if he was lying when he told me that he did everything while she was in school. She had him by his balls, and if they had had a child together, I knew there was no way I would have been entertaining him right now. She would have been controlling every aspect of his life, whether they were together or not.

Lazarus had a gentle spirit, and she knew that just like I did. I could definitely tell that she was caught off guard by his response to her, though.

As we sat there waiting for our food, I took a sip of my strawberry lemonade and glanced around the restaurant. That bitch had me on edge, and I didn't like that at all. I just wanted to enjoy an evening with the man I felt like could one day have my heart. Our evening had just started, and she'd put a sour taste in my mouth.

He reached across the table, and I slid my hands to his as he stared into my eyes. I could see the sorrow in them, and it pulled at my heartstrings. He had no reason to feel guilty about what that ho did.

"Would you like to take our food to go?"

"No. That's not necessary. I'm sorry. She just caught me off guard."

"I'm the one that's sorry. I wanted to enjoy being with you. I'm so busy during the week. This is crazy. She's trying to ruin me and make me unhappy. Excuse my language, but it's fucked up."

I saw a different man in that moment. His countenance was screaming defeat. While I wanted to encourage him and let him know that everything was cool, I found myself in a sunken place as well. We'd successfully allowed her to ruin something that felt so perfect.

I slid my hands away from his and just stared at my drink. I'd made him feel guilty because of how I let her get under my skin. I looked up at him to find him staring at me.

"I'm sorry, Lazarus. I feel like I pulled you to this sunken place with me. You seemed to be okay and ready to continue our date after you said what you had to say to her. You didn't do anything wrong. Actually, you did everything right. Let me go to the restroom and pull myself together. I'm a little angry about what she did, and I'm allowing that to ruin our date, which was going wonderfully, by the way. Excuse me for a moment, okay?"

He nodded and stood from his seat to assist me from mine. I clomped my way to the restroom like I was about to go fight someone. When I realized I was stomping, I took a deep breath and eased my steps. My inner Ki wanted to grab that heifer by the neck.

I pushed the door open and went inside a stall and relieved myself. As I sat on the toilet, I took a few deep breaths and prayed. God was the only one that could calm me down at this point. I was an easygoing person, but when I got angry, it took me a while to come back from it. It was something I needed to work on.

While I never went too far in my anger, my attitude stayed jacked up for a while. I needed to pull it together to salvage our date and my time with Lazarus. That gorgeous man didn't deserve this angry Kiana. He was able to dispel his anger quickly. I could see the anger flash in his eyes, but the moment that woman walked away, the Lazarus I was getting to know was right back with me.

After taking a few more deep breaths, I flushed the toilet and made my way to the sink to wash my hands. I wanted to put cold water on my face to cool me off, but I had worked too hard on my makeup, trying to make it look as natural as possible.

As I was about to head back to our table, that woman walked into the restroom. I stared at her for a moment as she somewhat cowered.

Suddenly, she said, "He's a good man, but he's still in love with me. I can see it. You're wasting your time."

"You're right. He's a good man. However, when he looks at you, I don't see love. I see anger, hurt, and hostility. If he weren't a respectable man, I believe he'd choke the hell out of you."

She chuckled, and that only made me frown harder. "Lazarus doesn't have that in him. He's not a fighter. He's soft and passive. Besides, you look too young for him anyway."

"Let me tell you something. You don't know me. If I didn't want to catch a case, I would choke the shit out of you in here. Your boldness and audacity is sickening. You're an evil person, and you never deserved him. He has a pure soul that has been blessed by God. When you try to destroy a man of God, you're signing your own death sentence. Be careful. If you ever cause him to snap, I feel sorry for you. You divorced him. You created the distance. Keep that same energy. He's doing well without you, and he's a better man now that he's dropped the dead weight." I walked away from her as I mumbled, "Bitch."

That was what I needed. I needed to get that shit off me. I felt better after going off on her. Hopefully, I could pull Lazarus out of the place I'd dragged him to.

When I got back to the table, our food was there. The moment he saw me, he stood from his seat to help me in mine. He was such a damn gentleman.

"Thank you, Lazarus."

I gave him a big smile, and he smiled slightly. Once he sat, I reached for his hand. "I'm so sorry for the mood I put you in. I gave her power that she shouldn't have. The mood of this date and our time together should be all that's important. I really love spending time with you, and I'm no longer allowing her to control how it goes. I released in the restroom, and I feel better now."

His eyebrow lifted slightly, causing me to chuckle a bit. "Released how?"

I released his hand after I insisted we bless the food first, and he grabbed his fork. He hadn't started eating yet because he was waiting on me to return. I appreciated that.

"I saw her in the restroom. I think she probably followed me there. This only proves how miserable she is. She wants others to be as miserable as she is, but we won't go there with her. I pretty much told her that much after she said that I looked too young for you and that you would always love her. After I told her my piece, I felt so much better."

I brought a piece of blackened fish to my mouth and savored the flavors from it. Cheddar's always seasoned their dishes well.

When I heard a slight chuckle, I looked back up at Lazarus. He was staring at me with a look of amusement on his face. That was much better than him being in the sunken place.

"What's funny?" I asked.

"The way you're making love to that fish."

I had to have turned red. My chocolate skin didn't stand a chance against this heat seeping from my pores. I hadn't had sex in a while, but just the mention of it had me imagining what it would feel like to have him hovering over me, filling me with joy. I couldn't maintain my gaze because of where my mind had gone, but I could see that he was still staring at me. It felt like he was pulling my clothes off with his eyes.

Dear Lord, keep me near the cross.

It was the prayer I'd prayed multiple times concerning Braylon, but it didn't feel as sincere this time. This man sitting across from me looked like he could be Black Jesus with all this wavy hair. I wanted him. There was no doubt about that.

When I looked back up at him, he was eating his food. I chose to change the subject so I could pull my thoughts from the very pits of hell.

"So, tell me about your mom. You've met mine already. I would love to meet yours."

He smiled slightly. I knew she was important to him. She was the only family he had here since he was an only child. He'd previously told me that all his other family members were in Alabama, so he wasn't close to any of them. I also knew that he didn't have any close friends. That had to be lonely as hell.

"She's a mess," he said, then chuckled. "She's extremely fun to be around. She's hard on me, but she's who helped me see that I needed to love myself more. That woman is my number one until another woman moves her back to number two." He smiled, and I could tell he was thinking about her.

"Is she cool with being number two?"

"Yeah. When I was married, she never interfered, although I knew she couldn't stand Jamie. She said she saw right through her, but I wouldn't listen. Probably would have saved me a lot of heartache had I took heed to her words, but I probably wouldn't have met you. So regardless of how things turned out, I'm grateful for the journey. It led to you."

I was a huge softie now. He had me feeling like mush. I pushed my plate to his side of the table and stood to sit next to him. After those words, I just wanted to be close to him. He stood from his seat and allowed me to slide in first. Once he sat next to me, he smiled then lifted my hand for a kiss. However, I had something different on my mind. I leaned in and kissed his lips.

God, they're so soft.

As I pulled away, he gently tugged my bottom lip with his. I stared into his eyes and food was the last thing on my mind.

He rested his hand on my thigh, then slid it to the inside, gripping it. His touch was strong but tender at the same time. It felt like I'd levitated. I almost wanted to lift my dress and let him do as he pleased right here in Cheddar's.

A soft moan left my lips, and his hand inched a little higher, then he slid it back down.

"I'm sorry, Kiana. I didn't mean to cross the line."

"Lazarus, look at me."

When he turned to me, I bit my bottom lip. His gaze was touching every part of me. This man was so damn sexy. I brought my hand to his cheek and slid my fingers through his beard.

"Did I seem uncomfortable?"

"Naw."

"Then you didn't cross the line. I enjoyed every moment of your touch and the way it makes me feel."

He leaned in a little closer and asked, "How does it make you feel?"

"Like I'm finally with a man that knows how to treat a woman . . . that knows how to treat me. You've been nothing short of a gentleman tonight, but now I'm giving you the opportunity to be less than a gentleman. You're free to disrespect my body any way you choose to."

Shit! What was I saying? That last line was supposed to stay a thought. I cleared my throat and turned away from him, stiffening slightly. I was in a Lazarus-induced haze, and it had my lips loose and my body even looser.

"Naw. Look back at me, Kiana."

I took a nervous breath in and looked at him. He bit his bottom lip. "I'm not in a hurry. I haven't had sex in almost two years. I don't want to rush that moment. If it naturally goes there, then I'm cool with that. I can see you're nervous, though. That's not something I have to have right now."

"I'm not nervous about what I said. I just didn't mean to say it aloud. That's exactly how I feel, and nothing about your touch makes me nervous."

He nodded repeatedly, then kissed my lips again. This time, he slid his tongue in my mouth for a second. I wanted to slide my hand through his hair and pull him on top of me. I was so damn horny it was ridiculous.

He turned back to his food for a moment and just stared at it. "Suddenly, this ain't so appealing anymore."

I chuckled. I felt the exact same way. He was the only thing I wanted to devour at this point. That fish could go to hell. I slid my hand to his, intertwining my fingers with his, and slightly leaned into him. He released my hand and slid his arm around me and kissed the side of my head.

"I guess I better ask for to-go boxes."

I smiled at him. "Yeah. Once my Lazacoma is over for the night, my stomach may be violent."

He laughed, almost choking. "Lazacoma? Girl, you crazy."

I chuckled as well, but that was what this felt like. It was like he'd completely taken over all my senses. I no longer had control of even my thoughts.

"You are all I can concentrate on."

"Same here."

When I looked up at him again, he kissed my lips. "You and these juicy-ass lips. I love your lips."

"I love yours too. They're so soft."

The waitress appeared to check on us, so Lazarus asked for two to-go containers. She smiled, noticing that we were now sitting on the same side of the booth.

"Kiana, this date was everything. We were able to see more than one side of each other. We got the angry sides, the emotional sides, and the sides we originally wanted the other to see. I'm attracted to all three. I think I got your petty side too when you came back from the restroom."

I chuckled and slowly shook my head. "You did. I can be petty at times. I haven't had to be in a long time, but I could clearly see that it was still there. That was probably why I was so angry. I was trying to restrain it."

"You don't ever have to restrain any part of yourself when you're with me. I want to know all of you, Kiana, even your petty side," he said, then grinned.

I rolled my eyes playfully as the waitress returned with our boxes and the check. I tried to get a glimpse of it, but Lazarus kept it tucked tightly to him. I'd come prepared to help with the check if he needed me to, but I knew better than to offer. Just because I was aware of his financial situation, I didn't want the burden of the date to be all on him. However, since he asked me out, I had to assume that he had it covered.

As he took out his wallet, I asked, "So, when will I get to meet Ms. Mitchell?"

"Maybe next weekend if she doesn't have plans. I'm not going to even tell her. I like seeing her face when I shock the shit out of her."

He chuckled, and it produced a chuckle from me as well. Hopefully, him shocking her didn't have the opposite reaction.

Chapter 8

Lazarus

If I was an abusive man, I would have gotten Jamie's contact information so I could strangle her ass later. I was so damn embarrassed when she approached our table. I just knew when Kiana came back from the restroom, she was going to be ready to go. I was prepared for that. While I didn't get Jamie's contact information, I was more than sure I would be seeing her again. I wouldn't even have been surprised if she followed me to the hood just so she would know where I lived. It was apparent that I didn't go much of anywhere if I was just now running into her again.

After our dinner date, I took Kiana home. I wanted to be respectful with the time since she still lived with her parents. While I had painted the walls at my place, I wouldn't dare bring her there. She'd given me permission to fuck her world up, and Lord knows I wanted to grant her wish, but I didn't want to spend the money on a hotel room right now. I still had bills to pay, and the fall semester was quickly approaching. Lamar was gonna rape me for nearly two grand for two classes. The shit was ridiculous. I didn't know who determined the costs for students, but they shouldn't have been able to sleep with themselves at night.

Kiana and I had only been able to text for the past couple of days, but I finally got off early enough to call before class. I was on my way home to take a shower and for once, I wasn't rushing. However, her phone only rang. Deciding not to leave a voicemail, I continued home and took a shower so I could get ready for class. She was probably tutoring someone. I knew she would call back whenever she had time.

Once I was home and had showered, I ate some food my mama brought by earlier for me. She'd put her foot in the smothered beef tips. I was just happy that she'd brought enough for tomorrow, too, along with potato salad and green beans.

After getting dressed, I called her to tell her thank you, then made my way to class. I was surprised I hadn't heard from Kiana yet, but I wasn't tripping. Maybe I would get to see her in passing since I was a little earlier than I had been the past couple of days. Usually, I got to class right on time, not a minute to spare. Today, I had fifteen minutes before class started when I parked.

As I walked toward the library, hoping to see her, I got jittery. I wasn't sure why. I checked my attire, and I was cool as usual. My hair was pulled in a man bun because I didn't have time to get it braided. Maybe that was what it was. I didn't know if she would like it. Surely, that alone wouldn't have me feeling jitters.

I tried to shake it off as I headed to class. When I got close to the library, I didn't see her. Just as I started to go in there, I saw her talking to a man. They were seated on the park bench, and he had his arm around her. She looked comfortable there and was giggling quite a bit. I wanted to still walk over there, but she was clearly preoccupied with someone else. We weren't a couple, nor did we discuss dating one another exclusively. Maybe we should have because this didn't feel right to me. My mental wasn't strong enough to handle no shit like this.

When I realized I'd stopped walking, I met eyes with the guy she was with right after he'd kissed her forehead. He nudged her and nodded in my direction so she would look. When she did, the smile fell from her face. It was like she felt guilty. That was all I needed to see. I walked off, and she didn't try to stop me.

What the fuck! I refused to be duped again. She couldn't answer her phone because she was busy entertaining someone else. It was cool. She could keep entertaining him. I was done. I was really starting to feel something for her, so it was probably a good thing that this happened now instead of later.

When I got to class, I sat at the back. I didn't know how focused I would be on the lecture, and I would hate to be in Professor Walker's face and not be paying attention. That was what I got for trying to be with a woman as young as she was. I supposed she was keeping her options open after the fiasco Sunday evening. I thought that she was over that, because the rest of our dinner had gone amazingly well. Her kisses tasted like chocolate and cherries, and her thighs felt like fluffy pillows that had me fiending to lay in between them. I'd done all that fantasizing over a woman that had already withdrawn from me. It just didn't seem right.

Maybe she was all in and told her sister or mom about what happened, and they convinced her to leave me alone. Jamie had brought the unnecessary drama and caused me to lose out on a nice woman. Although I wished Kiana had talked to me about whatever was going on, I had to respect that she was moving on. I also had to protect my heart. I refused to chase after a woman who clearly had other options. I had other options as well. After my speech yesterday, I had gotten plenty of attention. There were some women from an earlier class who

Professor Walker had asked to do their speeches in our class, since it was smaller. They'd all given me the eye at one point during the class. I'd ignored them because my sights were set on Kiana Solé Jordan.

Professor Walker entered the classroom, and she looked a disheveled mess. I stood from my seat and made my way to her. "You okay?"

She shook her head as a couple of other guys approached. "A guy knocked me down and fought with me for my purse. He won."

"I'll call campus police," one of the guys said.

"Do you need medical attention?" I asked.

"No. I'm okay. I need to get cleaned up. Class is canceled tonight, guys," she said as everyone began crowding around her.

I refused to leave her like this. Her clothes were dirty, her leggings were torn, and her hair was everywhere. She was always put together, so it wasn't hard to tell that something had happened to her. "I can't believe that no one saw this going down," I said.

Before she could respond, the campus police arrived. I wanted to make sure she was okay, but they asked for everyone to leave unless they'd witnessed the crime. We were all hesitant because we wanted to be sure she was okay. She was a good person and a great teacher. Everyone liked her.

I went to the back of the class and got my back-pack and left the class along with everyone else. However, I was quickly reminded of why I was in a funk when I saw Kiana once again, walking with that guy toward her car. I could only shake my head. I couldn't believe that she'd ignored me like I meant nothing.

"Lazarus!"

I turned to see who was calling my name, and when I saw it was her, I kept walking. The guy with her was frowning. Then he burst into laughter. I didn't know whether he was laughing at her or at my name, but I didn't give a shit. I walked to my car like I didn't have a care in the world and like she was a complete stranger, the same way she had treated me earlier. Had she spoken earlier, I would have assumed that what I saw was innocent. For all I knew, he could have been related to her.

Lies. I could clearly tell by the way he looked at her that they weren't related. He wanted her, and she was entertaining it.

When I got in my car, I called my mama. Since I was free, I could use her braiding skills. I'd have to be sure to pay her today. I'd taken them down early to impress Kiana. I usually kept them braided for a week, sometimes two when she put that foam stuff on them.

She answered on the third ring. "Hello? Why you ain't in class?"

"It was canceled. My professor got robbed. She came to class all messed up."

"Oh, wow. Was she okay?"

"She was shaken up, but physically she seemed to be okay. One of the other students called the campus police. But umm . . . can you come braid my hair?"

"Again, Laz? Boy, why the hell you take it down so soon? You know what? Don't even answer that. Probably from your li'l date Sunday that you won't tell me about."

"I'm gon' give you some ends, Ma. I appreciate you. I'm on my way home to wash it, so bring that foam stuff with you so it'll last longer."

"Ugh! Okay. See you in a li'l bit."

She ended the call, leaving me in my feelings. I was happy that I hadn't told her about my "li'l date" now. If I had gassed Kiana up and made her sound all perfect and shit, I would have to tell her that I was no longer speaking to her.

While I was thinking about it, I went to her contact information in my phone and blocked her, then deleted her contact information. *Gone without a trace.*

I went to our text thread and was about to delete our thread until I saw a new text from her. I opened it out of curiosity for what she had to say.

Can we talk?

I rolled my eyes and deleted the thread. There was nothing to talk about. I refused to be used again. So, if that meant I had to be single for the rest of my life, then I would. If I judged by her, it seemed the dating pool had shit in it anyway.

"Nigga, hold your head still."

I exhaled loudly. My mama was on my last nerve. She apparently had been busy when I called her, and she stopped what she was doing to come braid my hair. All she had to do was say she couldn't do it. I would have managed. But now I had to put up with her attitude.

"Listen, calm that shit down, Ma. What, you had a nigga you was entertaining or something?"

She quieted down, and that was a telltale sign that I had hit the nail right on the head. When I could feel that she was about to start another braid, I turned to her to see the smirk on her lips.

"Ma! You seeing somebody?"

"Boy, turn around so I can get through."

"Naw. You gon' talk about it. I ain't saying I gotta meet him, but I need to know who you canoodling with in case I gotta fuck somebody up."

"Lazarus, really? I'm a grown woman, and the last time I checked, I was the parent. If you need to know something, I will tell you. We haven't spent time alone yet."

I turned back around as I said, "Mm-hmm. Before you do, I need to know the particulars about that nigga. You mess around and come up missing, and I don't know shit about where you are or who you were with. And quit rolling your eyes."

"What makes you think I'm rolling my eyes?"

"'Cause I know you. Now say you weren't."

"Ugh. Be still so I can get through. What's up with you and your lady friend? How was dinner?"

"It was cool," I said, refusing to go into detail.

"That's it? It was cool? You must not like her that much."

I remained quiet because at the mention of her, I got a mental picture of her with that nigga, enjoying his company and seemingly enjoying his touch as well.

"Aww, shit! What did she do?"

It was my turn to roll my eyes. "Nothing. Chill out. We are just talking and getting to know one another. That's it. We aren't a couple, Natalie."

She popped my head with her rattail comb. She hated when I called her Natalie. We were damn near best friends, but she just couldn't fathom me calling her anything but Mama. She was old school and wouldn't hear of me calling her anything else.

"What I told you about calling me by my first name? Disrespectful ass."

I closed my eyes and exhaled, trying to keep my mind from going back to Kiana, but I couldn't help it. Since Mama had brought her up, my mind grabbed ahold of her and ran.

Maybe I had been too hard on her. Just because she was with someone else didn't mean she wanted them. He could have been flirting with her and she was just too friendly to tell him to move around.

"His name is Kirk, and we've been talking for a couple of weeks. I met him at the grocery store in the meat section."

I glanced up at my mama as she parted my hair. "Now, was that so hard? The woman I'm getting to know is Kiana. She's a graduate student, who's also in the pharmacy program and will graduate next year. She wants to be a pharmacist. I figured I'd offer you the same courtesy. What does Kirk do for a living?"

"He's retired. He was a refinery worker."

"How old is he?"

"Sixty-two. He said he goes back to work from time to time to help out when they are on a shutdown, turnaround, or whatever he called it."

Sixty-two wasn't too old. She was fifty-seven, so they were only five years apart. I was glad she was finally seeing someone. For her to even mention him, she must really be feeling him. It was past time that she be happy. When Jamie and I first got divorced, Mama had made a comment to the extent of being glad that she hadn't met anyone because she knew that I would need her. That I did, but it was time that she lived her life without worrying about me. I would be just fine.

"Mama, I'm glad you're living your life. You raised me to be a respectful and responsible man all on your own. I don't even recall you dating when I was young. You did what you had to do to make sure I was at my best, even when you were at your worst. I'm happy for you, and most of all, I'm proud to be your son."

"Lazarus, don't make me cry. I thought I babied you too much, but you grew up to be a strong man that loves hard. Jamie don't know what she fucked around on. Stupid-ass ho."

I bit my bottom lip and decided that I would give her the real about Jamie and what happened with Kiana. "I think Kiana is done with getting to know me."

"What? Why?"

"Jamie tried to fuck up our date Sunday. She saw me and approached our table. I gave her the business, something I've never really done, but I could tell that it bothered Kiana. Then she said Jamie approached her in the bathroom, saying bullshit, that I still loved her and would always love her. Today, I saw Kiana at school with someone else. He had his arm around her and kissed her forehead. She looked extremely comfortable."

"Oh, baby. I'm sorry."

I began counting down silently. *Five . . . four . . . three . . . two . . . one.*

"Jamie gon' get fucked up. I know just where the fuck I'm gon' catch her ass at."

"That's not necessary, Ma. I had thoughts of getting at her myself, but I can't give her power. If she thought for one second that she got to me, then that would make her statements to Kiana true. I'm done with that shit. I'm not in love with her anymore, and I just want to live in peace. So, I'm gon' be on my grind with work and school and stick to myself like I've been doing."

She continued braiding my hair and didn't say another word. I knew her wheels were turning, though. One thing she didn't play about was her son. I still believed she had tried to do something to Jamie when she kicked me out of our house. She was angrier than I was. Starting over wasn't easy, especially since I was broke from paying all the bills I'd created putting Jamie through school.

When I felt the foam on my head, I knew she was done. Since I hadn't given her any specific instructions, I was interested in seeing what she came up with.

Once she was done, she said, "Okay. Tell me what you think."

I stood from the floor and went to the mirror to see that she had done seven braids with zigzag parts between them. She was getting better and better at this. Before long, I would really have to pay her.

"Damn, Ma. This look good as hell."

"I know."

I went and got my wallet from the table, and she said, "I don't want your money. You finishing your degree will be all the thanks I need. I don't care how long that shit takes. When I see you walk across that stage, it'll be something that will make my soul happy. You finally doing what's best for you makes me happy, and I know you have always wanted to have a degree. A dream deferred is not a dream denied. I just wish you would take advantage of the help I'm offering so you can finish sooner."

I thought about her words and knew that I couldn't do that, especially now that she was seeing someone. "Naw. You need your privacy."

"If things get serious between me and Kirk and I need privacy, I can go to his house. Come home, baby. You won't have half the bills you have now, especially rent. Then, by the spring semester, you can take three classes instead of two."

I closed my eyes for a moment, knowing that this was what was best for me right now. Living with her would eliminate rent, renter's insurance, an electric bill, and a water bill. Not to mention, she lived closer to the school, the city yard, and the club. I opened my eyes to find her watching me, awaiting my answer.

I smiled slightly and said, "Okay. But you have to let me pay for something."

She rolled her eyes. "Boy, you'll rarely be there with as much as you work and now going to school."

"I pay the light bill, or I stay in my hellhole."

She rolled her eyes, then said, "Fine. So, when you moving?"

"Sunday good for you?"

"Sounds like a plan."

She was giddy with excitement, but I hoped I was making the right decision for me. While it would benefit me financially, I didn't want it to be a hindrance to me or her emotionally. There was only one way to find out, though. I would gradually start bringing my things to her house throughout the week and putting this damn furniture to the street. My mama wouldn't dare have me sleeping on a mattress that was on top of egg crates. As long as I got a good night's sleep, I didn't care.

I walked her to the door and began mentally preparing for her to be all up in my business. Shit, like she was now.

Chapter 9

Kiana

It was the second week of the fall semester, and I'd been in a funk for the past month. There was one reason for that: Lazarus "no middle name needed" Mitchell. I felt like I was going through the motions every day that I had woken up since the last day I'd seen him. After that day, he made sure to alter his route to his public speaking class to assure that I didn't see him. He'd probably blocked my number, and I felt like I was dying on the inside.

When he'd seen me with Braylon, I froze. The look in his eyes was something I could never imagine causing. He looked hurt beyond repair, like I'd stabbed him in his heart. I didn't know what to say, and before I could gather the nerve to say something, he'd walked away. Braylon's ass always pushed up on me, and me allowing him to do so that day was a huge mistake. Although his advances had never gone anywhere and things were totally innocent on my end, that wasn't how Lazarus saw it.

So, when I tried to speak to him as he was leaving, he ignored me. It hurt me more than I ever thought it could. We'd only been on one date, but I thought I had made it clear how I felt about him. There had been so much anger in his eyes when he glared at me. I was sure it didn't help that Braylon had laughed loudly when I'd called his name. His exact words were, *"What kind of muthafucka name their child Lazarus?"*

Then I thought about everything Lazarus had been through and realized he was in protective mode. He'd put up the wall around his heart and left me on the outside of it. I'd ruined things from a misconception. I thought about what I could have done differently and came up with a couple of things that had been haunting me all month. I had refused to speak to Braylon since that incident. It was like I couldn't find my joy anymore. While I wanted to blame him, I knew that I had to accept all of it. I should have put him in his place a long time ago, long before I met Lazarus, and this would have never happened.

Not speaking to Lazarus when I first saw him had been plaguing me for the past month. I believed that if I had spoken to him, things would have been okay. I looked guilty of something to him. I just didn't know what to say, because the hurt I saw in his eyes paralyzed me. After I saw his missed calls from earlier that day, I felt worse. My phone had been on vibrate since I was in the library tutoring, and I'd dropped it in my purse when Braylon joined me on the bench.

Although Lazarus and I weren't a couple, I felt like we were on our way to that, even after the disaster with his ex-wife. What we were building was worth crying for. I'd cried for days like we were a couple in love. Knowing that my actions had hurt him that way did something to me I couldn't explain.

When I explained what was going on to my sister, she wanted to go find Braylon and tear him a new asshole. She was totally impressed with Lazarus, and so were my parents. While my parents had no clue of his age, they loved him for me already. Kinisha had held me in her arms while I cried my eyes out. She thought Lazarus was being unreasonable until after I explained his situation with his ex-wife, since she already knew his age. She then understood why he'd gone into retreat mode. He was afraid of being sucked in again, being hurt like last time. She told me that she would have her eyes open on campus and would let me know if she saw him.

After leaving class, I headed to the library to tutor. Since it was the fall semester, my tutoring hours were different. I stayed much later than five in the evening. On Tuesdays and Thursdays, I was there until ten at night sometimes. I left a little earlier on Mondays, Wednesdays, and Fridays. I felt like I was a zombie as I made my way through the crowd, only to practically walk right into a show the Alphas were putting on. I quickly gathered my composure and rerouted myself. A step show was the last thing I wanted to see. I only wanted to see Lazarus.

Everyone had noticed the change in me. My parents were constantly questioning me about what was going on with me, and my advisor had been checking on me every day. Anyone that spent an extended amount of time around me knew that something was terribly wrong. I didn't know how I would pull myself out of this funk I was in.

After getting to the library and sitting at the desk, I looked around the library, hoping to catch a glimpse of the man that had me infatuated beyond belief. No such luck. Most likely he wouldn't be here so early anyway. It was only two o'clock. I should have been tired of looking for him. He'd perfected the task of avoiding me. He would see me whenever he felt like he could handle it. By then, it would be too late for me.

The library was bustling with activity, sounds of pages turning, copy machines going, and slight whispers of students talking to librarians and other students. Most of them wore earbuds, though. This was the only place on campus you could come to and be in complete quietness without anyone being in your business—well, except tutors. However, no one tutored on the first floor anymore. I had moved to a different floor. There were too many distractions.

When my first student arrived, I did my best to put my personal issues to the side. I had a job to do, and I wanted to give my students my best, no matter how I felt like I was dying on the inside. Surely, I should have been over him by now. It had been a little over a month! How was I so attached to a man that I had only kissed? It was like I was sprung off just his aura, and I didn't even understand how that was possible.

I supposed, mentally, I'd been making plans. I'd imagined that I would be his for the long haul, eventually becoming his wife. My thoughts were girlish and premature, but the feeling Lazarus gave me inside was something I never wanted to let go of.

My student and I made our way to the elevator so we could begin our session. I had all my students arrive five minutes before their session was to begin so we wouldn't waste time getting to our destination when I could be instructing them. The elevator was slow as hell. Getting from one floor to the next could take minutes. We could probably get to the desired floor faster if we took the stairs. If I were utilizing the second floor this semester, that would be ideal.

Since all the other tutors had made their way to the second floor, it was just as bad as being on the first floor. Students speaking to one another, interrupting sessions, was a common occurrence. I didn't have time for it, so I moved to the fourth floor right in the middle of the stacks. With the age of Google, Kindle, and electronic devices, people were rarely looking for a physical book, so the stacks were practically collecting dust.

Once we got to our desired location, the young man pulled out my chair. I smiled slightly and said softly, "Thank you."

He nodded politely and sat next to me so we could begin our session. Right at the beginning, I realized we were going to be spinning our wheels. He hadn't memorized the periodic table of elements. He had no clue what any of the abbreviations were. Who with any science background didn't know that hydrogen was H and oxygen was O? This boy questioned about H_2O and said that he never knew what it actually stood for, just that it was water. The only reason he knew it was water was because of the movie *Water Boy*. He'd watched it with one of his older cousins as a kid. Only God himself kept me from slapping that boy out of his seat.

Needless to say, our session was cut short because I wasn't about to deal with him not knowing the elements. I gave him pointers on how he could learn them quickly by separating them into groups and told him to research songs for kids to help him remember them easily, then I dismissed him. He apologized a few times before we reached the first floor, and I'd committed to helping him learn it. My heart was way too soft, but maybe that was why I was a good teacher. It was at that moment that I decided I wanted to change my field of study. I no longer wanted to be a pharmacist. While I was obtaining a Pharm D degree, I was also obtaining a master's degree in chemistry. It didn't make sense to abandon the pharmacy degree plan since I was almost done, but I knew what my calling was. Teaching was it for me. Maybe I could be an instructor in the pharmacy program. My advisor had been right when she posed the question to me before summer school had started. She saw it in me before I saw it in myself.

As I made my way back to the desk on the first floor, I stopped dead in my tracks. I was still in the foyer area near the elevators and hadn't walked through the glass doors yet when I saw him. Lazarus. He was inside talking to one of the tutors. He needed help with chemistry. He knew I was a chemistry tutor. I somehow trudged forward, and the moment I entered the area to fall to my seat, our eyes met. He had to have been able to see how his absence was affecting me.

I couldn't even force myself to smile. My heart felt like it had sunk to the pits of hell and my spirit only grew weary. He stared at me for only a moment, then turned his attention back to the tutor he was speaking to. His hair was braided nicely in about seven cornrows, and they looked to have grown since the last time I'd seen him. His beard was a little fuller, and he just looked great. I found myself staring at him, hoping that he would at least stop by my table and say hello.

The lump in my throat was practically restricting my airway, and while I wanted to cry, I knew I couldn't allow that . . . not in front of all these people.

I had twenty minutes until my next student arrived and nothing to do to distract me from his slender but well-defined body. He had the build of a typical basketball player. I could see his biceps and triceps were long and lean but definitely noticeable.

As he nodded a couple of times, I assumed wrapping up their conversation, he headed in my direction. He had a slight frown on his face, and that only further killed me. When he stopped in front of me, I stopped breathing.

"They said you're the best chemistry tutor. I wanna pass, so I guess I need to see if you have any availability on Tuesdays and/or Thursdays."

I swallowed hard and nodded, wanting myself to say something to him. I needed to explain what he had seen, but it had been a month already. Did he even care anymore?

I pulled out my phone and checked my schedule. "I'm available on both days from seven to nine. I'm here until ten p.m. on both days."

When I looked up at him, I continued, "Hi, Lazarus."

"I'll take seven. See you later."

With that, he walked away. My heart was hurt, and I didn't know how to deal with it other than to rush to the bathroom to cry my eyes out. I missed him so much.

As I tried to pull myself together in the stall, I heard a soft voice. "Kiana, are you okay?"

"Yes. Thank you."

I didn't know how in the hell I was going to tutor him without being able to be myself around him. Being that close to him without kissing his lips was going to be torture. No one else was probably available at the time he needed. That was the only reason I could imagine he would subject me to this. There was no other logical explanation. He had to be torturing himself as well. If he weren't feeling me, there was no way he would have looked so hurt and angry. He was still angry.

Him refusing to even speak to me bothered me. It hurt. I could imagine that he thought he was getting me back by being so cold. I was suffering enough without him. Being in his presence every Tuesday and possibly Thursday, avoiding our personal connection and brief history, would be a lot for me. I could refuse to tutor him, but I wanted to try to get through to him. I didn't have it in me to intentionally hurt anyone, not even Braylon's ho ass.

After leaving the stall, I went to the sink to wash my hands and pat my face with a cold paper towel as I noticed my sister looking on.

"What are you doing in here?" I asked.

"My friend told me that she saw you practically run in here. I take it that you saw him."

"Yeah."

"I saw him too. He's sitting outside on the bench, staring at his chemistry book. I can tell he isn't reading it."

I looked over at her and nodded. I supposed she wanted me to do something with that information. I couldn't go out there and try to talk to him. I had a student coming in a few minutes. Plus, I wasn't in the mood to be rejected twice within thirty minutes.

"You aren't going to go try to talk to him?"

"No. I'll see him at seven for a tutoring session. I tried to speak to him earlier, and he ignored me. He treated me like I was a damn robot. Strangers get more courtesy than what I got from him. I just want to go prepare for my student, okay? Thanks, Nisha."

Her sad eyes followed me to the door as I exited, heading to my table to wait on my next student.

It was six forty-five, and my nerves were going crazy. Lazarus would be here in ten minutes, and my stomach was in knots. I went to the restroom to pat my face with cold paper towels, then returned and took a huge gulp of the cold water in my LU thermos. I used this damn university thermos faithfully since I'd paid nearly thirty dollars for it. I closed my eyes and took a few deep breaths, then opened my eyes to see him walking through the door. Checking the time, I saw he was ten minutes early instead of the five minutes I required.

As he approached, I stood from my seat. "Hello, Mr. Mitchell. Thank you for being on time. Let's journey to the fourth floor."

I was doing my best to remain professional and treat him like he was treating me, but that was so hard for me. I could hear the tremble in my voice as I spoke to him.

He said, "Hello. Okay."

I walked away, and he followed behind me. When we got to the door, he quickly got ahead of me and opened it. Despite his qualms with me, he was still a gentleman.

"Thank you."

He nodded, and I continued to the elevator. Since it was so late, the elevator was there at the bottom, because there was little to no traffic. We walked on and stood on opposite sides as it slowly rose to the fourth floor. I could have probably used the second floor since hardly anyone was there, but I'd already gotten used to being on the fourth, away from everyone else.

When I exited, he followed behind me through the stacks to the desk positioned in the middle area. I set my bag on the floor, and before I could pull out my seat, he did so for me.

"Thank you."

He nodded as I sat. When he sat next to me and I got a whiff of his cologne, I closed my eyes. It was the same cologne he'd worn on our first date. When I'd gotten home that night, I refused to shower until the next morning because I wanted to feel like he was with me as I slept.

When he set his chemistry book on the desk, I turned to him and asked, "Have you memorized the periodic table yet?"

"Yes . . . mostly."

"Okay. Let's get started. Show me where you're having difficulties."

"I mainly need a slower instruction right now for certain areas. I'm not the greatest with science, so it takes me a while to grasp certain things."

"Understood."

He showed me the areas in his book where he was struggling to grasp the information, and for the next hour, I explained things in layman's terms for him to understand, using metaphors and relating the information to real-life situations. The entire time, I stared at the book on the table or one of the stacks of books we were surrounded by. While I could feel him staring at me as I spoke, I only gave him a glance here and there. I couldn't dare stare into his eyes without crying and showing him just how sensitive I was to him.

It was like being around me didn't bother him one bit. He seemed so relaxed, the total opposite of earlier. In this moment, I was simply his tutor. That was it. Once our hour was up, I closed my book and stood from my seat.

"Will your appointment be once a week, or should I put you down for twice a week?"

"I don't want to get behind, so let's do twice a week at seven. Thank you."

"You're welcome."

We walked to the elevator in silence. I was practically sweating under my breasts because he made me so nervous. However, I knew I needed to say something.

As I turned to him, the elevator doors opened. He gestured for me to go first. Once the doors closed, I turned to him once again.

"Lazarus, I'm sorry. What you saw isn't what it is. I've known him since I was six. While we don't have a brother/sister type of relationship, I'm used to his advances and his stupidity. When you saw us, I was frozen. What I saw in your eyes rendered me speechless. The hurt and anger swirling inside of you had my entire body on pause. What I feel for you is real. I promise it is. I've been depressed this past month not being able to see you or even hear your voice. I miss you."

He turned to me, but he didn't say a word. It was like he was allowing my words to go through a filter to see if anything pretentious would come out of them. I needed him in my life. Nothing about that was fake or phony. I didn't want to use him for any personal benefit. I only wanted to eventually love him and have him close to me. He was broken by his ex, and anything that resembled what she'd done to him was discarded quickly. I could understand that, but I also needed him to understand me.

When he slid his hand in mine, my entire body trembled. He still didn't say anything. The elevator had stopped, and once the doors opened, he escorted me off.

"Do you have another tutoring session?"

"No. You were my last since no one scheduled for the later hours."

He nodded, then pulled me toward the exit. I didn't know what to think. My brain was trying to make me believe that he had forgiven me and that he was ready to pick back up where we'd left off, but I didn't want to get my hopes up.

As we walked out, someone he'd befriended said, "What's up, Laz? You hooping tonight?"

"What's up? Naw. I'ma take it easy tonight. I'll holla at y'all Thursday."

"A'ight," he said as they slapped hands.

Lazarus began walking toward my car, and I was about to go insane waiting for what he would say. He turned his head to me as we walked, and he stared at me. I wasn't sure how to take this. Why was he torturing me this way?

When we got to my car, I turned to him to say thank you, but he spoke first. "Thank you for that apology. I umm . . . I think I'm just gonna chill out, though, and concentrate on my classes. I've made some changes this past month that I believe are going to be beneficial to me, but I need to get used to my new normal. Relationships can be risky and messy, and it's just not something I'm ready to deal with right now."

Despite me doing my best to hold it back, the tear slid down my cheek. I saw his gaze soften as I quickly turned and got inside my car.

"Have a good night, Mr. Mitchell." I quickly closed my door and started my engine. I needed to get as far away from him as possible. Rejection hurt, especially from him.

As I backed out, he stood there watching me like he wasn't the one who'd just crucified my heart, nailed it to a tree like it bore the sins of Jamie. Somehow, I would have to get past this and him. I just didn't know how, since I had to look at him every Tuesday and Thursday.

Chapter 10

Kiana

"God is a sovereign God who wants His children to come to him. The Bible says to trust in the Lord with all thine heart and to lean not unto thine own understanding. But it keeps going! In *all* thy ways acknowledge Him. All, church. Not just some, not just when you feel like it, not when it really gets bad, but *all* thy ways! And He shall direct your path! Proverbs chapter three verses five and six. What good is it to have a father that's all-knowing and all-powerful if you can't go to him? It's a slap in God's face when we try to do things on our own!"

I was sitting in church, half paying attention until this point. I needed God to heal my broken heart. Lazarus's Thursday session wasn't any better than Tuesday's. I struggled the entire hour and needed some relief. I was going to have to stop tutoring him. I couldn't handle it. It was one thing to ask God for guidance, but I couldn't continue being stupid and throwing myself in the line of fire, then have the audacity to ask for God's help. I didn't have to tutor Lazarus. I had fallen for a man that no longer wanted the things I did.

The admission of that was hard. The acceptance of it was just as difficult. Everyone around me was standing on their feet, praising God as Pastor preached his heart out. I was still seated and had been for the past six Sundays. I couldn't find my joy. This had never happened to me, and I had no idea how to climb out of it. Depression had engulfed me in its arms and squeezed me so tightly until it was practically suffocating me.

I glanced over at my mama to see she was watching me. Surprisingly, she hadn't asked any more questions. Most likely she'd figured out that it had to do with Lazarus. Otherwise, she wouldn't have given up so easily. She wasn't the type to leave something alone until she had answers. Dad left our issues to her to deal with. As our mother, she never took that role lightly.

The tears streamed down my cheeks as everyone continued praising God, some shouting, others dancing or running. Normally, I would have been in the number, giving the Lord a good dance offering.

God help me. Please . . .

That was all I could silently get out. This was what the older people meant when they said the

Lord knew our hearts. I wanted Lazarus, and I thought that he was the one God had sent me. Apparently, I was wrong, and now I was stuck on a man that had no desire to be stuck on me.

After wiping my eyes, I noticed my mama sitting next to me. I fell into her and released what I felt like was a ton of sorrow. She hugged me and cried with me as she prayed aloud for God to take control. It was these words that caused me to look up at her, though.

"God, if it's in Your will for Lazarus and Ki to be together, bring him back to her. Place him in her life for Your purpose and Your will to be done. If not, help her to be able to accept that and move on with the life You've given her. Don't allow her to forget about *her* purpose because of a temporary distraction."

She knew. I figured as much. Either she had figured it out, or Kinisha had broken code and told her. She'd been extremely worried about me over the past month, so I wouldn't have been surprised if she had. I'd barely been talking to her, and that was just as heartbreaking as me not being with Lazarus. It was like I withdrew my friendship due to no fault of hers. I'd withdrawn from everyone except my students that I tutored. I'd even withdrawn from myself. Whenever I wasn't at school or church, I was in my room in my bed, wallowing in depression and defeat.

As I laid on my mother's shoulder, she said, "We are more than conquerors through Christ, and it's time for you to start walking like a victor instead of a victim."

I lifted my head and nodded my acceptance of her words. She was right, and I couldn't help but thank God for speaking to me through her. After Lazarus's next tutoring session, I would have to reassign him. That alone was going to be a task because I had no clue who would be able to take him on at seven o'clock in the evening. However, it was time I put my mental well-being at the forefront. He would have to accept that—or not—but it was going to be what it was going to be, regardless of how he felt about it.

"Thank you, Mama. Please don't tell Daddy."

I knew that if he knew, he wouldn't be as forgiving as she was. The man that broke his daughter's heart would have no future in our family, no matter what role I played in the situation. He was my protector, even when I was wrong. He'd tell me I was wrong, but he always had my back.

She kissed my forehead and said, "Don't worry. Now, give God some praise for what He's gonna do."

I stood from my seat and lifted my hands, thanking God for a breakthrough, although it hadn't manifested yet. I had faith that it would, though, and that was all that mattered.

I felt a set of arms wrap around me, and I opened my eyes to see Kinisha. I lowered my hands and hugged her back.

"It feels good to have my friend back," she said in my ear.

I hugged her tighter as the music came to a stop. People were still shouting and praising God, so I was more than sure it would crank back up in a minute. Pastor hadn't preached yet, and if things kept going the way they were, he wouldn't be preaching at all. Sometimes it was like that. He would stand up there, getting the people in the spirit for a sermon, a word from God, and he never got a chance to speak it.

This time, they seemed to quiet down, though. We sat and got ready to hear a word from God. I was in desperate need of encouraging, and finally, my heart was ready to receive it.

I was shaking in my seat. Lazarus would be there in a few minutes, and I knew that today was the day I had to say goodbye to him. I couldn't continue tutoring him and torturing myself. While it seemed he was progressing and grasping information when I would explain it, he would have to find someone else.

I bid a couple of people a good night while I waited on the first floor. As I pulled my sweater on, he walked through the door with a smile on his face. My insides practically melted at the sight of it. I quickly turned my head as he entered and grabbed my things from the table.

"Hey, Kiana. We had a pop quiz today over the information you've been going over with me, and I made a ninety-eight. A ninety-eight! Can you believe that?"

"Hey. Congratulations. You're a smart guy, so I can believe that."

His excitement dwindled a bit as I walked past him. I was happy for him. I truly was. However, I couldn't pretend to be happy in his presence, nor was I happy about what I was about to do. He pushed the door open for me, and I walked through, straight to the elevator.

He remained quiet as we waited, but the minute we got on, he asked, "Are you upset with me about something?"

"No."

Again, Lazarus was a smart man. He had to know I was having a hard time with this, especially after I had poured my heart out to him last Tuesday, telling him how much I missed him. I was a step away from begging. That was something I had *never* done. This man had me losing control of myself. That was more of a reason why I had to end this.

He slid his hand in mine, and as hard as it was, I pulled away from him. I turned to him to say something, and he laid his lips on mine, causing my icy exterior to melt. I grabbed his beard and indulged in his kiss as his hands roamed my body.

When he grabbed my ass, I quickly pushed him away and wiped my lips. *What is happening?* I wanted to cry. Lazarus was taking me on a roller-coaster ride, and I just wanted to get off. I felt like I was about to throw up.

"Lazarus—"

"I'm sorry, Kiana. I let my past dictate my future. I trust you, and I believe what you said. I still want to be with you. Fear of being hurt again crippled me. You're not Jamie. I thought I was doing what was best, but last week was hard as hell for me. I can tell that it was hard for you too. This wasn't fair to you, and I apologize for being a selfish ass about it. So, if you still want to pursue something with me, I'm here. If not, then it's probably best that I find another tutor."

The elevator doors opened, and I slowly walked off the elevator, making sure I hadn't imagined everything he'd said.

I turned to him and said, "I'd planned to make this our last session. This has been extremely hard for me, Lazarus."

I walked between the stacks to our table and set my things on the floor next to it. He dropped his bag to his chair and took out his book. The chemistry in that book was the last thing on my mind. I was more concerned with the chemistry between the two of us. I looked up at him and offered him a small smile, then pulled his face to mine by his beard.

Something must have snapped within him because he lifted me to the desk, sitting me on top of it, and kissed me like he'd never done before. If I had been wearing a dress, my juices would have been flowing down my thick legs.

He pushed my legs apart and stood between them, continuing to woo me with his tongue. When he finally pulled away from me, I was so drunk with desire that I wanted to pull my clothes off.

He brushed his hand across my cheek while staring into my eyes. "I promise to never hurt you again, Kiana. I'm so sorry, and I'm going to spend the rest of my days proving just how much you mean to me already."

I wrapped my arms around his waist and laid my head on his chest for a moment. After taking a deep breath, I pulled away from him.

"Let's get some work done, shall we?"

He grabbed my hand, assisting me off the table, then pushed my chair in after I sat. When he sat next to me, I couldn't help but smile as I stared at him.

"Seeing the hurt whenever you looked at me was rough, too. I hope I never have to see that look in those expressive brown eyes again." Once he kissed my lips softly, I opened my book.

Before beginning, I quickly turned back to him. "And I'm extremely proud of you. Congratulations on your pop quiz. I meant it before, but I wanted to sound like I meant it, so that's why I said it again."

"I appreciate all your help, Kiana. Without you, I probably would have failed that shit."

I chuckled, feeling a sense of gratification from his words. "I don't want to be a pharmacist anymore."

His eyebrows lifted slightly. "Really? So you're going to teach?"

"Yeah. I believe it's my calling. It's what God has put me here for."

"*One* of the things He's put you here for, because that can't be it. He definitely put you here for me."

I lifted my hand to his cheek. "I truly believe that. My mama prayed Sunday that God would either have you come back to me or completely take you from me, because she couldn't bear seeing me so depressed any longer. I thought I'd lost you forever, Lazarus, and it was killing me inside. I'm so glad you're back."

"And the only way I'll leave again is if you want me to, and even then, you would have a problem on your hands. I'm not going anywhere. Just let your boy know that I'll fuck him up next time."

I chuckled. "There's no need. I haven't spoken to him since that day. We go to the same church and our parents are friends, so he has definitely noticed that I'm not fooling with him anymore."

"Good. Then we shouldn't have any problems." He looked down at his book, then back at me. "I moved in with my mother so I could take more classes. I'm still working a lot, but I don't have the bills I once had. I'm taking three classes a semester instead of two, and I'm off on Tuesdays and Thursdays."

"That's great. So we for sure have to make sure you do well this semester so we can apply for scholarships. If you have time, maybe we can go get ice cream when we're done."

He grabbed my hand and kissed it. "I'd love that."

He scooted closer to me and wrapped his arms around my waist as I began reteaching him the material. Not long after the first sentence, he nuzzled his nose into my neck, sending chills throughout my body.

"Lazarus, as good as that feels, you're going to have to stop, or you won't learn anything in this book."

He licked his lips as he stared at me. "What will I learn then?"

"What color my panties are. So stop."

He bit his bottom lip then chuckled. "Of all the times to move in with my mother."

"We'll have to either get a room or become extremely creative," I said, moving closer to him. I grabbed his bottom lip with my teeth and sucked it into my mouth.

When I heard the elevator door opening, I pulled away from him and cleared my throat. "That was a sign that we need to get to the reason why we're here."

"You're right. Let's pick up where you left off," he said as he scooted away from me some.

I immediately missed the connection, but I knew that the separation was best. "Before we start, let's set some definitions. I won't be seeing anyone else. I want to be yours, Lazarus. Only yours."

"I won't be seeing anyone else either, so consider it done."

He pecked my lips and tapped his book. I had my man back, and I felt one hundred times better than I had when I got here. I knew the road ahead could have its bumps, but my shocks were prepared to handle them all.

Chapter 11

Lazarus

If I thought we could have gotten away with it, I would have fucked Kiana right there on that table in the library. Although I had to get up early and work fourteen hours the next day, I didn't want to leave her. We were at Baskin Robbins enjoying our ice cream, talking about all the things we'd missed out on. I let her know that I made an A in public speaking, and we shared a celebratory kiss. I could barely keep my lips off her.

This past month had been hell. I'd put myself through it, but I'd convinced myself that she wasn't the one for me, that she was no different than the other women. I'd kept myself busy. I'd even befriended some guys at the basketball courts at school. My schedule had changed at work about three weeks ago, so every Tuesday and Thursday I was free, besides class. I found myself spending a lot of time at the basketball courts. They were short a man one day and asked if I wanted to play, and that was a wrap. Most times when I got to my mama's house, I was showering, eating, and going to bed.

However, I knew when the fall semester started, I would need help with chemistry. Although I had done okay, I hated that fucking class in high school all those years ago, so I knew I would need help now. I was expecting to be able to get someone else. I didn't want to torture myself, especially if Kiana had moved on. When I saw her the week before, I nearly went to the student services building and withdrew from chemistry and got my money back. I just wanted to do well, though. After I saw her, it felt like I couldn't breathe. Visions of her with that guy reentered my mind all over again. I'd done everything I could to avoid her during summer school.

That had been easy to do since I'd volunteered to walk Professor Walker to her car after class. Another guy in our class was able to get there early and walk her from her car to class. Doing that, I had to park in another parking lot. I was only parking in that other lot so I could see Kiana anyway. The other lot was a tad bit closer.

However, the first week of the fall semester, I was quickly reminded of the fact that I would need a tutor. When I mentioned it to my mama, she encouraged me to talk to Kiana, saying it could have all been a misunderstanding.

It indeed was. I was glad that she told me what happened, although I didn't want to believe her at first. I wanted to forget what was developing between us. That night at Cheddar's had brought us closer and had me feeling even more sensitive toward her, which was why I was so hurt about what I saw. Kiana was everything I knew I wanted, so when I saw her with that nigga, I was beyond done. She looked happy with him too, but until recently, I'd never seen her unhappy. Kiana was just a happy person, and there wasn't much that she allowed to throw her off her square. Even that situation with Jamie, while it had thrown her off slightly, she rebounded quickly, snatching her joy back.

The only time I'd seen her hurt was after I'd ghosted her instead of being a man about it and talking to her. It wasn't like she was trying to avoid me. She wanted to explain. I was the one that had behaved childishly and like the broken man I once was. Then I tried to play in her face and have her tutor me, knowing that it was killing her. The shit was killing me too, but I was able to hide it. She wasn't able to do that. Today, I knew I had to do something, say something. She needed to know that I still wanted to be with her. I was just grateful that she was receptive.

I leaned over the table and fed her the last spoon of ice cream from our bowl then stood to put the bowl in the trash receptacle. Once I came back to the table, I helped her from her seat and led her to my car.

"I hate our night has to come to an end," I said before closing her door.

Once I got inside, she said, "I know. Me too. But one good day, it won't have to end. We'll be going home together."

"I wish I could fast forward to that time."

She smiled at me as I started the engine and headed back to the school so she could get her car to go home. On the way, I held her hand the entire time, gently caressing the top of it with my thumb. We were quiet all the way there, and I noticed it was something we often found ourselves doing. Silence was never uncomfortable with Kiana when we were on good terms. Our souls were at peace.

Once we got to the school, I got out of the car and escorted her to hers. Before she could get inside, I kissed her lips and didn't want to let them go.

As she pulled away, I leaned in, causing her to giggle. "Damn. I love kissing you."

"I love kissing you too, Laz. Thank you for ice cream. See you Thursday."

"See you Thursday, Ki."

I kissed her once again, then stepped back so she could get inside of her car. Once I closed her door, I headed back to my car and watched her take off. I smiled the whole drive to my mama's house.

"Lazarus, come forth, boy!"

This. Was. The. Downside. Of living with your mother. She knew I'd had a long-ass day the day before and that I had to work at the club last night. Why she just didn't let me sleep was beyond me.

I hadn't gotten home until three o'clock this morning. I'd gotten to work at the city at four a.m. and didn't get off until six. I had to get to the club at eight. That was enough time to shower, eat, and get dressed. Here it was, ten in the morning. I worked twenty hours, and she wanted me to be okay with six hours of sleep.

I sat up in the bed, and as badly as I wanted to yell, *What the fuck you want?* I checked my attitude and got up. I brushed my teeth and washed my face, then made my way to the kitchen in only my basketball shorts.

When I walked in, there was a plate of pancakes, eggs, sausage, bacon, grits, and sautéed potatoes waiting for me. She set a glass of milk next to it on the table and said, "Good morning, baby. I wanted you to eat good. You always working and just eating what you can. I cooked all this for you."

I smiled slightly. "Thanks, Ma. I appreciate you."

"I'm just proud of you. I'm cooking dinner early.
Kirk is going to join us, and I'd like for you to
invite Kiana. What time do you have to go to work
tonight?"

"Eight o'clock. What time are you wanting to
have dinner?"

"Five."

I nodded, then went back to the room to grab
my phone. She'd never met Kiana, and I'd never
met Kirk, so things must have been getting serious
between them. Kiana and I had been back together
for two weeks, and things were great between us.
We'd spend time together on Tuesdays, Thursdays,
Saturdays, and Sundays. I had yet to go to church
with her, but it was planned that I would go tomorrow morning.

As I made my way back to the kitchen, I saw the
good morning text from Kiana. I smiled slightly
and responded to her.

Good morning, baby.

I glanced up at my mama to see that she was on
her phone. She had a big smile on her face, and I
loved to see it. She was always happy, but now
she seemed more than happy. It made me wonder
if she had even been happy before or if she had
been putting on for her entire life. Maybe what I'd
grown to know her happiness looked like was fake.
I just hoped this man was everything she perceived
him to be. After saying my grace, I dug into my
food before it got cold.

While I chewed, I sent Kiana another text.

Are you busy for a couple of hours this evening before I go to work? My mom wants to meet you, and she's cooking dinner.

I went back to my food as I waited for her reply. I glanced up at my mama and said, "It's good, Ma, but you know that."

"Of course I do, but it doesn't hurt to hear it from someone else to confirm what I already know. Thank you, son."

I chuckled as I demolished the buttery grits. I loved her grits. This whole debate about whether salt or sugar goes on grits was ridiculous to me. They were both delicious. However, I didn't use salt or sugar in their raw forms. I used either butter or syrup, never both at the same time. I didn't use just any syrup either. It had to be Steen's syrup. One of my mom's friends had shown me that when I was little, and it stuck with me.

My phone chimed, alerting me of a text, most likely Kiana's response. I picked it up and checked it.

I always have time for you. What time should I be there? And send me the address.

I smiled and sent her the address. Just as I hit send, I received another text message from an unknown number. When I checked it, I rolled my eyes. I didn't have time for her bullshit.

Hey Lazarus. This is Jamie. Can you please call me when you have time?

I responded a simple couple of words.

Hell no.

I proceeded to block that number. I'd never have time for her ass. I wasn't sure how she'd gotten my new number. If someone at Sprint gave it to her, I was gonna have their job.

"What's wrong, Laz?"

"Jamie just texted me. I'm trying to figure out how she got my number."

"What is so important for her to talk to you about? If solicitors can get your number, it can't be that hard. I told you to let me get at that bitch."

I rolled my eyes. "I ain't tryna bail you out of jail, woman. You'll go too far, and I ain't got time to be running to the jailhouse behind your bullshit," I said, mimicking her voice for the last part of my sentence.

She used to say that shit to me all the time when I was going out or hanging with the guys. *Don't be out there doing nothing stupid, Laz. I ain't got time to be running to that jailhouse behind no bullshit.* I slowly shook my head at the memory while she laughed and swatted my shoulder.

"Shut up, boy! I can handle Jamie Hightower and her bourgeois-ass mama. Act like she just been sitting in the lap of luxury all her life. That white heifer was trailer trash when you met Jamie. Oooh, I didn't like them people."

"Well, tell me how you really feel. Damn," I mumbled as she paced.

She was getting heated just talking about them. I knew she didn't like them, but after Jamie and I split up, her hate rose to unforeseen levels. I think she disliked them more than I did. I actually didn't have anything against her mother. She had never come at me wrong. My mama didn't like her because she believed that she was coaching Jamie. I didn't have proof of that, so I couldn't hold that against her.

As I ate my food, she said, "I have to go to the grocery store. You need anything?"

"No, ma'am. What are you cooking?"

"Don't worry about that. You'll see when it hits the table this evening."

With that, she grabbed her purse and left. I continued eating as my mind shifted to thoughts of Kiana. Mama would love her. I couldn't imagine anyone disliking her. She was so kind to everyone she met and extremely helpful. Her sister, Kinisha, was just as friendly. I saw her on campus sometimes, and she would stop and hug me every time. She seemed to be a little more outgoing than Kiana, though. I watched her on a couple of occasions interact with people on campus. She knew a lot of people, whereas Kiana would speak and keep it moving, similar to the way you spoke to a stranger in passing.

After I finished breakfast, my eyes were extremely heavy. I cleaned my plate out, then cleaned the kitchen. That was the least I could do to repay my mama for the meal I'd consumed. Once I started the dishwasher, I headed to my room to get more sleep. Before I could lie down, though, I needed to hear my baby's voice. Kiana had quickly become so much more to me. That was why my mama was so protective of me. I attached quickly.

Although we were taking things slow, since we were both still pure to one another, my heart was hers. She could have whatever she wanted from me, but this time, I was more than sure she felt the same way about me. Nothing between us was one-sided, or at least it didn't feel like it was. Jamie had been more like the damsel in distress that took advantage of everything I offered, although she didn't really feel as deeply for me as I had for her. Kiana was ready to give me all of her. I just didn't want to force things. I wanted it to be organic.

Me living with my mama and her living with her parents made it hard for that to happen. Getting a hotel room would be us planning it. I was cool with getting it in a car, public places, or wherever. I wasn't sure how she felt about that, though. I wanted to take her right in that library on top of that table. It seemed like she wanted me to, but when she stopped me so we could study, I agreed.

She answered the phone groggily. "Hello?"

"Hey. You fell back to sleep?"

"Yeah. I woke up at six to work on a paper."

"Okay. Get your rest. I was about to go back to sleep too. I'll call you when I wake up—if Natalie lets me stay asleep. Text me when you wake up if I haven't called."

"Okay, Laz."

She sounded like she was already sleeping. I was about to chuckle until I heard her mumble, "I love you."

I remained quiet until I heard the call disconnect. I wondered if she realized what she had said and just ended the call hoping I hadn't heard her. *She loves me?* That admission would have my mind going before I could fall asleep.

I lay back in my bed and stared at the ceiling, evaluating how I felt about her. I knew I cared for her deeply. Love wasn't something I took lightly. Once I admitted that, I would be ready to discuss marriage. When I gave love, I gave it freely and unfiltered. I didn't hold anything back. Until I knew I was sure about the depths of what I felt, I would keep those words under lock and key.

I pulled my comforter over my body and got comfortable, but my eyes stayed fixed on the wall. I was feeling soft inside. Her words, although she wasn't fully lucid, had touched me. I hadn't heard anyone other than my mama say "I love you" in a long time. Over the last few months of our marriage, I didn't recall Jamie ever saying it. If I were honest with myself, I didn't recall her saying it at all after we buried the baby, four years before our marriage's final demise. It was like when we buried him, she buried the love she had for me right along with him.

Hearing them from Kiana had me feeling emotional, but I knew that even if she realized what she'd said, she probably wouldn't bring it up again if I didn't. I also knew there was some truth to it. I could feel it in her words and her touch. I could even feel it whenever she stared at me. A slow smile spread on my lips as I closed my eyes, grateful to feel the very thing I'd always craved. Love.

Chapter 12

Kiana

When I parked against the curb at Lazarus's mother's house, I felt calm. Since it would be my first time meeting her, I thought I would be nervous. We'd talked through Lazarus a couple of times. She'd butted into a couple of our phone conversations with hilarious commentary about Lazarus. Of course, he didn't find it hilarious, but it was like gold to me, especially the story about how this li'l girl had him eating sand because she told him that she'd made spaghetti just for him. He was supposed to pretend to eat it, but because he liked the little girl, he ate it for real.

I laughed so hard when she said that by the time he'd finished throwing up and coughing, he had his own sandbox at home. It also let me know that when he was into someone, he was all the way in. He knew no other way to be. Surely, he knew he wasn't supposed to eat sand. He was five years old. Still, because the little girl that he had a heart for told him that it was spaghetti, he ate it. That was so dangerous, but with the right woman, it was beautiful. So, I was beyond ready to meet Ms. Natalie. She seemed extremely fun.

When I got to the door, I smoothed out my denim dress, then pulled some fuzz that had attached itself to my turquoise nails. I glanced at my matching toenails, then rang the doorbell. The door immediately opened, and I came face to face with Lazarus.

He licked his thick lips. "Damn, Ki. You look beautiful, baby. Come in."

I walked inside, and he pulled me in his arms and kissed my lips. We hadn't seen one another since Thursday evening, but one would think it had been two weeks instead of two days with the way we were behaving. After closing the door, he grabbed my hand and led me toward the back of the house where the kitchen was.

"Mama," he called out, getting her attention.

When she turned around, I smiled, because there was a huge smile on her face.

As she walked toward us, Laz said, "This is Kiana. Kiana, this is my mother, Natalie Mitchell."

She pushed him out of the way and hugged me. When she released me from her embrace, she held me back by extending her arms, giving me a once over. "Kiana, you are so beautiful, girl. Gorgeous."

She looked over at Lazarus and said, "You did good, boy."

I giggled as she pushed him in his arm. "Thank you, Ms. Mitchell. It's so nice to finally meet you."

"Girl, call me Natalie. Make yourself at home. The food is almost ready."

I'd arrived a little early because I was excited about spending time with Lazarus. He led me to the couch, and we had a seat. He brushed my freshly done braids over my shoulder as he stared into my eyes.

"I missed you," he said.

"I missed you too."

I could tell from his gaze that he had indeed heard what slipped from my lips earlier. When it did, I had woken right up. I sat straight up in my bed, ended the call, and started lowkey panicking. If he didn't mention it, neither would I.

I meant what I'd said. I was indeed in love with Lazarus Mitchell. This man was everything I wanted. He was kind, considerate, and sweet. He had an amazing work ethic, and he was extremely disciplined. It was like God had dropped him from the sky and said, *"Here you go, Ki. Enjoy."*

Although I'd never dated anyone his age, it was like it didn't even matter. Most times, I forgot he was twelve years older than me. He looked my age. I knew I would soon have to tell my parents. I didn't want Lazarus to be blindsided with their response, whatever that would be.

I stared up into Lazarus's eyes and asked, "What's on your mind?"

"You."

"What about me?"

"How amazing you look in this dress. How kissable your lips look right now. How I wish we could have some privacy."

His gaze never wavered, and I couldn't handle the intensity of it without losing all restraint. I lowered my eyes to my hands only for him to lift my head by putting his fingertips beneath my chin. He kissed my lips, and I wanted to moan into his mouth.

When he pulled away, he said, "My feelings run deep for you, Ki. When I get to where you are, you will be the first to know. Okay?"

That was confirmation that he'd heard me. "I didn't mean to say that aloud. I didn't want you to feel pressured."

"I don't feel pressured, baby. It actually made me feel light. I haven't heard those words from a woman in years, long before Jamie and I got a divorce." He slid his hand to my face. "Please don't stop saying it. I love how it makes me feel. Your touch, your words, your gaze, I feel it in everything you do. You're an amazing woman, and I'm going to do my very best to keep you happy."

We were interrupted when we heard a male voice in the kitchen. It sounded vaguely familiar to me.

Lazarus frowned. "Must be my mama's new boyfriend. I guess he went through the back door. I wonder how many other times he's snuck in that way."

I chuckled. He sounded like the typical protective son.

He stood from the couch as he continued. "I haven't met him yet, so I'm not waiting for him to come in here. You coming?"

I shook my head. "I'll wait until she escorts him in here."

He twisted his lips, then said, "I'll be right back."

I giggled as he made his way to the kitchen. Today was going to be great. Knowing that he welcomed how I felt about him made me less nervous about it. His past had made him cautious, but I totally understood that. He wasn't the same man that ate sand because a woman he loved said it was spaghetti. I chuckled at the thought of it.

When I heard the gentleman speak again, my curiosity was piqued once again. I was fidgeting, trying to decide if I should just invite myself in the room or wait until Lazarus came back to escort me to the dinner table. The wait was killing me.

Just as I was about to stand, Lazarus appeared. "Dinner is ready, baby. Come on."

He extended his hand, helping me from the couch, then escorted me to the dining area. When I got to the table, I noticed the man was still in the kitchen with Ms. Natalie. I couldn't keep still, and Lazarus noticed.

"You good? You cold?" he asked.

"No . . . I mean, I'm okay."

That voice was so damn familiar. I needed to know who that was. Ms. Natalie emerged with a platter of what looked to be beef roast. Lazarus stood and took it from her, placing it in the middle of the table. She left again and came back with two bowls. One had rice in it, and the other had mustard greens.

It was smelling so good I wanted to start eating without them. However, when the man emerged from the kitchen holding two containers of food, I lowered my head, not believing what I was seeing. Mr. Greer was Ms. Natalie's boyfriend, as in Braylon's happily married father. He was my dad's best friend, and his wife and my mother were friends that worked together. I'd known the man since I was six.

I felt like I was going to throw up. He hadn't noticed it was me until he sat down. His face turned to stone as Lazarus said, "Mr. Greer, this is my girlfriend, Kiana Jordan. Kiana, this is my mother's boyfriend, Kirk Greer."

He stretched his arm across the table and said, "Nice to meet you, Ms. Jordan."

I nodded and said, "Same here."

I couldn't believe he was pretending like he didn't know me. *That jackass! How dare he?* I wanted to blow up his spot so bad, but I knew I couldn't do that right now. I was definitely going to tell Lazarus once we were alone. My entire body was trembling, and I'd lost my appetite. This fraud-ass nigga was making my inner Ki emerge, and that was the last thing I wanted to happen here at dinner.

Lazarus grabbed my plate. "How do you feel about pinto beans, baby?"

"I'm good with everything on the table. It looks and smells so good, Ms. Natalie."

"Girl, what I told you? Na-ta-lie."

"That is going to be hard for me. I was raised to respect my elders . . . until they did something not to deserve it," I said as I glanced at Mr. Greer.

She huffed loudly and rolled her eyes. "I understand. I raised Lazarus the same way. So I guess I'll be okay with Ms. Natalie."

I chuckled quietly as Lazarus stared at me. He'd set my plate in front of me.

"Thank you, Lazarus."

He licked his lips and nodded. He could see that I was bothered. *Ugh!* It was always hard for me to hide how I was feeling.

"So, Ms. Jordan, what do you do?"

I looked over at Mr. Greer, and I wanted to slap the spit from his mouth. He was really trying to play the part and engage in conversation like he didn't know me.

I tilted my head to the side slightly. "I'm a full-time graduate student at Lamar. I'll graduate after next semester."

"What do you plan to pursue?"

"I thought I wanted to be a pharmacist, but that has changed. I'm keeping my same degree plan, but I realized that I enjoy teaching so much more. Tutoring students has given me joy."

"Is that how you and Lazarus met?"

"No. We met at a club. I was going to a bachelor-ette party, and he was working."

Any more questions, you lying sack of shit?

I was steaming. I wanted to blurt out what my issues were with him. However, his next question made me frown hard.

"You seem really young. How do your parents feel about you dating an older man?"

"I'm young, but I'm grown. What Lazarus and I have is pure. It's not filled with lies and deceit. That's hard to find these days, no matter the age bracket. So when you find it, you shouldn't take it lightly. I suppose what I'm saying is that it doesn't matter how they feel about it. *I'm* in a relationship with Lazarus Mitchell, not them."

"Whew, baby! I felt the heat in that answer. They have a problem with Lazarus's age?" Ms. Natalie asked.

"They don't know his age. They've never asked, and I haven't volunteered that information. It doesn't matter. It's not like he's their age or something."

"Okay. Can we chill out on twenty-one questions? Since you're retired Mr. Greer, what do you do to keep yourself busy, besides sneaking in back doors?" Lazarus asked with a frown.

"Laz—" his mom started.

"It's okay, Natalie."

Lazarus grabbed my hand as he mugged Mr. Greer.

Good. Take that shit, jackass!

Lazarus was defending me, and that made me love him even more.

Mr. Greer said, "I do carpenter work and cut some of the older folks' yards in my neighborhood. I also volunteer at the food bank occasionally."

Lazarus turned his attention to me. "You okay?"

I nodded as he rubbed his thumb across my cheek. He picked up my fork and filled it with greens and brought it to my mouth. I opened my mouth as he fed me in front of his mama and Mr. Greer like they weren't there, and it made me tune them out as well. I only saw him.

I grabbed his fork and began feeding him as well. I wanted to straddle him so bad right now. He was taking his time with me, but most of the days I was around him, he had me so horny I would have sex with him in front of an audience. I'd transform into Janet Jackson and be on some anytime-anyplace type of behavior.

When Ms. Natalie giggled, Lazarus turned to see what she was laughing at. She and Mr. Greer were sitting extremely close, and he was saying some things in her ear.

I was really struggling to keep my cool. "Lazarus, can you show me to the bathroom?"

"Yeah, baby."

"Excuse me, y'all."

The moment I stood from my seat, Lazarus put his hand at the small of my back and led me to the front of the house.

"He almost got the fucking business. If I didn't respect my mother, he would have gotten cursed the fuck out. I'm sorry about his questioning, baby."

"It's okay. It made me angry too."

"I can tell. The bathroom is right here. I'll wait for you."

"Thanks, baby."

I went inside and wanted to pull all my braids out. I pulled my phone out of my purse and sent a text to Kinisha.

Guess who Lazarus's mother's boyfriend is . . .

I set my purse on the vanity, then relieved my bladder while I waited for her response. I didn't have to wait long because she was at home doing nothing. She was taking the day off and away from everyone. She said she needed time to herself. We all needed that from time to time. The message came through as I was still sitting there.

Who?

Kirk Greer.

I know you fucking lying!

After handling my business and washing my hands, my phone was ringing. I knew it was her. I answered quickly.

"I can't talk right now, Nisha."

"I just need to ask one thing. What did he do when he saw you?"

"Acted like he didn't know who the hell I was. Now bye."

I ended the call as I heard her gasp. I opened the door to find Lazarus standing there, leaning against the wall with a frown on his face. I pressed my body against his and pulled his face to mine to kiss his lips. He glanced down the hallway and backed me back into the restroom. When he stooped and his hands slid up my thighs under my dress, my body shivered. He kissed my neck as his hands roamed to my ass. He pulled my dress up and looked at my bare ass in the mirror.

"Man, you don't play fair, Ki. Where yo' drawers at?"

"At home."

He turned to the sink and washed his hands, then turned back to me and lifted one of my legs as I quickly grabbed ahold of him. When he slid his fingers into my paradise, my eyes rolled to the back of my head, and I felt like I'd levitated.

He leaned over and kissed my neck and said, "When I finally get to this shit, I'm gon' fuck you up for this."

His aggressiveness had turned me on, and I didn't know how to respond. He slowly pulled his fingers from me and brought them to his mouth. The way he sucked them clean had my clit throbbing.

After fixing my dress, we headed back up front. Before returning to the table, he sucked his fingers once more and moaned softly. If that didn't calm my nerves, I didn't know what would. I was so on edge, though. I needed to feel him inside of me ASAP. The bulge in his pants told me that he couldn't wait either.

Once we sat, he began feeding me again, using the hand that carried my scent. I felt like I was being tortured, but I knew that as soon as possible, Lazarus was going to be taking good care of me, and I couldn't wait.

As I chewed, Mr. Greer said, "I apologize for my questioning earlier. I was out of line. Please accept my apology."

I didn't want to accept shit. He was trying to threaten me. If I told on him, he would tell my parents how old Lazarus was. I'd planned to tell them anyway. There was no way I would have Ms. Natalie looking like a fool. While it would hurt her, I had to tell her. I would also tell my mom. His wife was her friend. If she wanted to tell her, she could. I could see where Braylon got his whorish ways from. Like the old people said, the apple didn't fall far from the tree.

I nodded at him as his phone rang. He silenced it as I glanced at him. I wondered where he'd told Ms. Reneé he was going. Turning my attention back to Lazarus, I smiled at him. I could see he still wasn't really feeling Mr. Greer's apology. I wasn't either, but I didn't want to cause confusion. I would endure the rest of my time here and tell Lazarus about his trifling ass later. In the meantime, I would have to spring on my parents just how old Lazarus was. That was a conversation I wasn't looking forward to.

Chapter 13

Lazarus

It was something about that nigga I didn't like. Besides the bullshit he did to Kiana, asking all those fucked up questions, something just didn't sit right with me. I kept looking him over, and I couldn't figure it out. He seemed phony in a way, and I didn't know why I felt that way about him. I didn't know him. However, I also noticed Kiana's nervousness when he entered the room. It was like she was familiar with him or at least knew of him. If they knew one another, it was obvious that he wasn't supposed to be here.

Her nerves seemed to be eased right now though, since I was stroking her thick-ass thighs under the table. I wanted to slide my fingers in her honey pot again while I fed her. My dick was begging to feed her. Her taste was still on my tongue, and I was already addicted. I wanted more. My body craved her taste already, and my dick was fiending for

something he'd never had. The higher I slid my
hand up her thigh, the more nervous she got. I
could feel the tremble in her thighs.

My mama stood from the table and began clearing dishes and putting food away. Mr. Greer was
helping her. I glanced at him as they walked to the
kitchen. I didn't like his ass.

When I turned back to Kiana, I said, "I want to
feel your insides, baby. Are you ready to proceed
to that level?"

"Been ready, Lazarus."

"Good. How umm . . . do you feel about sexing in
a car or public places?"

"You get me horny enough, anything can happen."

I nodded repeatedly as I tried to feed her more.
"You full?" I asked when she held her hand up.

"Stuffed."

When my mama rejoined us to get the leftover
meat, Kiana said, "Ms. Natalie, the food was delicious. I enjoyed the meal."

"Thank you, sweetheart. Kirk and I are gonna
take a ride to give the two of you some privacy. I'll
finish cleaning the kitchen when I get back."

I frowned slightly, then said, "Okay, but let me
talk to you before you go."

I kissed Kiana's cheek and let her know that
I would be right back, then led my mama to the
front room. I turned around to her, and before I

could say anything, she said, "You really look like your father when you're upset."

My frown seemed to dissipate at her words. She knew what to say to have me eating out of the palm of her hand. I pulled her in my arms and hugged her tight.

"Be careful, Ma. It's something about him that doesn't sit right with me. It has nothing to do with Kiana. He seems fake to me. I don't even know who the man is, but I don't know. Just be careful. Make sure you have your gun and Mace in your purse, and please don't forget your phone."

"Lazarus, everything is okay. Concentrate on that beautiful woman you've been rubbing all over at my damn dinner table."

I frowned as she rolled her eyes. "How many times I gotta tell you? I know yo' ass because I'm yo' mama. Just make sure you protect yourself and only do that shit in your room. She's a nice woman, very mature for her age. I like her."

"Thanks, Ma."

I kissed her cheek, and she walked away from me, bypassing her purse. "Woman, you don't listen. Get your purse."

She huffed, but she came back and grabbed it, putting it on her shoulder. "Happy?"

"Not happy, but I feel better now."

She slowly shook her head then made her way to that fake-ass nigga in the dining area. However, I saw him give Kiana a pointed look like he was low-key threatening her about something. They knew each other, and she was gon' tell me the fuck how.

When they walked out the door, she stood to her feet and took our plates into the kitchen. I could see that she was bothered again.

"What did he say to you? How do you know him?"

She turned to me and lowered her head. I hoped she wasn't about to say that she used to fuck with him or something. How would he know to ask about how her parents would feel?

"Ki, for real. What's up?"

"He's married. The guy you saw me with that day at school is his son. He's my dad's best friend, and I've known him since I was a kid. Him bringing up my parents was him low-key threatening me. I planned to tell my parents before they saw you again, because I didn't want them to find out by your answers to some of their questions. I was going to tell you, but I was going to wait until he left."

I could feel the anger building inside of me. I pulled my phone from my pocket and called my mama, only to hear her phone ringing in the bedroom.

"Fuck!"

She irritated the hell out of me when she left without her phone.

Kiana's nervousness made sense now, and my assumption of him was right. He was a fake-ass, lying-ass, deceitful-ass, punk-ass nigga that needed somebody to knock him off his high horse on his ass. My thoughts were on the same energy as the words of the rapper Bun B at the beginning of the song "Sippin' on Some Syrup" by Three 6 Mafia. Anyway, I was just the man for the job.

I glanced at the clock to see it was already six thirty. I only had an hour and half before I had to be to work. Kiana stepped closer to me, and I roughly pulled her in my arms. She laid her head against my shoulder, and I could feel her relax beneath my touch.

I stooped slightly, then picked her up as she screamed. "Lazarus! Don't drop me!"

"Girl, I got'chu," I responded with a chuckle.

I refused to focus on that shit when I only had an hour left to enjoy her company. I took her to my bedroom and set her on the bed. She took off her shoes as I closed the door, then I watched her scoot back on the bed. Her eyes stayed on mine as she did so. That shit was so sexy. I pulled my polo shirt over my head, revealing my bare chest to her for the first time. She licked her lips as she untied the denim belt around her waist.

I wished I had taken my braids loose so she could grab my hair and run her fingers through it. I wouldn't dare waste time doing that now. As

I unbuckled my belt and dropped my pants, her eyes widened at the sight before her. My shit was painfully hard, and there was some leakage on my boxers.

When I saw her eyes dip there, I said, "You did that shit to me when I found out you weren't wearing underwear."

She smiled slightly as she slowly unbuttoned her dress, making me hot with anticipation. I could feel the heat surrounding my ears as she revealed skin. She didn't have on a fucking bra either. I took off my boxers, stretching the waistband over my erection, and made my way to her. She moaned slightly as she stared at my digging tool. Giving her a show, I grabbed it with my hand and began stroking him.

"Take that dress off, Ki. Unfortunately, time isn't something I have a lot of right now, but I need to experience all this sex appeal you serving."

She stood from the bed and allowed the dress to fall to her feet. My God, she was beautiful. I loved how confident she was, not a shy bone in her body.

"Got damn, you fine."

She put her hand on her hip and asked, "So, what are you going to do to show me how fine I am?"

"Mm. First, I'm gon' suck that pussy. I'm already a fiend. Then, I'm gonna go on an excursion for buried treasures. I plan to touch every part of your body in a short amount of time, so I hope you ready for how fast this shit finna go."

She sat on the bed, scooted to the middle, and lifted her legs and spread them wide. *Shit!* She was ready as hell. I went to the nightstand and strapped up, then made my way to her perfect body. I was ready to get to that cream-filled chocolate between her legs, though.

Easing my way to the bed, I slid over her and kissed her lips as she wrapped her legs around my waist. While I wanted to just shove my dick inside of her, I knew I had to take things a little slower than what I'd told her. It had been a while for her just like it had been for me.

The tip of her nose was red, and her dark nipples were hard as fucking rocks. Just feeling them on my chest was about to drive me crazy. Feeling her nails drag across my back was about to take me to the king. The passion I'd been missing was right here. It was what I had been missing for so long.

As I made my way to her nipples, I pushed her breasts together and sucked them into my mouth simultaneously, teasing them with my tongue as her moans filled the room. They were so sexy. Her soft, airy voice sounded just as passionate as mine did. We were compatible so far, and that only propelled me forward.

I eased my way down her body, kissing and licking every inch along the way. I wanted to make her feel just how much I desired her. When I reached her center, I went in tongue first. I wasn't about to sample shit. I was all in—nose, mouth, and part of my chin. Her fat pussy served like a damn muzzle on my face. She tasted so damn good.

Feeling her nails on my scalp was sending me over the edge, and I knew I needed to stop playing with her and just make her cum so I could have more time for the main course. The appetizer was so damn appealing, though. The shit was delectable. I went to her clit and sucked it like my life depended on it and slid two of my fingers into her paradise, prepping her for the main attraction.

She began squirming and calling out my name like I was the best thing since sliced bread. Hearing my name with so much emotion and love behind it nearly had me cumming in the condom before I could feel her walls crowding my space.

"Lazarus, oh my God! I'm cumming!"

That she did. My beard was soaked, and while I wanted to take my time to indulge in her goodness, I pulled away as her body still spasmed, and I slid inside of her. Her back arched, and she hissed as I allowed my dick to get comfortable in his new home. I kissed her lips, then went to her cheek, ear, then neck.

"You good, baby?" I asked.

"Mm . . . yeeeessss."

When I began stroking her and hearing the sloshing noises, I could barely handle it. "Oh, fuck, Ki. Fuuuuck!"

I lifted her leg in the crook of my arm and dug deeper into her paradise, thankful to be getting this glimpse of what it felt like to be an inhabitant.

"Lazarus, this was worth the wait. Shit!"

Her nails dug into me, causing me to release a growl that rumbled through my body. I was doing my best to restrain my nut, but there was almost nothing I could do at this point. Her pussy was sucking the shit right out of me. The grip it had on me was threatening to end it all. I lifted her other leg and brought her knees as close to her shoulders as possible, then plunged into her shit.

I watched the action as her pussy lips grabbed ahold of me. Watching my dick slide in and out of her was a torment that I wanted to feel forever. It was such a beautiful sight I didn't want it to end. The screams coming from her didn't help the situation.

"Kiana, I'm about to nut, baby. Fuck!"

"Give it to me, Laz! Shit!"

I fucked her harder as I listened to our bodies slap against each other, that clapping sound that said someone was getting fucked. My nut was right at the edge. I started getting dizzy and somewhat lightheaded. It felt like I was about to see stars as my seed exploded into the condom.

Damn. I surely didn't want to go to work now. I wanted to give this shit to her as much as she wanted it. I stroked her cheek with my thumb as I hovered over her.

"I hope it was as good for you as it was for me. Damn, Kiana. I wish you could come to work with me."

"I can't go to work with you, but you aren't going to deny me the right to put in work."

I frowned slightly, trying to figure out what she was talking about as I pulled out of her and pulled off the condom. After getting up and taking the used condom to the wastebasket, I made my way back to the bed.

When I lay next to her, she rolled on top of me and worshipped my dick like it was the only one God had ever made. She slurped it into her mouth and sucked it into a hardened state, then began teasing my shit with her tongue. She caressed my balls with her hand as she stroked the base of my dick with the other.

She can put in work all night.

This shit was fucking me up, for real. She was bringing back the Lazarus of old that knew what he was worth, and I loved that. She began a slow rhythm, sucking my dick like it was leaking honey.

I lifted my head so I could watch the action, and that was when she sacrificed the back of her throat for my satisfaction. The way my dick twitched in excitement, I knew it was going to be a heavy load. When she began gagging, I pulled out of her mouth and shot cum all over her breasts. It was like I was cumming uncontrollably. It was a good thing I didn't let all that fill her mouth.

I squeezed the head of my dick as I stroked it, being sure I'd gotten out every drop while she watched. She licked her lips, then brought her fingers to her chest and smeared it in her skin. She brought her fingers to her mouth and slowly tasted my flavor, making me hard all over again.

I checked the clock to see that it was already seven. I had thirty minutes to get cleaned up. "As much as I want to indulge in you again, I gotta shower."

"I'm going to shower with you. We can make time."

She went to my nightstand and grabbed a condom, then headed to my bathroom before I could take the first step in that direction. I'd unlocked the freak in Kiana, and I couldn't wait to experience even more of her.

I followed her to the bathroom, and when I walked in, she'd turned on the shower. Watching my cum inching its way down her body was sexy as hell. I licked my lips and pulled her to me while we waited for the water to get hot.

"One day, we'll be this way all the time in our own place. I can't see myself ever getting enough of you. I hate that our first time had to be rushed. I'm going to make it up to you."

"Lazarus, it's okay. I know our time is limited. We have responsibilities that we can't throw to the wayside. I get it, baby."

I kissed her lips, then got towels for us. Once we got in the shower, she grabbed my dick and began stroking him back to life. My nigga was practically stuck to my thigh, thankful for the action he'd finally gotten. I hadn't given her all of me yet because I didn't want to destroy her cervix until she'd gotten acclimated to my size. In this shower, I would give her a little more to digest.

She tore the condom open with her teeth as I began washing my beard. I had to multitask. This shit wasn't planned, so I had to do everything over. I couldn't have people getting close to me at the club and smelling my baby's pheromones, getting all excited and shit.

When she sheathed me, I immediately grabbed her by her hips and spun her around and bent her over. Looking at all the ass on her back had me in a trance. I just wanted to see it jiggle. I entered her swiftly and pulled out, seeing her cream practically cover me. I had never seen no shit like that. It was almost like someone had sprayed some damn whipped cream down there. Well, not that much, but fuck. I couldn't concentrate on anything but adding to it.

"Kiana, you so fucking sexy. Damn, baby."

I gave her more of me, and her gasp halted me for a moment.

"Please keep going, Laz. Don't stop, baby. Pleeeeaaase don't stop!"

I began stroking her at a medium pace, then smacked her ass. The way it was twerking on me had me ready to say fuck that job. I dropped my head back as I growled, doing everything in my power to hold my nut.

I pulled out of her, then pulled her up by her braids and kissed her neck. My hands journeyed over her skin, gripping her love handles and rubbing her stomach until I reached her breasts. I cupped them, then toyed with her nipples with my thumbs. Her body was trembling against mine, and I loved every moment of it.

Her desire for me was over the top, and I couldn't wait until I could take my time. I spun her around and stooped to lift her.

"Laz, no. I'm too big for that shit."

I frowned at what she said. "Says who?"

I picked her up and lowered her on my dick as I made my way to the corner for support. "Look at me, Kiana." I slowly stroked her pussy as she opened her eyes and stared into mine. "You're my woman, and there is nothing I wouldn't do for you. Let me determine what I can and can't do with this beautiful body. Just because I'm slender don't mean I'm weak. This definition you see ain't for nothing. If I can bench press four hundred pounds, I can surely bench press your beautiful ass. You hear me?"

"Yes. Yeeeesss, I hear you."

"Good."

I began stroking her faster, giving her more of me while she scratched the fuck out of my back. She might have drawn blood with that shit, but at the moment, all I cared about was getting her to relinquish her final orgasm for the evening. I was about to explode at any minute.

"Ki, cum on my dick, girl. Give me that shit. Talk to me."

"I love you, Lazarus. Oh, shit! I love you, baby. I'm about to cum all over your dick. Fuuuuck!" she screamed.

That shit was filled with so much passion and intensity. The moment her walls tightened around me, she squeezed all the fucking goodness out of me. I fired off without warning as her body convulsed like Satan himself had inhabited her.

As we both panted, I released her legs, and she allowed them to slide down my body while her eyes remained closed and her teeth sank into her bottom lip. The tremble in her breathing told me that her body wasn't done, so I brought my hand between her legs and gently patted her pussy right over her clit. She nearly fell to the floor as her body contorted and squirted out its ultimate satisfaction with the performance.

"Got damn, baby. That was some sexy-ass shit."

"Jeeesuuus. Laz, what are you doing to me?"

"I hope I'm adding to the reasons why you love me."

Grabbing the towel from the metal rack, I squirted a bit of shower gel in it and began washing her body. She quickly did the same for me before getting out so I could rinse off and finish maintaining my beard.

This had to be the best night I'd had in a long time. Kiana was more than I thought she would be. She wasn't as inexperienced as I thought she was. I wasn't disappointed about that shit one bit.

However, my mind had shifted back to Kirk Greer. I couldn't believe he actually thought he would get away with making my mama his side piece. He probably would have gotten away with it longer than this had Kiana not exposed him, but he would have eventually fucked up and exposed himself. The only thing on my mind now was how I was gonna fuck him up on sight the next time I saw him.

Chapter 14

Kiana

Last night with Lazarus was something I would never forget. Although we didn't have a lot of time, every second was filled with passion, desire, and love. Whether he wanted to say it back to me or not, I felt his love for me. He didn't just fuck me. He made love to me, and I couldn't get that shit off my mind.

I was getting ready for church, trying to take my time to make sure I looked my best. Lazarus was supposed to be with me, but I didn't know how this would go. Mr. Greer would be at church because he served on the deacon board with my daddy, and it was communion Sunday. I knew he wouldn't miss it. I was hoping that Lazarus would be able to contain himself.

I was planning to tell my parents about his age after church today. I was scared shitless because the last thing I wanted was a confrontation with my parents. They'd had my respect for my entire life, and they'd given me their respect as well. I didn't want things to get so bad that either of us lost that.

There was no way in hell I could give up the priceless treasure I'd discovered in Lazarus Mitchell. He was the man I wanted, and if for some reason things didn't work out, then at least I would have the experience. I was experiencing grown-up, mature love, and his age didn't have shit to do with that. As long as he wasn't abusive or using me, then I didn't see what the problem was. He wasn't *that* much older than me.

I took a deep breath as I looked at myself in the mirror, and I decided that I should tell them now, before they left for church. I left the bathroom and nearly ran right into Kinisha.

"Girl, where you going in such a hurry?"

"I'm going to tell them about Lazarus."

"Oh, shit. Let me go with you."

I made my way down the stairs, my nerves on edge. My parents were in the kitchen, preparing to leave for church.

"Mama, Daddy, before y'all leave, I have something to say."

They both halted their forward progress. The smiles had gradually fallen from their faces as they stared at me. I knew they were probably thinking the worst, so I quickly blurted, "Lazarus is thirty-six years old."

I swallowed hard as Kinisha held me at my waist. My dad's face hardened, and my mama's jaw dropped.

"Are you serious? He doesn't look a day over twenty-five," my mom said softly.

She was in shock. My dad, however, was steaming.

"What does he want with you then? You're only twenty-four, Kiana. You're barely a grown woman."

"No disrespect, Daddy, but I've been a grown woman since I turned eighteen. I've always been responsible and mature for my age. We mesh so well. He's been through a lot, and he's had to start over in life. His heart is open to me, though, so I know he had to be sent to me by God."

"If he was sent by God, this chaos wouldn't have accompanied him. What has he been through? Drugs? Alcoholism? What?" he yelled.

"He's been married before. His wife took everything from him after he put her through school for ten years. She wouldn't offer him the same courtesy after the sacrifices he made for her. She divorced him."

"Drama. So he's on the rebound. Great. We'll talk more after church, Kiana, but I can tell you now that I don't want you with him. Period."

"I'm sorry, Daddy, but that's not your decision to make. I'm not a child, and I love Lazarus."

He dropped his keys to the countertop as he glared at me. "Love? Girl, are you crazy? So you're willing to settle for a man that has nothing when Braylon is dying to be with you? What kind of judge of character are you?"

"A good one! Braylon has sex with women at *church*! Is that what you want for me? He's the church whore! What kind of judge of character are *you*?"

"Kiana! That's enou—"

"And better yet, your best friend and his father is the archetype! He's cheating on Mrs. Reneé!"

They both stood there stunned as the tears fell down my cheeks. I wasn't giving up Lazarus. If I had to get a better job and move out, I would. They weren't going to keep me from him. I was too grown for this bullshit. I'd never gone against them, but there was a first time for everything. Lazarus was worth every bit of this.

My mother stepped closer to me as she slowly shook her head. "God isn't pleased with your disrespect, Kiana, and neither am I. You owe your father an apology. And . . . that's a bold accusation to make about Kirk."

"I saw him with my own eyes. The woman he's fooling around with doesn't know that he's married because they just met a month or so ago. I will apologize for my tone, but I can't apologize for what I said because I meant every word of it. Lazarus is the man I love. I won't stop seeing him."

"If you wanna throw your life away, that's on you, but you won't do it under my roof. You bringing Kirk into this was the ultimate disrespect, Kiana. I'm hurt that you would do something like that. It pains me to give you that ultimatum, but I cannot allow you to do that from my doorstep," my dad said, breaking my heart.

"I'll start looking for a place then."

I turned to walk away and forgot Kinisha was standing there. When I bumped into her, I saw her tears. I hugged her tightly and was about to walk past her until my mama asked, "Where did you see Kirk?"

I turned back to her as I wiped my face. "At dinner last night. He was with Lazarus's mother. Her first *real* boyfriend since her husband died nearly thirty years ago," I said, throwing up air quotes when I said the word *real*. "He pretended not to know me and asked me a bunch of questions, low-key threatening me, insinuating that he would tell Laz's age if I told on him. I planned to tell you guys about Laz today after church. However, I figured I had better beat him to the punch. It would be much better coming from me than him, even though I didn't know how he would have gotten away with telling y'all that without y'all questioning him about how he knew that information."

I walked away, feeling the lowest I'd ever been. I wasn't going to church today. Leaving my parents' home an entire year before I was ready was going to be scary. I had to do this on my own because asking Lazarus for help was out of the question. His last relationship had started this way, and I refused for ours to be reminiscent of that. He would run in the other direction.

When I got to my room, I sat on my bed and cried my eyes out. My dad had pretty much put me out if I didn't leave Lazarus.

There was a knock on my doorframe, and I looked up to see my mother. She had a look of sympathy on her face as she entered my room.

"This is a lot, Ki. I can't believe you're willing to sever your relationship with us over a man that broke your heart not too long ago."

"Mama, that was a misunderstanding. He saw Braylon with his arm around me and thought I had moved on, like his ex-wife. Because I didn't say anything right away, I looked guilty. I broke his heart first and reminded him of the worst heartbreak of his life."

"How long was he married?"

"Fifteen years. His wife is now a psychologist. Her first name is Jamie."

"Jamie . . . Hightower?"

"Yes. You know her?"

"Yes. She was interning with the psychologist I was seeing. She wasn't very friendly."

"See? Lazarus isn't a bad man. He loved that woman, and she spit in his face. I refuse to do that to him. My heart longs for him. I wish y'all could look past his age and see how happy he makes me. I could see if he were your age."

She slowly shook her head. "We just want what's best for you, Kiana, and I don't believe that he's it. I don't want to see you struggling your last year in school, but your father isn't budging on his ultimatum, and I don't expect him to. He's the man of this house, and if you don't like his decisions and rules, then you need to be the woman of your own place."

With that, she walked out of my room. She didn't make anything better. I thought she'd come in here to say that she was sorry and okay with me being with Lazarus. I stood from my bed and pulled out my duffel bag. I had money in my account that I'd made from tutoring. The only thing I paid for was gas for my car, so I could afford a night in a hotel. I knew staying here until I found an apartment would be like being in prison.

Grabbing my phone, I sent Lazarus a text. I didn't want him to show up at church only for me not to be there.

Hey, Lazarus. Sorry I'm messaging so early, but I'm not going to church.

It was only seven thirty. Since my parents were so involved in church, they attended both services.

As I packed some under garments and clothes for the next day, my phone chimed. I went to it on my dresser to see Lazarus had responded.

Good morning, baby. Why? You feeling okay?

I didn't want him burdened with my shit, nor did I want him to try to talk me out of my decision, so I responded like everything was okay.

I feel fine. I'm just skipping today. I'll call you a little later.

The tears continued to stream down my cheeks as Kinisha appeared next to me. When I looked over at her, I saw that she was fully dressed, but she didn't have on a stitch of makeup. That was unlike her. I knew why, though. She was feeling just as depressed as I was.

"Ki, are you sure about what you're doing? You know I love you, and I always have your back, but I don't want you to make a wrong decision. How well do you know Lazarus? Do you think you can handle living on your own right now?"

I remained quiet as she fired off question after question. When she quieted down, I said, "It's scary, but I have to follow my heart. It may not make sense to you or to them, but it makes perfect sense to me. I'm not breaking any laws by being with him. I'm not dropping out of school or changing who I am to be with him. I'm still smart-as-hell Kiana Solé Jordan. Sometimes matters of the heart aren't so clear cut. But guess what? I don't care.

Y'all can't see it because God didn't give him to you. He gave him to me, and I have twenty-twenty vision."

I walked away and grabbed some shoes from my closet as she remained silent and looked on.

"Ki, where are you going?"

"I don't know. Daddy said I can't stay here, remember?"

"I don't think he meant you had to leave today. Wait until you find a place."

"Kinisha, he's trying to bully me into staying. He knows I can't afford to live on my own. But I'll live in my car before I go without seeing Lazarus."

"But would he do that shit for you? Are you sure that he feels the same way for you?"

"Yes. His mom questioned him about my age also, but guess what? She allowed him to be a man and make his own decisions despite his horrible marriage. Lazarus is a good man, Nisha. I refuse to be controlled. I'm not a teenager."

I threw more clothes in my duffel bag, knowing that I had made a difficult decision look easy. Grabbing another bag, I loaded it with toiletries, makeup, and more undergarments. When I came out of my bathroom, I looked around my room to make sure I had everything I needed. I quickly noticed my laptop and went to it and put it in the carrying case. After grabbing all my chargers for my phone, laptop, and iPad, I stuffed them in my bag.

Kinisha pulled me in her arms as she continued to cry. I had expected her to understand if no one else did. I was wrong in my assumptions.

I grabbed my purse and bags and headed to my car. After loading it, I went back inside to get a blanket and a pillow just in case my car had to be my residence for a while. Kinisha was heading down the stairs, looking like she'd lost her best friend. It felt like that to me too. I didn't know if they would keep paying my phone bill, so talking to her would be out of the question.

What was I doing? I didn't know how I would make it, but loving Lazarus was worth it.

"Since you didn't go to church, you ought to come chill with me at the house."

I'd just gotten settled in a hotel room for the next two nights. My nerves were on edge, and Lazarus had called me before I could call him. I'd been trying to budget the money I had in my account. I had enough for maybe one month's worth of rent and a deposit. That was it. I didn't have any furniture, so I wouldn't have a thing to sleep on. I was going to have to tell him what was going on.

"Okay. I'll be there in a little bit. Have you told your mother about Mr. Greer?"

"Not yet. When I got home from work, she was asleep, and when I woke up, she wasn't home.

That's something I need to tell her face to face. Don't worry. I won't do it while you're here. Are you sure you're okay? You don't really sound like your normally chipper self."

"Chipper? That's a word you use?"

He chuckled. "I couldn't think of anything else other than bubbly. You aren't bubbly, but you *are* happy usually. You don't sound happy, baby."

"We'll talk when I get there."

"Aww, shit. Did I do something? I can't take that kind of pressure."

"No," I said as my voice quivered.

"Okay. Just get to me. Would you prefer I came to you?"

"No. I'm on my way."

I ended the call feeling worse than I already did. Staying in Motel 6 wasn't where I saw myself, but after I realized how much money Residence Inn was going to cost me, I'd quickly made my way up the highway. Love was definitely a damn battlefield. I had no idea that the man I chose to love would cause all this simply because of his age. It wasn't because he was disrespectful or doing anything illegal. I wouldn't date someone like that anyway.

As I made my way to my car, I saw several transients hanging around outside. That shit scared me more than a little bit. I realized just how sheltered I'd been. What if something happened to me in the name of love? This was crazy.

When I got in my car, I took a deep breath, then pulled down my visor to look at myself in the mirror. My eyes were red and getting puffy. At first sight, Lazarus would know that something was seriously wrong.

I couldn't leave him in the dark on this, though. I'd done my best to avoid drama at all costs and be the mature adult my parents had raised me to be, but look where it had gotten me—homeless and not knowing where to go from here. I was in a situation that could break me if I allowed it to.

After backing out of my parking spot, I said a prayer, asking God to please take control. The last thing I wanted to look like was a fool. Nor did I want to hear the "I told you so" that would come from my family.

Chapter 15

Lazarus

I didn't know what was going on with Kiana, but whatever it was had to be serious. She sounded like she wanted to cry, and I didn't like the way it was making me feel. Someone had caused her to be that way. That alone was making me angry, and I didn't know what the problem was. I paced back and forth as I waited for her to get here.

Between her and my mama, I was gonna blow a gasket. Natalie Mitchell was so damn hardheaded. I didn't have a clue what time she had gotten home last night because she never texted me. However, I knew she was home because there were biscuits on the stove when I woke up.

When I heard a car drive in the driveway, I peeked out the window to see Kiana. She was wiping her face like she'd been crying. I didn't have a good feeling about this shit. She said this wasn't about me, but it sure in the hell felt like it would affect me.

I went to the door to open it. The minute I did, she swallowed hard and said, "Hey."

"Hey. Come in."

My heart was soft as shit now, and I only wanted to make her feel better. She went to the couch and sat while I closed the door. When I joined her, I grabbed her hand and kissed it, immediately thinking about how much I had enjoyed last night with her. I was so happy at work they thought I was about to quit. My coworker said a nigga only came to work that happy when he was about to tell some people to kiss his ass. I had to laugh at that shit. Maybe my serious demeanor at work had been because of my drought. I was the happiest I'd ever been. Judging by the look on Kiana's face, I knew that wasn't going to last much longer.

"What's up, baby?"

"My dad put me out."

I frowned. That shit caught me off guard completely. "What? Why?"

"They don't want me dating you. He believes I'm gonna throw my life away by being with you, and I couldn't do that from their house. So, it was either leave you and stay there, or keep you and leave. I chose the latter."

"What did I do to—" I stopped mid-sentence when I realized what had happened. "You told them my age, didn't you?"

"Yeah."

I slid my hand down my face and took a deep breath. I knew where this was going. We hadn't been together long. I couldn't go there again and rescue another woman for her to turn around and bite me. *She's not Jamie.*

"Damn," I whispered. "Why are you leaving? I can't have you going against your family for me, Kiana. You've known them your entire life. I can't let you put yourself through so much heartache. You have a degree to finish and goals to reach. That shit will only defer your dreams."

"What are you saying, Lazarus? Don't break my heart. Please don't prove them right. I'm not asking for help, if that's what you're thinking. I'm going to finish my degree, even if I have to sleep in my car. But I love you. I can't stop seeing you."

"Baby, I don't want to see you struggling. I want what's best for you, just like they do. If they are against us this way, then I'm willing to let you go. I don't want you suffering on account of me."

She stood from the couch and walked down the hallway to the bathroom. My heart was crushed. Letting her go was the last thing I wanted to do. My heart needed her. She was the woman I wanted to build with, but I couldn't allow her to suffer like this.

Her parents were on some bullshit. They were willing to put their daughter out of their house because she wanted to date an older man. They had me sounding like a fucking pervert for pursuing her. Kiana was a grown woman.

She came out of the bathroom and was walking to the door. I quickly stood from my seat and made my way to her.

"Ki, where are you going?"

"Back to my motel room. You're breaking up with me, Laz. What do I need to stay here for?"

"Baby, please don't be like that. I care about you so much. This shit is hurting me too, but I can't allow you to suffer that way."

"Laz! I'm going to suffer regardless! I'm going to suffer without you!"

I pulled her to me and kissed her lips. This shit was so hard. She already had a motel room. I didn't like the sound of that. She was at a motel . . . not a hotel, but a motel.

My heart and mind were at fucking war. I would ask Natalie if she could stay here before I let her sleep in her car. My mama would blow a fucking fuse. She was happy that I was moving on with my life, but I didn't think she would be cool with me moving a woman into her house. It was bad enough I was living there.

My tongue eased into her mouth, and she allowed it. She slid her hands over my cheeks, pulling me in deeper. What kind of man would I be if I allowed her to live in her car? I knew she was thinking at this moment that I had changed my mind, but I had not. I just needed her to calm down for a minute.

When I pulled away from her, I asked, "Where are you staying?"

"Motel 6."

I cringed inside. Homeless people hung around that place all the time, and it just looked dirty from the outside. I swallowed hard, then said, "Kiana, listen to me. You can't stay there, baby. I can't allow that. Go get your money back, and I will pay for you to get a better room for the night. However, after tonight, I need you to make things right with your parents."

She jerked away from me, seemingly in shock. "You're still breaking up with me, Lazarus?"

"Yes, and it's killing me, Ki. I care about you too much to see you suffer, even if that means I have to let you go."

"So this is your only option? You're not going to even fight for me?"

"Baby, how am I supposed to fight for you? You want me to confront your parents? If they won't listen to you, what makes you think they will listen to me? Your dad probably wants to kill me right about now."

"Fine. Stay away from me. I can't tutor you anymore either. I can't believe you're doing this."

Seeing the tears fall down her cheeks was killing me. It didn't help that Natalie was walking in the back door. When I turned to look to see where she'd gone, Kiana bolted out of the front door, running to her car. Before I could get to her, she got in and slammed the door. Just as I reached for the handle, the locks engaged.

"Kiana, please understand."

She put the car in reverse, causing me to take a step back as she sped out of the driveway and burned rubber in the street. I stood there in the same spot for a while, not believing what was happening. I was in shock about what her father had done to her. To us.

I just wanted her to achieve her goals and be successful without worrying about where she was going to live or what she was going to eat. I couldn't be everything for her right now. It was too soon. Although I knew she wasn't asking me for anything, I felt like it was implied. She expected me to step up and say that I would take care of everything. I'd been there, done that, and got burned. It was way too soon.

I walked back inside the house, feeling like shit. My heart was dragging behind me like a tail, holding on by a single blood vessel that could burst at any moment.

The minute I walked through the front door, my mama asked, "Was that Kiana? What's going on?"

"Her parents don't agree with her dating me and told her that it's me or them. If she chooses me, then she can't live there."

"What the fuck?"

"Same thing I was thinking. But I told her to go back home. I can't have her choosing me and suffering. She has shit to accomplish, and that will be damn near impossible to do if she's living in her car. I can't allow that. It's bad enough she's staying at Motel 6 tonight."

"Why is she staying at a motel? They didn't give her time to make a decision?"

"She chose me, Ma. But I can't do this shit again. Not right now. I can't take care of anybody else. I can barely take care of my damn self. This shit is heartbreaking. I broke her heart, and that shit is eating me alive."

"Damn. This is a tough situation. I think you did the right thing, son."

"That isn't all that's bothering me. You know that nigga married, right?"

"Who?"

"Kirk Greer. He's married. He goes to church with Kiana. That's why he felt so comfortable asking her those questions. He was threatening her."

She lowered her head, and I nearly blew a gasket.

"You knew?"

"Not at first. I found out about a week ago. He said that they aren't getting along and that he would be filing for a divorce soon."

"I know you ain't falling for that shit!"

"I'm not, but I'm lonely, Laz."

"Listen. You're a beautiful woman. I assure you that you can pull a nigga that ain't married. You need to send that nigga packing. I would hate to fuck him up on sight. That ain't a good look, Ma. Imagine yourself being in his wife's shoes and finding out some bullshit like that about your husband. You would be hurt like hell. I'm shocked at you. For real."

"I'm sorry. You're right."

"I'm going to my room to lay down. It's been a rough day. I could have lost my forever a minute ago, and I don't know how I'm going to cope with that shit."

The moment I got to my room and flopped on the bed, I called Kiana. I needed her to understand why I was doing this. I would have to make a trip to her parents' house to let them know that I couldn't allow her to struggle that way. It wasn't because they were right. It was a no-brainer for me. I would never want anyone to suffer the way I had when Jamie left me. If I didn't have my mama, depression would have killed me. Kiana didn't need the added stress that me being in her life would bring. I was falling for her, but I was surely going to have to put the brakes on that.

She didn't answer her phone, and everything in me wanted to go to Motel 6 and find her. I couldn't do that. Instead, I knew I needed to talk to her parents. I wasn't going to get any sleep anyway. I got up and put on more presentable clothing and grabbed my phone and keys. I wanted to cry, but I refused to do that right now. My heart was hurting worse than it had been when I left her the last time. I knew I shouldn't bail at the first sign of trouble, but knowing what was at risk was too much. This could very well affect her future. I couldn't have that on my conscience.

When I got to the kitchen, my mama was in a heated conversation with who I assumed was Kirk's punk ass. That muthafucka was bold as fuck to cheat openly in the same city. They'd gone to the movies and out to dinner. For him to be that bold, he'd been cheating for a long time. It was like he had no fear of getting caught. Maybe he'd gotten caught before and his wife stayed. Who knew what the situation was? But I knew it was fucked up on this end of it. I refused to allow my mama to settle for some you-can-have-a-piece-of-my-love type of nigga.

As I proceeded to the back door, she looked up and asked, "Where are you going?"

"To talk to Kiana's parents. They've destroyed our possibilities for right now. If she can wait until she's living on her own, then maybe we can try again. I just don't want to see her struggle, nor do I want to put myself in the same situation all over again."

"She's not Jamie, Lazarus. You can't live in fear that way."

I nodded as she went back to her phone call only to find out he'd disconnected it. She put her phone on the table and huffed.

"What did he say?" I asked.

"That he loved me and would be back for me when his divorce was final."

"Lying muthafucka. I gotta go, Mama. I'll see you when I get back."

"Okay, baby. Be careful and control your temper."

I nodded and walked out the back door. I didn't have a bad temper, but if I was pushed hard enough, I could become volatile, which was why it was perfect that Jamie wasn't home when I'd gone back and found all my things in the garage two years ago. I refused to allow them to take me there. I would leave first. However, I didn't want them to think that I didn't want Kiana. I needed her, but I was willing to do without her if it meant that she would have everything she needed. My woman was staying in fucking Motel 6 because of their bullshit, and I hated that.

When I got there, they were just getting there too. It was nearly two o'clock, so they'd probably gone out to lunch. I got out of my car and headed in their direction. Mr. Jordan looked up and frowned at the sight of me. Mrs. Jordan didn't seem as bothered by my presence.

Once I was close, I said, "Hello, Mr. and Mrs. Jordan. Can I speak to you inside?"

Mr. Jordan walked away from me without a word, but Mrs. Jordan said, "Come on in, Lazarus."

I wondered if she agreed with his decision, or if she was just going along with it because he was the "ruler" of their household, like her opinion didn't matter. She seemed too welcoming to say she shared his sentiments concerning Kiana and me.

After he unlocked the door, we walked inside, and Mrs. Jordan led me to the dining room table. I stood there until they both sat, then I sat as well.

"I'm here because I need you to know that I told Kiana to come back home." I closed my eyes and took a deep breath. "I care for her so much. I'm falling in love with her. But I can't watch her suffer. I would never want anyone to have it as hard as I have. Had I not had my mother, I would have died of depression. She needs y'all. Her giving up your support and practically your love to be with me doesn't sit right with me. I care too much to watch her struggle. I have my hang-ups, and I may not be what or who's best for her. So, you're right about that. She's just right for me, though. It's killing me to do this, but I'll let her go to assure that she's able to finish school without the added stress of where she's gonna live and what she's going to eat."

"So, you aren't man enough to take care of the woman you're falling in love with? Why would she have to worry about anything like that if she has you?"

"I can barely take care of myself right now while putting myself through school. That's something I can't throw by the wayside again. That's my hang up. I did all that for my ex-wife. I dropped out of school after my freshman year to put her through school and take care of her. The deal was that once she was established in her career, she would do the same for me. I don't want to be picking up trash for the rest of my life. Although I make a decent living doing so, I saw more for myself. I should have been a finance director somewhere by now."

Their faces were like stone. There was no emotion in their eyes about my dilemma, but I needed them to understand why I was making the decision to leave Kiana. The last thing I wanted to do was break her heart, or my own for that matter. It felt like I was setting myself on fire by letting her go, but I knew it was something I needed to do for her.

While they didn't seem to be the least bit concerned, I continued anyway. "When it was my turn, she refused to honor her end. She put me out of our house and divorced me, saying that she deserved better. I gave her the best that I could. I'm still trying to recover from that financially. I had to start all over. I can't survive another hit like that. Kiana may decide that she doesn't want to be with me anymore the same way my ex did. I want her to make things right with you and assure that she will be able to finish school and has everything she needs to do so."

I stood from my seat as they stared at me. "Although it hurts me to my heart to let her go, it would hurt me more to watch her struggle. I can't do that to her. She's staying at Motel 6. Please go get her."

I walked out of their house, my heart heavy as hell. The lump was in my throat, and it wouldn't go down. The moment I got in my car, I allowed the tears to fall. My time with Kiana was done, and I could barely live with myself and my decision.

As I left, I saw her sister turning in their driveway. She stared at me with wide eyes, probably wondering why I was there. I was more than sure her parents would give her the wrong perception of why I was there. They would make her believe that I didn't want Kiana and that this was my perfect out.

This shit was painful, and I could barely bear the guilt and hurt of it. Instead of going home, I drove out to the school library. Going to the fourth floor, I found the table in the middle of the stacks of books and just sat there, wishing that things were different, that her parents could see me for the man that I was. Did I think that I deserved Kiana? I didn't. She deserved so much more, but

I was dedicated to proving myself worthy and showing her that I could be all the man she needed and more.

I dropped my head to the table and stretched my arms out in front of me, knowing that I would have to move on from here. *Somehow*. I just couldn't fathom it right now. This shit was eating me alive.

I was susceptible to depression, and I believed it was because my body didn't know how to handle it. It was time to make another counseling appointment. This hurt almost as bad as the divorce had, and that was something I wasn't expecting. I knew it would hurt, but I didn't foresee it being *this* difficult. Maybe Kiana had dug deeper in my soul than I wanted to admit. Maybe I already loved her.

Chapter 16

Kiana

Seeing Lazarus at tutoring with someone else was hard as hell. My heart was aching, and I didn't have the strength to make it stop. While I loved teaching and helping students grasp information that seemed so foreign to them before, I quit. I could no longer tutor, because every time I did, I thought about Lazarus and how our past couple of sessions were filled with affection. The way he wrapped his arms around me while I was explaining something or the way he kissed my lips as his response, saying he understood what I was saying, flooded my soul whenever I was in the library.

Knowing that he had come to my parents' house to explain himself didn't help matters. My dad only condemned him for it and tried to make Lazarus out to be a man that I knew he wasn't. Since he'd left me a month ago, I had barely uttered a word to anyone. I felt like I was dying. My soul had sunk into the depths of depression, and I felt like I was only going through the motions. I wasn't living. Life was "life-ing" the hell out of me without him. He'd become my everything and made me feel emotions that were foreign to me. I still loved him, and I wanted nothing more than to lay in his arms like none of this had ever happened.

The times I'd seen him on campus, he looked just as depressed as I felt. He still played basketball on campus with his friends on Tuesdays and Thursdays, but every other time I saw him, he was alone.

The only friend I had was my sister, but I felt so distant from her right now. When they had showed up at Motel 6 to get me that Sunday evening, I knew that Lazarus had told them where I was. I willingly went back home, knowing that I didn't have a choice. There was no sense in struggling financially if I didn't have Lazarus. He was my whole driving force, the reason I was willing to go through it in the first place.

No matter how much they talked to me, I couldn't seem to verbalize a thing. I only ate once a day, and I had lost fifteen pounds. If I wasn't at school or studying, I was asleep. I just didn't have the energy to do much else. This breakup seemed so final. Last time was bad, but we weren't even a couple back then. This time felt like someone had stolen the breath out of me. All the praying I was doing didn't seem to help. I was a living, breathing, empty shell. My insides had been gutted out like a pig to the slaughter.

I'd cried more than the law should have allowed, and I was surprised that I could still function enough to even go to school or study. At first, I was angry with Lazarus. My brain wanted me to hate him for breaking me this way, but my heart wouldn't allow it. He did what he felt was best for me and him. I knew he was still struggling with some things, and I didn't expect him to take care of me, but as a man, *my man*, he couldn't just watch me struggle. I got that. I understood it more than I wanted to initially.

It was almost time for our Thanksgiving break. I wanted to go to his mother's house just to see how he was doing, although I'd refused his calls. He was calling a lot at first, but now it was sporadically. He hadn't called in two days. It had been over a week since I'd last gotten a glimpse of him, and I missed him like hell. I didn't know what was God's purpose for sending the man of my dreams and allowing him to leave me, but I was doing my best to trust that He was in control. I couldn't wait for His plan to manifest, because this was hard.

As I headed home, I decided to stop at Subway to get something to eat. Eating at home meant that I had to sit at the table and pretend to be happy to be there. I felt like I was living in hell without

Lazarus, and being there only reminded me that it was their fault. The less time I spent with them the better.

When I went inside, I saw a familiar face that made me want to throw up. Mr. Greer and Braylon were sitting there having lunch. I pretended not to see either of them and went to the front to order turkey on wheat.

By the time I got to the cashier, Mr. Greer was standing next to me. "Let me take care of that for you."

I rolled my eyes as he paid for my food without saying a word, then found a table to sit at alone.

Braylon came to the table and said, "You can sit with us. We ain't gon' bite."

I stared at him for a moment, then put my food back in the plastic and walked past him and out the door. *Fuck them*. They were the last people I wanted to be caught fraternizing with. I would sit with the devil himself first.

I got in my car and headed back toward the school. Going home was out of the question. It was still too early. I got out of the car and headed to the bench outside the library. Other than being inside of Gray's Library, this was my place of peace. Although my memories of Lazarus sometimes got the best of me, it was the only place I could go where I could think about my life.

I took small bites of my six-inch sandwich and prayed for stability, peace within, and self-content-ment. I needed to be okay with being alone again. I'd gotten a taste of heaven, then was kicked out to go straight to hell. I bypassed Earth altogether. Nothing about it was gradual either. I went from one extreme to the next.

As I ate my sandwich, I stared off at nothing in particular until I caught a glimpse of Lazarus heading to the library. His tutoring sessions were earlier now. As I stared at him, he looked up and saw me.

Quickly packing up my food, I tried to make a beeline to my car, but he caught up with me.

"Kiana, wait. Hey. How've you been?"

I rolled my eyes only for a tear to fall. I hated not being able to control my emotions, especially around him. Choosing not to respond, I tried to walk away from him. He grabbed my arm and pulled me to him for a hug. What was supposed to be a friendly hug became something totally different when I burst into tears as I inhaled his cologne.

"I miss you so much, Laz. I feel like I'm dying without you," I said hoarsely through my tears.

"I miss you too, baby, but this is what's best, okay? I need you to be strong. You have to gradu-ate and do all the things you planned to do. I'll be waiting. I promise. I ain't going nowhere. I love you, Kiana, and life ain't shit without you."

He held my face in his hands as he gently wiped my cheeks with his thumbs, staring into my eyes. I wanted to kiss him so badly, but I felt like we were being watched. I backed away from him and nodded, then turned to walk away.

He said he loved me.

I looked back to find him still standing there, watching me walk away, but I also saw Kinisha watching us too. I wiped my eyes, then got in my car and tried to finish my sandwich. I felt weak, and I knew it was because I hadn't eaten a full meal. It seemed like I just couldn't eat my meal in peace.

Although I was happy to see Lazarus, interacting with him only made me feel worse. By the time I got home, I'd eaten half of my sandwich, but my appetite was gone. I couldn't stomach anymore of it. I felt like I had to throw up, and I just wanted to go to my room and sleep the rest of the day away. I'd pulled out of all the activities I was involved in at church, so I literally had nothing to do but study. Since I'd had two tests today and two yesterday, I had nothing to really study.

After walking inside, I threw the sandwich in the trash. I glanced around to see that no one was home yet. I was extremely grateful for that. Going straight to my room, I dropped my purse and bag and fell to the bed.

I was so tired of feeling this way. Why couldn't my parents see how miserable I was? It was like they didn't even care. I hadn't said a word to my dad in over a week. I was always sure to be asleep before I knew he would get home. Today he had a deacon's meeting, and my mama would be meeting with the deaconesses. They usually came home before they went to church. Hopefully they wouldn't this time because I could use the peace and quiet.

Getting up from the bed, I went to my ensuite bathroom and started the shower. The weather had been amazing, so I wasn't a sweaty mess like I usually was. It wasn't cold, but it wasn't hot either. There was a breeze blowing. In the shade it was a little nippy, but other than that, I was enjoying the weather and could have stayed in it all day had I not been interrupted. Seeing Lazarus wasn't the interruption. Seeing Kinisha see us was. I could have stayed in his arms forever.

After fully disrobing, I heard the back door closing. I hurriedly made my way to the shower, wishing I could stay in there until they left for church.

Within a couple of minutes, there was a knock on my bedroom door.

"Kiana, I'm coming in."

It was my mother's voice. She knew I wasn't going to respond, so she announced herself before invading my privacy. She then knocked on the bathroom door.

"I just wanted to let you know that Braylon is here to see you."

I couldn't hold my peace. "I don't want to see him."

"He said you were really rude to him and his dad earlier and he knew that wasn't like you. He came to check on you, Kiana."

"Okay. Tell him I'm fine, and I didn't want to keep company with them."

She huffed and said, "You know, ever since you got involved with that man, you've become more disrespectful. I don't like it."

I closed my eyes as I let the water hit me in the face. I hadn't become disrespectful until they did. They disrespected the love between Lazarus and me. He finally told me he loved me at a time when I was unable to experience it.

When I heard the door open, I froze. Why in the hell was she in my bathroom? And while I was taking a shower?

"Kiana, I have a question. Were you a virgin before meeting Lazarus?"

"No."

She exhaled loud enough for me to hear her. There was no sense in lying to her. She had been assuming all these years anyway.

"Have you slept with Lazarus?"

"Once."

"Damn it! He was quick to give you up because he's gotten what he wanted from you. I've told you and Kinisha over and over the importance of saving yourselves for your husbands."

I remained quiet. I didn't care to hear anything she had to say. She needed to be concerned with Braylon and why he was here.

"What do you have to say for yourself?"

"That Lazarus was my forever. The moment I graduate, get a job, and move out, I will be with him again."

"Girl, please. That man is going to move on. He's already gotten what he wanted from you."

"I can't wait to prove you and Daddy wrong. You are two controlling and hateful individuals, and guess what? God isn't pleased with neither of you either."

She snatched the shower curtain back and turned the water off as she glared at my naked body. "You will watch your mouth. I'm two seconds from throwing you out of here."

I slowly shook my head. "Just do it. Save me the misery. To know the people I love don't care a thing about me or the things I want and need in life is depressing. I'm better off alone. I'm tired of being without him. I'm tired of feeling like my world has fallen apart. If you don't want me here, put me out. All because I want to love a man that's thirty-six. He's done nothing to deserve this treatment. We love each other, and no matter what the two of you do, it won't change a thing. So don't act like you're doing me any favors. Put me out if you don't want me here."

She stormed out of the bathroom and slammed the door. I was more than sure I would be out of there by tonight. There was no way they would allow me to stay after this exchange. It didn't matter since I felt alone anyway.

I quickly washed my body and got out of the shower. My dad would probably be home soon, raising hell about what my mom would most likely tell him I said. I was over it.

I had relatives, but I wasn't close enough to any of them to ask to crash with them. My paternal grandparents lived in Louisiana, and my maternal grandmother was in a nursing facility. Her husband died before I was even born.

After getting dressed, I began packing. This time, I was taking my time, packing neatly so I could take more clothes with me. If they didn't put me out, I would be surprised.

As I sat at on the floor folding clothes, Braylon appeared at my bedroom door.

What the fuck is he doing up here?

He walked into my room, slowly shaking his head. "I can't believe you about to let that nigga cause you to lose your family's support."

"I can't believe you're in my bedroom trying to offer your two cents."

"This fly. I always wondered what your bedroom looked like," he said, then chuckled as he looked around.

My room was filled with lighter shades of pink and white. I loved light pink. My ceramic dolls were still sitting on my cedar chest, and there was a huge picture of me standing in front of the Eiffel Tower above my bed. The floors were a rustic white wood, and my walls were white as well, except for the accent wall. It was pink with small gray stripes. I had plenty of figurines, from ballerinas to ponies. I loved dainty things when I was younger, and I chose to keep them.

I rolled my eyes at Braylon's remark. "Why are you here?"

"Slow down, calm down. I'm here to offer you a solution."

He glanced out of the room to make sure no one was in the vicinity. "We can move in together."

"You done lost yo' damn mind. Why would I move anywhere with you?"

"Because I know you in love with Jesus's uncle or friend or whoever Lazarus was to him. I mean, I know there were two of them in the Bible, but from what I understand, he's poor like the one in the parable Jesus told too."

I rolled my eyes and chuckled quietly. "So you know the Bible, Satan?"

"Girl, I'm crushed. But yes. I know the Bible. For the record, I think it's fucked up what they doing to you. Why are parents stricter on their daughters than their sons? My pops knows how I get down and don't have shit to say about it. But Ramsey? He give her hell."

Ramsey was his sister. She was twenty-two, around the same age as Kinisha.

"First of all, your dad isn't perfect."

"I know. I know he fuck around. I caught him. That was what our li'l luncheon was about at Subway today. I may be a lot of things, but I ain't about to get into a relationship if I ain't ready for the shit. He married my mama, so he needs to honor the commitment he made to her and God. He told me that you knew at lunch. While I knew it was nothing for you to blow me off, you weren't usually that way with him."

"I lost all respect for him, Braylon. I couldn't believe what I was seeing."

"Hmm. Me either. He said it was your boyfriend's mother. She broke it off with him. I wanna tell my mama, but for some reason, I think she already knows."

"That wouldn't surprise me. Your mother is so sweet. I hate that she's being subjected to that."

"Me too. But listen, I'm serious. Me and Ramsey are talking about moving out together. She's sick of the tight rope, and I'm sick of that shit for her."

"I can't do that. Laz knows that you're into me. If I moved in with you guys, he would have an entire fit. He said he could tell by the way you looked at me that you wanted me. Thanks for the offer, though, for real."

He nodded as he watched me fold clothes for a moment, then he sat on the floor with me and began rolling my pants up to make room in my duffel bag. I gave him a tight smile and a shoulder bump to show my appreciation. Sometimes comfort came from the most unexpected places, and Braylon was the last person I thought I would receive it from.

As we folded clothes, Kinisha appeared in the doorway. "You're leaving again?"

I shrugged but didn't offer any more words.

She slowly shook her head. "Why you gotta buck the system? Do what you have to do out of their watchful eye and do what they want you to do in their face."

Braylon looked up at her and said, "Shut the fuck up, Nisha. You can do that when you don't have nothing meaningful in your life. When you dick hopping, that shit don't matter."

Kinisha turned red as hell.

"Kiana found something worth fighting for, and I'm envious of the shit, honestly. You ought to be too," Braylon said.

I had no idea she was getting it in like Braylon insinuated. My eyes widened slightly as she stormed off.

He put his arm around me and said, "I got'chu. Don't worry about a thing, okay?"

I wanted to cry, but instead I nodded and thanked God for choosing to bless me by way of Braylon Greer.

Chapter 17

Lazarus

"I don't know why you come to tutoring if you're not going to pay attention, Lazarus. You haven't answered a question I've asked today."

"I apologize, Genesis. My mind is just somewhere else."

She huffed loudly and started packing up her things. It didn't make me no never-mind, since the only thing I could think about was the sadness and depression that was all over my baby. Fuck the past. I had to do something. The way she fell against me earlier, crying her eyes out, had hurt my soul. She was the woman I loved, and I refused to go another day without her. This shit was destroying us both. Maybe after seeing me today, she would answer her phone.

As Genesis made her way out of the library, I gathered my things and did the same, only to walk right into Jamie. When was I going to get a break?

I frowned hard as she stared up at me with sad eyes.

"Hi, Lazarus."

"What's up?" I asked as I moved past her, doing my best to make it to my car before she could answer the question.

"A lot, and I would appreciate it if I could talk to you."

"It seems like you were on bullshit at Cheddar's. If you wanna talk about the same shit you were talking to Kiana about in the restroom, you can miss me with that."

She shook her head rapidly, then led me to the bench— the same one Kiana loved to sit on at times. She angled her body toward mine and said, "I have a dilemma. Actually, I have a couple of dilemmas."

I stared at her, waiting for her to continue as she cleared her throat. I glanced at the time on my cell phone, wishing she would hurry the hell up with whatever she had to say.

"My mama is dying. She lives in Austin now, and I need to move there to take care of her. The house is in both of our names. I never had it changed. So, I took the liberty of drawing up papers to where you could have the house."

I frowned. "So, you just gon' hand it over like that, huh? I would prefer you put it up for sale. You and I both know I can't afford the three-thousand-dollar mortgage. So you just gon' up and leave your practice, huh?"

"No. I lost my practice. I was sued, and I lost my license. I'm surprised you didn't see it on TV."

"I don't have time to fucking watch TV. I'm trying to put myself through school, remember?"

"Lazarus, why are you so cold?"

"Isn't this what you wanted? You said the old Lazarus was too soft. My soft side is reserved for someone else now. Is that all?"

"Yes. I'll let you know when the house sells and provide you with documents to sign and give you a cashier's check for half of the profit. You'll have to answer your phone."

"Leave a message, and I'll call you back if necessary. When you divorced me, it took a long time to get over you, but I did it, so now I need you to respect where I am in my life right now. You had access to all of me and still would have had you not divorced me. I need you to respect that I belong to someone else now. She appreciates me and loves me just the way that I am. I don't really care to see you again unless it's unavoidable or one hundred percent necessary."

I stood from my seat and made my way to my car. The quicker I could get away from her the better. Just the sight of her made me sick to my stomach.

When I got to my car, I couldn't help but think about Kiana. The way she looked earlier had bothered the hell out of me. She appeared to have lost weight, and she looked like she was on the verge of passing out. She needed me, and I needed her as well, because I wasn't doing much better.

I called her, and her phone went straight to voicemail. That was weird. Her phone had never done that. She'd never powered off her phone.

I cranked my engine and headed home so I could pack some clothes for us to stay in a hotel room for the night. I wanted to be there for her in every capacity. I couldn't keep living in fear and neglecting the woman I loved. Her parents would just have to accept the fact that we would be together, or they could kiss our asses.

I called her again and I received an automated message saying that the number was no longer in service. I frowned hard, wondering what in the hell was going on. I knew there was only way to find out, and that was to get to her parents' house and get my woman.

I threw my duffel bag over my shoulder as my mama stood in the doorway.

"Hey, Lazarus. What are you doing?"

"I can't take another day without her, Ma. I promise I won't give up on school, but I can't go on without her, and more importantly, she needs me. I'm going to her parents' house to get her, and we'll stay in a hotel tonight."

"Lazarus, she can stay here. She can be my company when you aren't here. I don't mind. I know y'all are trying to make a way for yourselves. I mean . . . y'all can't be all loud and shit or I'ma kick y'all asses out, school be damned."

I hugged her tightly as she fought me. "Boy, let me go and go get your woman!"

"Come with me."

I grabbed her hand, not waiting for her answer. I knew that if she was with me, I wouldn't take things too far with Kiana's parents. Kiana was suffering big time, and I wondered if her grades were suffering as well. I couldn't have that.

After getting in the car, I decided to tell my mama about Jamie. "Jamie is moving to Austin. She lost her practice, and her mama is dying."

"How you know that?"

"She tracked me down at school."

"What the hell? You know what? It's good for her ass. She used you to get everything she has, and now that shit done been taken away from her. How did she lose her practice?"

"She said she got sued. Apparently, she had to pay some type of settlement, and she lost her license to practice, so all that shit I paid for was for nothing. Thousands of dollars wasted."

"That shit was wasted the moment she put you out of that house. So she's giving you the house?"

"Yeah, but I told her to sell it. We can split the profits. I can't afford that mortgage, and she knows it. That was the house she wanted. I didn't too much care for the house in the first place, but because she liked it, I went along with it. Plus, I didn't want to jump into a mortgage that soon into her career. I was supposed to be going to school, but she wanted that house probably because she was planning to kick me out that bitch as soon as possible."

"You trust her to give you what she owes you?"

"Yeah, because she didn't have to tell me. She could have sold the house and been on her way, and I wouldn't have ever known. I think she's starting to feel guilty about how she treated me now that karma is paying that ass a visit."

"You right, baby. Although I fussed about how you let that woman walk all over you, I'm proud of how you handled that situation. Look at you now, going to fight for the woman you love. This is beautiful. I'm glad I'm here to witness it."

I frowned slightly as I glanced at her. She was fidgeting, and I knew that couldn't be a good sign. She was withholding something from me. It was easy to do because the only day we usually spent an extended amount of time together was on Sundays. I couldn't deal with that right now, though. I needed to stay focused on getting Kiana; then I could shift back to her once this was done.

I parked on side the curb, as I had done before, then got out of the car to head to the front door.

Before I could even get to it, her dad stepped out of it and yelled, "Get the hell off my property! You are not welcomed here."

I frowned, trying to figure out why he was so damn hostile. I didn't go there with that attitude. Kiana's mother came out behind him and grabbed ahold of his arm. She had tears streaming down her face.

I held my arms out to my sides, palms up as I said, "I only came here for Kiana. She's the woman I love, and I can't do this to her anymore. I can't honor your wishes, and I'm sorry. She needs me, and I need her."

"She's already gone. Braylon took her out of here an hour ago. I guess he was more man than you if he's willing to take care of her."

My face had to be red. There was no way Ki would give up on me like that, not after what we shared today. It didn't make sense. I had no rebuttal for his words because my mind was working overtime. Why would she leave with him when she knew that I was waiting for her? Had it gotten that bad around here? Was I too late?

"Now get off my property before I call the police!"

I backed away slowly, my mind doing one hundred miles a minute, trying to make sense of what he said. Kiana had left with Braylon. Was she that desperate to get away from here? Why didn't she call me?

I slowly made my way back to my car and something happened that I'd been trying to avoid. A couple of tears made their way down my cheeks. I let my past ruin my future. My hang-ups had cost me dearly. I lost her.

Before I could get in my car, Kinisha came running down the driveway. "Braylon took her to a hotel. They wouldn't let her take the car. He came over because he found out about his dad's philandering ways and that Kiana knew. She'd gotten into with my mother, and they were putting her out again. He just happened to be here when it happened, so he offered to get her a room. They turned off her phone, but I have Braylon's phone number."

I took a deep breath. *Thank God.* "Thank you. I thought I lost her."

"She loves you too much to forget about you that easily. I love my sister, and I want to see her happy. If that means being with you, then I'm all for it. Take care of her," she said as she handed me a slip of paper with Braylon's phone number on it.

"I'm glad he was here for her. As a friend, right?"

"Absolutely. Not the same Braylon I grew up knowing. I suppose knowing what his dad was doing to his mother matured him in the moment."

She smiled slightly, and I did too.

"Thank you."

She glanced back at the house, then turned back to me. "I don't know who they are right now. They've always been the best parents, but I suppose it was because we always did what they wanted us to do. Now that Ki is trying to make her own decisions, they have a problem with that. She's a grown woman, and she's smart, cautious, and mature as hell. They should trust her judgment. Although I questioned it at first, I trust her."

I nodded, then got in the car and dialed the number as my mama looked on. I could tell she was angry, but she remained quiet, which was so unlike her.

"Hello?"

"Braylon, this is Lazarus, Ki—"

"I know. I took her to Residence Inn. Her suite number is 328. Listen, you're a blessed man to have a woman so strong-willed and beautiful. I told Kinisha if she saw you to give you my number so I could let you know that nothing I did was in attempt to get at her. I know that you saw us a while ago. I always tried to take it there, but she always refused. Above all that though, I know what kind of a person she is, and I knew she needed a friend at this moment. No ill intentions or ulterior motives involved.

"What puzzles me is that her parents know what kind of person she is. They're making it seem like she makes horrible decisions all the time. I'm glad her love for you is this strong. It makes me want the same thing for myself."

"Thanks, man. I appreciate you being there for her and looking out for me. While I know everything you did was for her, you didn't have to talk to me about it. So, thank you."

"No problem, bruh. Go get your woman."

I ended the call with a slight smile on my face. That was maturity at its finest, and I appreciated his honesty in this situation.

"Take me back home, baby. Go spend the night with Kiana. I'll go home and make sure the house is warm and welcoming for when y'all come home. Okay?"

"Thank you, Ma, but what's up with you? You've been unusually quiet, and you've been fidgeting a bit. You've always been a straight shooter. Don't stop now."

She took a deep breath as I drove away from the curb. I assumed she was trying to build up the courage to say whatever it was she needed to say.

"I've been filled with so much grief and hate. It's caught up with me after my last couple of stunts."

I frowned as I glanced at her from the corners of my eyes. "What do you mean, your last couple of stunts?"

"The person that sued Jamie and won was one of my acquaintances from the book club I'm in. I

hated Jamie for what she did to you. So much so
that I was having chest pains. When Tomorrow
told me what Jamie had advised her to do, I knew
she had her ass."

"Tomorrow? That's her name?"

"Yes."

I rolled my eyes and shook my head. Sounded
like some ratchet-ass shit to go along with whatever they did.

She continued. "Jamie advised that woman to
get revenge on the person that had hurt her and
said that it would make her feel better. Then she
would be able to focus on her own healing. The
problem is that Tomorrow ain't all the way right
in the head. The girl needs medication if you
ask me. Jamie failed to diagnose her. The story
Tomorrow had told her about her stepfather was
true. She took Jamie's advice and fucked that man
up with a baseball bat. He's clinging to life. I told
her to sue Jamie. Tomorrow had no idea about my
scheme, but I was hoping Jamie was the quack
that I thought she was."

I took a deep breath, knowing that Jamie had
issues with her real father that she'd told no one
but me about. She'd refused to go to the author-
ities. Whatever Tomorrow had to say about her
stepfather had probably triggered Jamie.

Instead of telling my mother about that and
making her feel worse, I remained quiet. I was

somewhat disappointed in her, but I knew she was looking out for her baby. I should have known that she didn't just let it go like I'd asked her to.

I glanced over at her and asked, "What else?"

"I messed around with Kirk to get back at his wife. She works at the Social Security office and was rude as hell but had the nerve to have all her Christian signs on her desk. She denied my benefits and told me that I just needed to go back to work. She had pictures of her family on her desk as well that I thought I didn't pay that much attention to until I saw her husband in the grocery store. I knew he was married from the beginning. He obviously had no clue that I knew. It just worked in my favor that he was a ho."

My mama was the perfect picture of "hurt people hurt people." Her grief had consumed her and made her bitter, something I was too busy to even notice.

She shook her head and said, "My chest pains got worse. I went to the doctor, and he said I was suffering from high blood pressure and on the verge of congestive heart failure and had I not gone in, I would have eventually had a massive heart attack. That's why I've been cooking lighter and healthier lately."

"I know I've had a lot going on, but don't ever keep no shit like that away from me. You hear me? I need to know what's going on with you, Ma. For

real. I'm gon' always be there for you, no matter
how wrong I think you were for exacting revenge
on Jamie and Mrs. Greer. That wasn't right. I think
you probably had issues before all that bullshit,
but it didn't help matters, that's for sure. I need
to know what's going on as it happens. If I have to
take off work, I will. That shit ain't as important as
you. I love you."

"I love you too, baby. I'm sorry. You know some
of that B-ham ratchetness is still in me."

"Yeah, I know, but it sounds like you need to see
a grief counselor, Ma. Dad has been gone for thirty
years. You have to let go and live."

She nodded as I turned in her driveway. "You're
right, Lazarus. I'm going to get better. I have to if I
wanna be here for when you and Kiana get married
and start having my grandbabies."

I slowly shook my head. I couldn't disagree with
her on one thing she said. I wanted Kiana to be
my wife one day, and I definitely wanted her to
have my children. We would go slow, if possible. I
would start with going to her now and promising
to never neglect her need for me or anything else
again.

Chapter 18

Kiana

If someone had told me Braylon would be the one to understand me and have my back against my parents, I would have never believed it. We hadn't had a serious conversation with one another in years. He was always clowning around and trying to get in my panties. I'd forgotten just how easy he was to talk to. Him knowing about how my parents, mainly my father, were trying to control me had infuriated him. He went toe to toe with my father like it was nothing.

"Mr. Jordan, I'm saying this as disrespectfully as possible. You and Kirk Greer need to get your heads out of your pompous, religious asses and realize that your relationships are lacking. If you can't control a situation, you think there's something wrong with it and everyone that disagrees with you."

My dad walked closer to him with rage in his eyes. I'd never seen him as angry as he seemed to be. The frown lines on his forehead were deep, and his piercing gaze had me stuck in place. I thought he was going to hit Braylon for a moment with the way he balled up his fists. However, Braylon didn't cower in his presence.

"How dare you stand in my house and disrespect me, boy?" my dad asked.

"And that's the problem. Y'all don't see us as adults. Yes, we still depend on y'all to be there for us while we're in school, but we are adults and expect to be treated as such. Kiana is a wise and brilliant woman, not a naïve teenaged girl. If she's making a mistake, let her make it and learn from it. She loves that man. She's a year away from a doctorate, fucking Pharm D degree, and you acting like she still in high school. She's twenty-four, not fourteen!"

"Get the hell out of my house, and since you're so concerned about my daughter and her well-being, take her with you. Let me see how you will support her. She is our responsibility, and as long as she lives under our roof, she will do what she's told. If she wants freedom to live her life on her terms, then she needs to move. That's a very simple concept. You don't like something, then do something to change it."

"I'll gladly take her with me. Y'all don't deserve this angel." Braylon turned to me and said, "Get your shit, Ki."

I didn't hesitate to move. Before I could get to the staircase, my dad yelled out to me. "Since you're so independent now, the car that's in our name will stay here, and so will that phone. You will see just how good you have it here and just how much we do for you. I'm hurt that you are behaving this way, but as parents, sometimes we have to teach hard lessons."

"Daddy, as parents, you should still be willing to be taught lessons as well. You are the be-all and end-all around here, and no one else's opinions or beliefs matter. That's not right."

I continued up the stairs, noticing that Braylon and Kinisha were right behind me.

As I lay in bed, staring at the ceiling, trying to decide what I would do after tonight and what I would eat, there was a knock at the door. I didn't feel like talking to my parents or Kinisha, nor did I feel comfortable with being alone with Braylon for too long in this hotel room. He'd gotten me a nice one-bedroom suite, and I'd thanked him a million times for his generosity. I was just hoping there wasn't an ulterior motive to his kindness. Despite his sexual advances, we'd been semi-close over the years and knew one another well.

Knowing that I didn't have transportation or a method to communicate had me feeling depressed. There were food places in the area that I could walk to, but not being able to call Lazarus was killing me. My cell phone had spoiled me, and I didn't know his phone number by heart. That had me feeling depressed as hell. Maybe I would see him at school tomorrow and could tell him. I had packed as much as I could because I had no intention of going back to my parents' home. While I knew I couldn't afford this hotel, I just felt like God would provide.

Someone knocked on the door again, and the curiosity of who it could be propelled me out of the bed and to the door to look through the peephole. When I saw Lazarus, I nearly flipped my lid. I couldn't open the door fast enough.

"Lazarus!" I screamed as I swung the door open.

He rushed inside with a bag on his shoulder and picked me up, swinging me around. His happiness made me extremely happy.

When he set me on my feet, I asked, "How did you know how to find me?"

"I went to your parents' house looking for you. Kinisha gave me Braylon's number. He told me where to find you. He's a good dude. You're going to come live with me and Mama until we can get our own place."

I chuckled. I had never heard anyone say that about Braylon; however, in this situation, he was definitely a good dude.

"I didn't know what I would do after today, but Braylon told me not to worry. Maybe he was going to contact you if you didn't contact him first. I was praying for a miracle and trying to trust that God would provide. I'm so happy you're here."

I brought my hands to his cheeks and held his face in my hands as I stared at him. He leaned over and kissed my forehead.

"I'm going to stay here with you tonight, but tomorrow you'll come to the house. I have to go to work so, unfortunately, we'll have to get up super early to get your things to the house before that, and my mama will drop you off at school. Get your tutoring job back if you can, and I'll pick you up when I get off work. I usually get off around five. If you're ready before then, I'll ask Mama to scoop you up for me until we can get you some wheels."

"Okay. I don't care about getting up early. I'm going to be with you. That's all that matters. I'm letting go of all that bullshit I've gone through because I have who I want and need in my life. I feel so happy and excited, Lazarus."

"Me too, baby. I had to put aside my hang-ups. I love you, and I refuse to neglect you any longer simply because I was fearful of my past repeating itself. Enough was enough."

"I love you too, Lazarus. So much." I fell against him and hugged him around his waist as he rested his cheek on my head.

"We gon' make this work. I promise. You gon' graduate at the top of your class, and I'm gon' make the dean's list. We're going to prove them wrong. Okay? We know how we feel about each other, and it has nothing to do with age or our backgrounds. It's about our hearts. My heart needs you, Ki. No matter how I tried to move on without you at first, I couldn't. You are the woman I've craved my entire life, and I refuse to let twelve years come between that."

I took a deep breath and relaxed in his embrace for a moment, then lifted my head and led him to the couch. I couldn't believe that we were about to live together. I had wanted it to happen eventually, but not this way. However, maybe being forced into it was a good thing. I didn't know how it would be a good thing, but only time would tell. It was meant for me to be with Lazarus at this very moment.

He wrapped his arms around me, and I relaxed in his embrace. I'd always wanted to just lay in his arms. We'd never really had this opportunity. We were always at school or on the go when we saw one another.

"This feels nice, baby," I voiced.

"It does. We'll get moments like this all the time now. Sharing a bed with you is going to be so amazing. Spooning you at night and waking up to your beautiful face every morning will be like a dream come true. But listen, we gon' have to be extra careful in order to make sure you don't end up pregnant. I've been thinking about our first and last time since you left the house that night."

I chuckled. "Maybe birth control would be a wise investment. I just hope they don't drop me from their insurance."

"They can't until their reenrollment period. When that time comes for me at my job, I'll add you to mine somehow. I don't know if they will accept you being my live-in girlfriend."

"Hopefully, I'll be done with school by then and have a job. If not, then I can always use the clinic at school."

I refused to let any of the small details make me lose focus. While I knew insurance was expensive, I couldn't focus on that. My focus was on finishing school, getting a job, and falling more and more in love with Lazarus as each day passed.

"Ki, they are digging through all my shit, asking if I'm hiding anything. I'm so pissed right now. I don't know what they expect to find by digging through my dresser drawers. I'm disgusted with them, and I swear I can't look at them the same anymore. I find myself doing like you and waiting until the last possible moment to go home. I miss you so much."

I was sitting on the bench outside the library. Kinisha knew exactly where to find me. I'd been gone from home for a few days, and things couldn't be better. Lazarus and I were getting along and adjusting to our new normal, and I was trying to get used to his schedule. Being that we lived together, I just wanted to be under him the entire time. However, I had enjoyed spending time with Ms. Natalie while he was at work this past weekend. When he woke up Saturday, he took me to Sprint so I could pick out a new phone to add to his cell phone plan. I was able to text Kinisha and let her know that I was okay.

We'd gone out to lunch, and he'd loved on me until it was time for him to head to the club. I was so crazy attached to him already that I wanted to get dressed and go to the club with him. I even thought about applying for a job there as a waitress or whatever they called them at the club. I was never a club goer, so the whole vibe was kind of interesting to me. Although the smoke worked my nerves, I had to admit that the time I went when I first met Lazarus wasn't *that* bad. It could be that I was just making excuses to apply there. Working there was only appealing because he was there.

I stared at Kinisha as she rubbed her temples with her fingertips. "Do you have anything to hide? Will they find anything?"

"No. There is never any evidence of what I do behind their backs," she said with huff.

"Then stay calm and let them drive themselves crazy thinking there is. They are the ones with the problem, not you."

"Easier said than done, but I'll try. I'm thinking about moving out and living with Braylon and Ramsey. They have a three-bedroom apartment available at the place they are moving to. Ramsey said they could change the unit they wanted, but I would need to let them know soon. I put in a couple of applications at grocery stores, so hopefully one calls me back. What twenty-two-year-old you know that isn't rich that has never had a job?"

"You'll be fine. Anyone would be blessed to have you as an employee. As far as you living with Ramsey and Braylon, do you think that's a good idea?"

"Not really, but what options do I have? I don't have a Lazarus to come and scoop me up," she said as she nudged me with her shoulder.

"I know, sis, I know. You *can* come spend time with me, though. I think Mama and Daddy are just angry with me and my decisions. Once that wears off, things will go back to normal. They'll get used to me not being around."

I lowered my head for a moment and swallowed the lump in my throat. The thought of them getting used to me not being in their lives hurt. While I was still angry at them, my love for them would never change.

I lifted my head to look back at Kinisha as she said, "Well, I won't. I miss you so much."

"Again, you can come spend time with me and Ms. Natalie when Lazarus is at work."

"That reminds me. Ms. Reneé came to the house yesterday after church. She knows about Mr. Kirk's philandering ways."

"Does she know who he's been seeing?"

"She didn't say she did. I hope she doesn't because she looked like she was ready for war. She said God had her back on this one. If that means what I think it does, somebody's ass is grass. Mama just sat there and cosigned, what she does best. Sometimes I wonder if she even has a mind of her own. I miss the old her when she would take us to the mall and let us buy the stylish clothes before we started getting a body."

I chuckled slightly. The minute my dad saw how my butt was starting to really poke out, he put a stop to that. I didn't understand back then. I was only eleven years old. I'd matured fast, but hopefully I would slow down as I got older, because I looked older than twenty-four.

I grabbed Kinisha's hand. "You're going to make it. You only have a year left of school, right?"

"Yeah, and that shit can't come fast enough."

We sat on the bench hand in hand as the breeze whipped through our hair. It was getting cool outside, and the cooler temperatures were becoming more consistent each day.

I glanced at my phone and noticed my first tutoring session would be starting in thirty minutes, and I needed to call Lazarus before it started. We checked in whenever we could, since we didn't get to see one another as often as we would like, which would be all damn day.

"Kinisha, I have to go, sis. Hang in there. I need to call Lazarus before my tutoring session starts."

"Okay. I love you, and I'll talk to you later."

She hugged me tightly then left. I called Lazarus only for him not to answer the phone. He was probably in the middle of something, so I would wait for him to call me back.

I had twenty minutes before I needed to step inside. It was my first day back tutoring, and I wasn't sure what the student looked like, so I needed to be in a place where they would know that I was a tutor.

As I played a game on my phone, I received a message from Lazarus.

I'll call you in just a few, baby. I love you.

I smiled as I read it, knowing that God was definitely good and loved His children. He proved that when He sent Lazarus to me.

Chapter 19

Lazarus

I'd been at work all damn day, and I was as tired as I-don't-know-what. I was in desperate need of a vacation, and I planned to take one soon. Kiana and I had been working so hard. On Tuesdays and Thursdays, she spent her free time helping me study, and I appreciated every minute of the time she took away from her studies to help me with mine, even after tutoring people nearly all day. Most of her classes were on Mondays, Wednesdays, and Fridays, opposite of mine. We'd been living together for a little over a month now, and the semester was just about over. I couldn't be more grateful. I was more than sure she shared my sentiments.

There had been radio silence from her parents, and I couldn't understand it. She missed them. Although she hadn't said so, I could tell by looking into her eyes that there was some sadness there.

Kinisha would come over on Saturday evenings while I was at work to spend time with Ki and my mama. I felt like that only made Ki long for them more. She'd constantly question Kinisha about their well-being.

Her friends, Braylon and Ramsey, had moved out of their parents' house for the same reason she left. They felt controlled and not allowed to make the decisions they felt were best for their lives. They'd been communicating with her by phone. Kinisha was still hanging in there. I didn't know how she was doing it, but she was. She said the end was right around the corner since she'd be graduating at the end of next year.

Kiana only had one semester left, and I was extremely proud of her. She'd shared with me just how hard she worked to finish her degrees in record time. She took as many classes as she could in undergrad so she could finish sooner. That was impressive as hell. I was struggling with three classes. However, I supposed it was because I was working my ass off, especially on Fridays. I knew the time would be coming for me to quit the club because I was getting worn out. My mama had stressed that I quit a long time ago, but the extra money was helping pay for school. I wouldn't be able to go to school if I killed myself from stress and fatigue, though. I'd been heavily considering her words.

Her journey to health had been going well. She'd been eating as healthily as she could and exercising a bit. I was beyond proud of her. I'd noticed that she seemed a little happier as well. I felt like that was because of the time she spent with Kiana. No one could consistently come in contact with her and remain the same. She was a bright light, full of so much joy and potential. Being around her motivated me to keep striving for my goals, because there were a couple of times this semester that I wanted to just say, *Fuck it*.

To try to help remedy my burnout, on Sundays, they'd let me sleep as late as I could, then Kiana would give me a full body massage. I couldn't forget about the other method of stress relief. Sex with her was off the charts. Although it drained me, it replenished me at the same time. The way she loved me was something I'd never felt. It made me realize that Jamie had probably never loved me. While I understood that people loved in different ways, in my relationship with Jamie, the love I put out was never reciprocated. It didn't feel nearly as strong as this felt.

So, I thanked God daily for bringing Kiana to my life. Despite her youth, she was as mature as they came and somehow, she knew exactly how I needed to be loved. She treated me with respect, and nothing about taking care of her felt odd. Financially, the burden was on me, but what she gave me in return, emotionally and mentally, was worth so much more. She contributed financially too. That tank of gas every week helped tremendously.

I'd gotten to the club an hour ago, and I already wanted the night to be over with, so I could lay up with my baby. Sleeping next to her at night was the ultimate peace after dealing with some of the foolishness I ran into on the weekends. She'd even offered to come sit at the club and chill while I worked just so we could be near each other. I knew that shit wouldn't be a good idea. As beautiful as she was, I knew that someone would have me losing my damn job in there. Niggas would be approaching her left and right, and I wouldn't be paying attention to shit, just her. I was extremely territorial and protective of my queen. Her aura had me stuck. I'd fallen in love with everything about her, even the soft snore that came out of her when she was extremely tired. She was the woman that I wanted to live the rest of my life for, so seeing another nigga all in my territory wouldn't be good.

As I shifted my weight slightly, I noticed Jamie coming through the door. *Aww, shit.* I didn't know what she was up to, but whatever it was it had better be on the up and up. She wore a short, tight-ass dress that dipped low in the front, barely covering her nipples. I had to close my eyes and take a deep breath. This was a woman I once loved, but she was also the person in life that had hurt me the most. With knowing this, I still couldn't make my body aware of that fact. When I saw her, my dick stood at attention.

That pissed me off because his ass was being greedy. Every part of me belonged to Kiana, and just this moment made me feel like I was cheating on her. I didn't know what the hell Jamie was doing here, but I knew I was about to find out as she made her way to me with a slight smile on her face.

When she got close, she said, "Hey, Lazarus."

I gave her a head nod as she cleared her throat. "I'm in town because the house sold. I was going to text you in the morning. We have paperwork to sign at the realtor's office on Monday if you can make it before five."

"I'll make arrangements. Text me the realtor's phone number because I forgot to save it," I said dryly.

"Don't you want to know what it sold for?"

"I figured I would find out when I signed the papers. I can't really be talking to you like this. I'm working."

"I apologize," she said as she shifted her weight, poking out her hip. She wasn't the least bit sorry. It felt like she was fucking with me, and I wasn't appreciative of that shit at all. "We get to split sixty grand. So, that ought to help a lot with your tuition."

I nodded. If she was telling the truth, that would help tremendously. Quitting this job would happen as soon as I got the cashier's check. However, I wouldn't get my hopes up until I spoke to the realtor for myself. I didn't trust Jamie as far as I could throw her ass.

She took her phone from her clutch and sent the number through text. Afterward, she stepped closer to me and said, "I can tell that you still love me and that I turn you on, although you're trying to deny that. She's no match for that."

Taking my eyes off the crowd, I stared down at her. "I fell out of love with you a long time ago. I'm sick of you trying to make it seem like you have some kind of hold on me. I did love you once, but that ship fucking blew up. My woman gives me everything I need, things you never gave me. She knows how to treat a man, a man that loves her. She deserves my love and so much more. You didn't deserve shit, and I gave it to you freely. You bit the hand that was feeding your ass, and now you're miserable because you have to live with that shit. Now get the fuck on before I put yo' ass out of here."

"You know what? Your dick says you still want me, Lazarus. Deny that shit."

"I can't control his ass. Your physical is attractive, but your core is rotten. He does that often when I see something appealing to the eye. However, you didn't nurture my soul. You stabbed me in the heart and left me to bleed to death. Fuck you. Now, let's go."

I grabbed her arm, leading her to the entrance. She snatched away from me.

"Fine. I'll leave. I'm done. When she breaks your heart, don't come running to me."

"I'll run to hell first," I said as my boy, Aaron, approached.

She turned and stormed out of the door as he asked, "Who in the fuck was that?"

"My ex-wife."

"I know you fucking lying. She fine as hell. What did you do to fuck that up?"

I glanced over at him and said, "Everything right."

I walked away, heading back to where I had been standing when she arrived. I wasn't about to get into my past with Jamie. I wanted that shit to stay exactly where it was, in the past. Nothing would make me happier than for her to leave me the fuck alone and disappear the way she'd done when she kicked me out of our house. Once this house business was done, that was what she would have to do. It was the only thing tying me to her evil ass.

***

When I got home, I snuggled up to Kiana and went straight to sleep. The rest of the night had gone okay, but I was tired as hell.

Before she could get out of bed the next morning, I'd indulged in the nutrients her love provided me with. She was ready and willing to give me what I needed from her. The moment my dick slid into her, the memories of the night melted away, and I was once again at peace. Immediately after, I fell back to sleep, not even bothering to get cleaned up.

I woke up two hours later to the smell of food, so I took a shower and was getting dressed to head to the kitchen. It was nearly noon, and I felt rested. I wanted to treat Kiana to a nice dinner at Longhorn Steakhouse. I knew that was one of her favorite places.

Before going to the kitchen, I decided to text the realtor. Although it was Saturday, I wanted to send it before I forgot and blocked out all memories of last night.

Good afternoon. This is Lazarus Mitchell, and I was contacting you about signing documents for the sale of our home. I hope to hear from you soon.

Hopefully, she would message me this weekend, but if not, I knew I could expect to hear from her first thing Monday morning. I needed to text my superior as well to let him know that I would need a day off. I didn't want to miss an opportunity to get Jamie out of my fucking life like she had been. I still had all my vacation time and personal days because I hadn't missed a day. All year, I had been on my grind, trying to make as much money as possible, so there shouldn't have been an issue with me taking a day. Hopefully, he wouldn't give me any flack about it being last minute.

As I opened the door and headed down the hallway, Kiana was making her way to our room. She smiled big as she said, "I was just about to wake you up. I know I usually don't, but we cooked and wanted you to eat before it got cold."

"Thank you, baby. What did y'all cook? Smells like breakfast food."

"It is. That's why we didn't want it to get cold. It doesn't taste so great rewarmed. You can go back to bed afterward."

I pulled her in my arms and said, "Naw. I'm up for good unless you're going to be busy today."

"Nope. I'm all yours, Laz."

"That's good to know. I want to take you to dinner tonight. Although we have finals starting at the end of next week, I wanted to celebrate the end of the semester and a job well done. Plus, I have some other shit I want to talk to you about."

"Okay," she said as I kissed her forehead.

She looked up at me and puckered her lips for another kiss. I obliged her as my phone alerted me of text message. Pulling it from my pocket, I saw it was the realtor. I quickly opened the message as I followed Ki to the kitchen.

Hello, Mr. Mitchell. If at all possible, I was hoping you could come in Monday morning first thing, so we can get this handled. Ms. Mitchell wants this to be done as soon as possible.

That made two of us. I continued reading.

I'm happy that we were able to sell the house above what you owed so you will be due a refund that we will split between the two of you once we've retracted our fees. I hope to hear from you soon.

When I got to the kitchen, I couldn't stop the smile that made its way to my lips. The women in my life had a full spread. While I was happy about the news in the text, I was extremely happy to be treated like a king. My plate was on the table, along with a glass of apple juice.

"Hey, Mama. Thank y'all for this breakfast. It looks good," I said as I took a seat at the table.

I wanted to dig in immediately because I was starving, but Mama pushed my head and said, "So I can't get a proper greeting, nigga?"

I chuckled, then stood from my seat and kissed her cheek as I normally did. She gave me a hard-head nod as I chuckled. That food had sidetracked the hell out of me.

I sat back down, and the two of them joined me as my phone chimed again. It was probably my boss. When I looked at it, I nodded.

He sent: Why don't you just take the week? You work hard, man, and I know you have finals to prepare for. You have the time. Use it and replenish yourself.

I smiled hard, then looked over at Kiana. "I hope you don't get sick of seeing me next week. I'll be on vacation."

Her eyebrows shot up, and she instantly wrapped her arms around my neck. That act alone let me know that we needed this. While we knew we had things we were trying to accomplish, we needed the time together. That was important.

As soon as she released me, I sent a text agreeing with him and thanking him. I also sent a text to the realtor, letting her know that I would see her first thing Monday morning.

I hadn't expected my boss to be so understanding and offer me the week at the last minute. He was never that easygoing. My mind immediately began trying to decipher the tone of his text message, which was damn near impossible. Something had to be up. I'd heard him bitch about people calling out all the time. Most days, he had a bad-ass attitude. If I wasn't such an introvert, I would know more. I stayed out of people's way and didn't really make friends easily. Aaron at the club was different. He wouldn't let me be great in that department. Everyone else just kind of let me be.

Although I had been working for the city for years, most of the guys that I was cool with had long ago moved on. Either they had changed departments or left the city altogether. A nigga named John and I were the only ones that had been there over ten years, and we worked opposite shifts. His long days were my off days.

"What are you thinking about, Lazarus?"

I turned to Kiana. Seeing the concerned look on her face had my words falling from my lips instantly. I never wanted her to think I was keeping anything from her. I truly believed she was my soulmate, and who better to share my dreams, struggles, and concerns with than her?

I frowned slightly and said, "My mind is starting to work overtime, trying to figure out why my boss suggested I take the week off work when I'd only asked for Monday."

"Why did you ask for Monday?" my mama interjected.

"Last night, I had to put Jamie out of the club. She came up there telling me that the house sold and that I would need to sign paperwork. But then she started talking out the side of her neck, and I had to boss up on her ass," I said as I glanced at Kiana.

I could tell that she was thinking hard, so I knew we would be talking about this privately.

My mama rolled her eyes and said, "Stupid bitch."

I ate some of my bacon, then said, "There was a profit that we will get to split. I should supposedly end up with thirty grand. I won't have to work as hard to put myself through school if that's the case. But back to the original subject—"

"Back to the subject my ass. Thirty grand? That's good, right?"

"Yeah, it is. I just don't know how true it is. I won't know until Monday when I go to the office to sign the paperwork. I hope one of you will be able to go with me. I have to go at eight."

"We can both go. Right, Mama Nat?" Ki said.

Whenever she called my mama that, it made me smile. Although this wasn't really a moment that called for a smile, I couldn't help it.

"You damn right, baby," my mama responded as she grabbed her plate and stood. "Y'all need privacy, so I'm gonna go eat in front of the TV."

She walked away as I turned to Ki. I could clearly see that she was uncomfortable. I grabbed the hand she was using to push food around on her plate with her fork. She dropped it and turned to me.

"Talk to me, baby. You know I'll never keep anything from you. I'd planned to talk to you about this tonight, but I suppose it's best if we talk now."

"What did she say to cause you to kick her out of the club?"

"That she knew I was still in love with her and extremely attracted to her."

"Do you still love her?" she asked softly.

I placed my hand on her cheek. "No, baby. You are the only woman I love. I promise you that. You're the only one that has my heart."

She lowered her head, and her hand began trembling. We'd gotten to know one another well, and I knew her nervousness was because she was feeling somewhat insecure in this moment. Me going back to Jamie was her greatest fear. I knew that her parents had thrown that in her face before she left. There was no way I would go back to Jamie. However, I knew that there was another question brewing in that mind of hers. I was nervous about answering because I knew the truth would hurt her.

"What else, baby?"

"Are you extremely attracted to her?"

"I'm extremely attracted to you. Do I still think she's physically attractive? I do, but her insides ruin that."

"I know you well, Lazarus. So tell me straight," she said as she looked up at me.

My heart seemed to drop to my feet as I looked away for a moment. When I looked back at her, I could see her eyes watering.

"She was dressed scantily. When I noticed, my dick got hard," I said softly, being sure that my mama didn't hear me. Although she'd gone to a different room, I knew she was ear hustling.

Kiana turned forward as she swallowed hard and began playing with her food. My appetite was ruined now as well.

I turned forward too as I said, "I'm sorry, Ki. I don't want her. I want and need you. I can't control him at times."

"Then maybe you should wear looser pants."

"As if that would help," I said, trying to get a smile out of her.

I failed miserably. She glanced over at me and slightly rolled her eyes, then stood and grabbed her plate. I stood as well and took her plate from her, setting it on the table. I slid my hands to hers and grabbed them, squeezing gently.

"Baby, please don't be angry, and definitely don't feel insecure. I'm sorry my actions made you feel that way."

"You have a lot of history with her. How am I supposed to feel if just the sight of her still turns you on? I mean, are you reminiscing when you see her? I won't be a part of any back and forth or feeling less than, Laz. It would be different if she was a stranger. I wouldn't feel as threatened. You were married to that woman for fifteen years, in love with her for damn near twenty. How do I compete with that?"

My heart was breaking in two as I listened to how what I said had affected her. I brought my hands to her face and forced her to look at me.

"Baby, you don't have to compete with no-damn-body. You hear me? No woman fucking compares to you. The way you love me is something I've never felt, not even from her."

"Maybe my immaturity in love is finally showing, but I can't believe that you didn't share with her what you share with me at some point in the relationship. Why would you stay married to a woman you felt neglected by for fifteen years, Lazarus? I'm sorry, but that just doesn't sound believable to me." She pulled away from me and picked up her plate again, scraping the remaining food in the trash.

I slid my hand down my face and tugged at my beard as I tried to explain. "I didn't know what love was supposed to feel like, Ki. I just knew how I felt for her. Since she accepted me, I thought that meant that she felt the same way. No one plans to divorce when they get married, and I wanted that shit to work. I didn't realize that I was wrong about how she felt about me until she divorced me. Although we had been having issues, I thought I was sure in the fact that she loved me. When I felt the love you freely gave, I knew that this was different. It's more intense, and it feels like my cup is full all the time. Please don't ever take that away from me, baby. I love you so much, Ki, and I know that no one else will do for me."

She rinsed her plate and put it in the dishwasher, then walked past me, heading toward the bedroom. I scraped my plate out as well and loaded it in the dishwasher as my mama appeared next to me.

"You better fix that shit. That woman is my daughter-in-law and the mother of my grandbabies. I'm not letting her go, so you better hold on tight too."

I huffed because I knew she had been listening. *Nosy ass.* However, she was right. Kiana would have to drag me like dead weight or call the cops to get rid of me, because at this point, we were like Siamese twins. She was stuck with my ass whether she wanted to be or not.

Chapter 20

Kiana

My feelings were hurt. Maybe I was overreacting. I knew he loved me. I knew without a doubt, but what I doubted was how he truly felt about her. It was very possible to love two people at once for different reasons, and the last thing I wanted to be a part of was a fucking love triangle. Although he said he didn't love her any longer, I felt as if he did. Now that she was back, wanting to be with him again, it made me feel nervous and inadequate. It was easy to go back to what he knew instead of trying to continue learning me.

I flopped onto the bed and stared at the ceiling, trying to convince myself that my feelings weren't valid in this moment, that they were extreme and ridiculous. That was extremely hard to do, though, because I deeply felt like they were warranted. However, Lazarus had given me no reason to doubt him. Despite how I felt, the thought of leaving him had never crossed my mind. I couldn't leave at the first sign of trouble. I wouldn't be any better than my parents. That acknowledgment didn't stop me from feeling a certain way.

When the door creaked open, I turned to face the wall. I was nervous about what he would say. The door closed, and then I felt him get into bed with me. The tears left my eyes as I realized how stupid I had been. No man wanted an insecure woman or a woman with trust issues. I trusted Lazarus with my life. Why couldn't I trust him with this?

I quickly wiped my face and turned to him. "Lazarus, I'm sor—"

His mouth collapsed on mine, taking my breath away. I quickly wrapped my arms around his neck. When he tried to pull away from me, I followed him, offering him more of me. He gently separated us and dragged his finger over my lips.

"Ki, I love you. Shit, I love you so much. I would never intentionally do anything that would cause me to lose you. You are my everything, baby, and I don't have a problem reassuring you of that every chance I get. No woman, and that includes Jamie, has the power to pull me away from you. You're the woman I want to marry and have my babies," he said as he slid his hand down my chest all the way to my honey pot.

A soft moan left my lips as I closed my eyes and allowed my head to drop back. I was obsessed with him, and that obsession had made me crazy. I couldn't even bear the thought of another woman turning him on.

After massaging me there for a moment, he brought his hand to my waistband and slid it inside my leggings and underwear. When his fingers slid inside of me, before I could moan, he again covered my mouth with his and offered me his tongue. I sucked it like it was giving me eternal life as he stroked me feverishly with his fingers.

Lazarus had me getting to the point of no return quick as hell as I bucked against his digits. I loved when he got me this heated. However, lovemaking was the last thing on my mind. I needed him to fuck me like I owed him my very existence.

He stopped right before I could cum and brought his fingers to his mouth and sucked them clean. I sat up and quickly pulled my clothes off. It didn't take him long to get on the same wave I was on. He stripped his clothes off, then went to the nightstand drawer to get a condom.

I was so damn horny, I spread my legs and began fingering myself, trying to achieve the orgasm he'd abandoned. My legs were trembling as he pulled my hand from me.

"That's my pussy, Ki. Let *me* get her excited."

I lifted my hips, thrusting his shit at him, desperately wanting him to put me out of my misery. I was so wet it felt like I'd messed up the bed already. My clit was getting all the air she wanted, so I knew she'd emerged without even touching her.

"Lazarus, please," I whispered.

He quickly got between my legs and pushed my knees to my head, entering me at the same time. He released my legs and leaned over me, letting them drop to his shoulders as he began stroking me roughly. My mouth formed into an O, and he quickly covered it with his hand as his pace increased. My legs felt like Jell-O already, and my nipples were hard as hell. I gently pinched them as Lazarus killed my kitty and resurrected her repeatedly.

When my orgasm ripped through me, I nearly bit his damn hand off. The wet noises had filled the room and were bouncing off the walls as Lazarus whispered harshly, "Fuck, Kiana. Shit!"

Once it subsided, he pulled out of me and rolled me over to my stomach. When I felt his tongue in my asshole, I came almost immediately. Whenever he did that, it made me cum in seconds. Although I'd just orgasmed, it didn't disappoint, because I came again. Burying my face in the pillow, I screamed into it, wishing we had our own place so we could freely express what we were feeling.

Lazarus went up on his knees and lifted my hips and slid back inside of me. I bit the pillowcase as I tried to stifle my excitement. The way my walls held on tightly to him, I knew he had to feel the extreme pleasure just as I did.

The smack to my ass caught me off guard, but the sting of it excited me, especially when he said, "This the only pussy I want. The way this thing creams for me, why would I want another? This the shit right here. Every man's fantasy."

He gripped my ass tightly as he wound his dick into me expertly. Seasoned dick was where it was at. His sexual experience made our sessions far better than any other I'd ever had. While I didn't have much experience on the subject, I had enough to know what I liked, and I loved the hell out of Lazarus's dick. His girth filled me perfectly without it being painful. His length took me to ecstasy every time. It was like it was created just for my pleasure.

As he plummeted me, his finger breached my asshole, and I tensed up.

"Relax, baby, and enjoy the ride."

I did what he said as he slowed his pace, taking his time to make sure this experience was memorable. As he stroked my ass, I could feel another orgasm building. I didn't know if I would be able to keep quiet after this one.

"Lazaruuuuus . . . Ooooooh shiiiit!"

He stroked me harder and faster, causing my ass to bounce against him until his orgasm slammed into him as well. "Fuck!" he yelled.

Apparently, he wasn't worried about Mama Nat either. I couldn't hold that in if I tried. As he fell next to me panting, he pulled me to him.

"I love you, Ki. It's me and you forever, baby. I can't wait to start our family."

"Me either," I said as my cheeks heated up uncontrollably.

Knowing that we had the same vision for where our relationship would go was refreshing. This was our first argument, and it wasn't even a real argument. The way we were able to squash it and move past it like adults spoke volumes.

He gently stroked my back as I lay on his chest, watching it rise and fall. Knowing that he would be off next week and we could do this nearly every day made me smile.

"I hope Mama Nat not too mad at us for making noise."

"She'll be a'ight. She told me to come in here and fix it, so she can't be mad with how I chose to do that."

I chuckled at his explanation, then looked up at him. "I really am sorry, Lazarus."

"You don't owe me an apology, Ki. Those feelings were warranted and normal. Never apologize to me for how something I did made you feel. You have every right to feel how you want to feel. If you told me your pussy got wet when you saw your ex, I'd be ready to kill somebody. I understand what you were feeling. I just have to be sure to prove my love every day so there's no room for doubt. I prove it by how I treat you. It's my job to always make sure you feel loved, respected, and cherished. If a time ever comes when you don't, check me about that shit."

I lay on his chest and smiled. He was definitely meant for me.

"Mama Nat was pissed."

"Like I said, she'll get over it. She wasn't as pissed as you think. That's how she plays at times, especially when she fucking with me about something."

"Well, it's a good thing I know how to braid hair because she may decide to not braid your hair next week."

"Naw, she ain't that petty."

I chuckled as Lazarus drove. He was taking me to dinner, and I couldn't wait to see where we were going. Normally, he worked on Saturday nights at the club, but he was off that night since they'd called him in Thursday night. After we had made love, we took a nap, then we studied some before leaving to go eat.

As soon as we had come out of the room, Mama Nat was cutting her eyes at both of us. I was somewhat embarrassed, until Lazarus started picking with her about it, telling her the same thing he'd told me in the bedroom about her saying to fix it.

When Lazarus turned in the parking lot of Longhorn Steakhouse, I nearly came unglued. I wiggled in my seat as he laughed. I loved Longhorn. A good steak always put me in my happy place.

"If I didn't know any better, I'd think you were excited to be here."

I giggled, then leaned over and kissed his cheek as he parked. "Thank you, baby."

"It's the least I can do to show you my appreciation for all that you do for me. I know tutoring me after you've been tutoring nearly all day on Tuesdays and Thursdays has to be taxing."

"It is a little bit, but when you show me your grades, it's worth every minute. Just like it's your job to make me feel loved and all the other things you stated, it's my job to be your helpmeet and make things easier for you to handle. Although we don't have our own place, you are still the man of the house. You work hard, extremely hard. It's the least I can do to show you how much I appreciate you."

He smiled at me and killed the engine. "You can show me how much you appreciate me when we get back home."

"It will be my pleasure, baby."

He got out of the car and walked around to the passenger side to help me out. The moment I stepped out in my jeggings and asymmetrical, sheer shirt, he licked his lips and pulled me into his arms.

He grabbed my ass and said, "You so damn fine. I have to be the luckiest man alive."

"Blessed, baby. Not lucky. Blessed."

"Touché. I agree."

He grabbed my hand and led me inside only for us to come face to face with my parents. It felt like I stopped breathing when I saw them. It had been over a month since I last saw them or even spoke to them. They'd written me off and refused to answer any of my phone calls. It was sad and pathetic. I supposed since I wasn't following their turn-by-turn instructions for my life, I was unworthy of their love.

"Hi, Mama. Hey, Daddy," I said softly.

My dad nodded at me like I was a stranger, but my mom walked closer to me and smiled softly. "Hey, Ki. You look great."

"Thank you. So do you."

She hugged me like one of those Christian hugs, not like a mother would hug her daughter that she hadn't seen in over a month. She nodded at Lazarus as he extended his hand to shake hers. She slid her hand into his and pulled it away quickly when my dad eyed her.

"Hello, Mr. Jordan," Lazarus said.

My dad turned his head and ignored him. I took a deep breath as Lazarus rubbed circles on my back, trying to soothe me. I almost wanted to leave, but there was no way I was going to let them run me away from my favorite place to eat because they couldn't get over themselves. I was tired of kissing people's asses. What I wanted to do with my life was my decision and no one else's.

"How's school going?" my mama asked.

"Great. Never better. I seem to be able to focus better now."

She nodded and accepted the slug I'd just shot as my dad rolled his eyes. I was so hoping that the hostess would escort them to their table soon. I was surprised they were even here tonight. They usually went there on Sundays after church. Whatever the reason for the change, I was sure Kinisha was happy for the reprieve. She said they had calmed down some.

Lazarus and I sat at the far end of the bench to wait for a table, while they stood close to the hostess desk.

"You okay, baby?" he asked as he rubbed my hand.

"Yeah. I just wish my daddy could stop acting like a spoiled child and grow up."

"One day, he'll come around, baby. Just continue to prove him wrong."

"I'm almost afraid that he never will unless I prove him right. Then he'll be able to say that he was right." Lazarus stared down at me as I said, "You don't have to worry about that, though. I would never trade in our happiness for his. Never."

I puckered my lips, and Lazarus smiled, then kissed my lips. When he pulled away, he gently caressed my face. "I don't know how he can ignore such a beautiful creation. God outdid himself when he made you."

I could feel my cheeks heat up as I leaned against him. "You are so good to me."

"And you to me, Ki."

We sat quietly as we waited for our pager to go off. My parents had been escorted to their table. My mama kept stealing glances at us, and I was sure to let her see just how happy I was. It was like she wanted to say something more, but she didn't want to say anything in front of my father. If she wanted to be controlled by that man, that was on her. I hadn't even realized he was controlling me until I wanted to be with and love Lazarus. I only wanted to share my world with the man I felt was sent by God directly to me.

When the pager went off, we stood and went to the hostess desk to be led to a table. As luck would have it, we were seated within view of my parents. We weren't close enough to talk to them, but I could clearly see them and read their lips, something I was really good at. I didn't know why God gave me that talent, but He did. It saved me from many whippings and punishments during my childhood.

My dad again rolled his eyes and said, "Great." Seeing us together was making him miserable for some reason. I couldn't understand what was so wrong with what Lazarus and I had. It was perfect for the both of us.

After the hostess left, the waitress appeared almost immediately and took our drink orders. Once she left, Lazarus grabbed my hand and kissed it.

"So, besides school, what else are we going to do next week?" I asked Lazarus.

"Whatever you want. I mean, I can think of a couple of things," he said with a slight smile.

I giggled. "I bet you can. Maybe we can go to see a movie. I'll have to look up what's playing. I haven't been to the movies in years. Netflix has me ruined."

"You and everyone else."

We continued to talk amongst ourselves as my mother continued glancing at us. I wanted to go and ask her why she was doing that. It was driving me crazy. If she was afraid of Dad, that was her problem, not mine. It was something she chose to put up with, but I almost wanted to believe that she was jealous of me. She didn't have the courage to go against him or stand up to him. I almost wondered if something had happened to cause her to be overly submissive to him.

I wouldn't mind submitting if a man was doing everything he was supposed to as a husband and made me feel like the most blessed woman in the world. But no man, husband or not, was going to keep me from communicating with my kids. She was afraid to even hold a damn conversation with me because of his watchful eye and constant throat clearing. Maybe someone needed to punch him in it to help get whatever was in there out.

The waitress returned with our drinks, then took our orders. I came here often when I lived with my parents, so I already knew the exact cut of steak I wanted and the infamous fried okra. It was seasoned well and was to die for. I had never tasted fried okra so good. When I first saw that it wasn't cut, I was worried that it would be slimy, but to my surprise, it was delicious. I'd been hooked ever since. I convinced Lazarus to order it as one of his sides. The baked sweet potato was my second choice.

I looked up to see my parents in what looked to be a heated discussion. I couldn't see my mom's mouth, but I could clearly see my dad's when he said, "*Tough love never hurt anybody.*"

She was trying to fight for me. That was what I wanted to believe. I continued watching them, waiting for my dad to say something else, so I could at least get part of the conversation. In my peripheral, I could see Lazarus staring at me. I hated that this was taking attention away from him, but I wanted to know what was going on over there. The only thing that kept me seated was me not wanting to make a scene in this restaurant.

"If she wants to throw her life away with that nigga, that's her business. I don't have to have a front row seat. Now, I don't want to hear another word about it, Lisa."

I was about to stand from my seat and go to them, but my mom stood. When my eyebrows shot up, Lazarus turned around to look as well. My mama picked up her plate and walked right toward us. I cleared my throat as I glanced at my man to see him staring at me.

When she got to us, she asked, "Do you mind if I dine with you two?"

Lazarus stood from his seat, and said, "No, ma'am. Have a seat." Since there were four chairs at our table, it was easy to oblige her. He pulled out her chair, and she stared up at him.

"Thank you."

The very moment she sat, she grabbed my hand. "I'm so sorry. Seeing you happy makes this façade hard to keep up. I miss you so much. I was worried about the decision you were making, but it was never my intent to block you out like you didn't exist. You are my first-born child, and this whole ordeal has been painful."

She looked over at Lazarus and said, "Thank you for taking care of my baby. Seeing the two of you so happy and in love makes me happy."

He nodded at her as I squeezed her hand and glanced over at my father. He didn't appear to be bothered, but I could tell that he was. I looked back at her as she awaited my response.

"It's okay, Mama. I miss y'all too."

She stood from her seat and pulled me from mine and gave me a proper hug, one that felt like love. This was what I had been expecting the first time.

She said softly in my ear, "I love you so much, Ki."

I released her and said, "I love you too."

Once we sat, the waitress was arriving with our food. She glanced at my mama, probably wondering where she came from with food already. "Ma'am, will you permanently be at this table?"

"Yes, ma'am, but my bill goes to him over there. I'll take care of their bill."

Lazarus looked at my mother with a slight frown, but before he could say anything, she said, "Don't take it as an insult, Lazarus. It's an apology. We were wrong for what we did to you guys and what we put you through. Whether we agreed or not, we should have supported y'all or at least supported our daughter. We put a hardship on the both of you. An unnecessary hardship. Kiana, you can come get your car."

"What about Daddy?"

"Don't worry about your father. I know it has to be hard trying to make do with one vehicle."

"It's a little inconvenient, but we've been making it work. Mama Nat has been helping us a lot by letting me live there. Honestly, Mama, she's been everything that I've been missing from you. She made the transition so easy. Of course, Lazarus has been amazing. He's the man I'm going to spend the rest of my life with. We're so deeply in love. Even with all of that, I've been missing something. You and Daddy. Kinisha sees me at school, and she comes to the house to visit sometimes, but that's not the same as seeing her every day."

My mama grabbed my hand as I continued. "I miss going to church, but I didn't want to make things awkward since y'all weren't speaking to me. Y'all were so angry, especially with what I said about Mr. Greer. I just . . . it's going to take time to heal from it all. When I think of you and Daddy, the first thing that comes to mind is the hurt. But I know we can change that."

The tears fell from her eyes, but she quickly patted them away with her linen napkin. Once she composed herself, she said, "We will definitely change that. Don't worry about your father. I will work on him. I can't go on like this. I need you in my life, Ki, no matter what decisions you make. You're my daughter, and I need to act like it."

I smiled softly at her then grabbed Lazarus's hand. This dinner had turned out to be more than a celebratory dinner. It had become so beneficial to my relationship with my parents. I was grateful to at least have my mama back. Oh yeah, and my car.

Chapter 21

Lazarus

"That ho better not say nothing to me, or I'm gon' fuck her up. You won't be able to stop me from doing it this time," my mama said.

"If this the type of time you on, I'm gon' leave you here. I'm there to get my money and that's it. All bullshit gon' have to ride."

My mama stared at me for a minute, then turned to Kiana. "I'm going to support you mainly. Lazarus can handle himself."

"Mama Nat, I can handle Jamie if need be. If you feel like you won't be able to stop yourself from strangling her, then stay home. I appreciate you for wanting to support me, though. She got one time to flirt, though. If she does, Laz is going to wish he would have left me home too. I try not to go there, but if I feel even the slightest threat, I go into defense mode and become someone else."

"Lazarus gon' marry a real one this time!"

I stood there shaking my head at them as they laughed and continued to chatter. They were talking about me like I wasn't standing there listening to them. It seemed like the longer Kiana was here, the more she was taking on the attributes of my mother. They were like two peas in a pod. I knew she was clinging to my mama even more because she missed her mama. Thankfully, they were on a journey to healing.

When her father was done eating, he'd come to our table and just stood there, waiting for her mother to join him. That man was stubborn as hell. Hopefully, Mrs. Jordan would be able to talk some sense into him.

"Are y'all done? Ki, you letting Mama's attitude rub off on you. I need my sweet angel back," I said.

"Aren't we going to fight with the devil? Why would a sweet angel be present at a time like this? I'm an angel of war right now."

"That's my girl!" my mama yelled as she high-fived Kiana.

These two were a whole-ass mess. Kiana would probably cool out, though, once we left. My mama had her all gassed up. She was good at that.

"I think you missed your calling. You probably should have been a hype man," I said to my mama as I rolled my eyes.

She pushed me in my arm as I grabbed Kiana's hand. "Don't get dealt with in front of your woman, boy. I'm still the woman that birthed you."

"Come on, baby, before Natalie has me late."

"I got yo' Natalie, nigga!"

I dodged the wooden spoon she threw at me as I laughed and pulled Kiana out the door. Once we got to the car, the smile on Kiana's lips faded a little bit. I didn't address it right away. I wanted to get away from my mama's watchful eye. She rode so hard for Kiana that the slightest frown Kiana made, Mama was jumping all over me, thinking I did something to upset her. I chuckled at the thought of it as I walked around to my side and got in the car.

After cranking up, I turned to her and asked, "Are you nervous?"

"A little. I'm trying to get my guard up and calm my nerves. I'm hoping she doesn't do anything stupid. I don't want to black out on her ass."

"Nat Junior, chill out," I said as I chuckled. She sounded just like my mama. "I'm not going to let her disrespect you without consequences. You are the woman in my life, and she will have to respect that. I got yo' back always, baby. If she deserves to get popped in the mouth, I'll let you handle it." I glanced at her as she frowned.

When we got to the traffic light, she asked, "So you would let me just fight in a public place like that?"

"If she deserves to be handled, then I'm gon' let you do it. That would be way better than me handling her and ending up in jail for sure. As a man, I would suffer swifter and harsher punishment than you would. I don't hit women. So yeah, I would let you handle her, but I wouldn't let you go too far."

She shook her head slowly. "Well, hopefully we won't have a thing to worry about."

"Hopefully we won't," I agreed. "I know I was clear about how I felt about her advances both times that she approached me. I thank God I found you, baby. I don't even want to think about what could have possibly happened had I been single. Being with you . . . shiiiid, a nigga feel like he on top of the world. My confidence was lacking for a long time, and she nearly destroyed me. Knowing that you felt as strongly as you did for me was a confidence booster like none other."

"Have you looked in the mirror lately? Have you evaluated your personality and characteristics? You're perfect, Lazarus, like God stepped out of heaven, molded you perfectly, blew breath into your lungs, and said, 'There will never be another one like this.'"

I laughed as I grabbed her hand and kissed it. "No, baby. You're the one that's perfect. Everything about you makes me swell with happiness. I love you so much."

She smiled and said, "I love you more, Laz."

Within a few minutes, we were turning into the parking lot of the realtor's office. I got out of the car and walked around to help Kiana out. Before I could close the car door, Jamie pulled up a couple of parking spots away from us. The reason I knew it was her was because she didn't have tint on her front windows. She had traded in her Mercedes and was driving a Kia Optima. That was a huge-ass difference. I didn't know how long she'd been without a job, nor did I have a clue about her finances, but clearly, things weren't great for her.

I briefly thought about my mama and how Jamie had lost her license. I couldn't tell Jamie, or else she would really be trying to resurface in my life. I felt sorry for her in the same instant because I knew what she had gone through. I knew without a doubt that conversation had triggered her. I didn't understand how she could become a psychologist and not handle her own trauma. She should have gone to counseling at the very least. That had to be a hard pill to swallow for her.

Her own father had sexually abused her, and she had refused to tell her mother about him. I wanted to believe that her mother knew and that was why she divorced him. However, had she known, it seemed like she would have called the police or taken Jamie to a hospital or doctor's office to be examined. Jamie had told me that it happened when she was ten and that it had only happened a couple of times. A couple of times was two times too many. I remembered holding her quite a bit when she would have nightmares about it early on in our marriage.

As Kiana and I headed to the entrance of the nearly all glass building, I glanced back at Jamie to see her staring at us with a slight scowl on her face. I didn't want to acknowledge that I saw her, but just as I focused my attention straight ahead, Kiana turned to look at her.

"Jesus, be a fence all around me every day. Help Jamie to stay in her place, so I can stay in mine. In your son's name. Amen."

"Amen," I agreed. "When I first met you, no one could have ever told me that you were somewhat violent. You didn't even fit in at the club. Your spirit just didn't gel with everyone else's. Your vibe was floating on top of theirs. But now . . . shit, I think my mama done corrupted you. I feel like I might be dating baby Sugar Ray or something."

She rolled her eyes and pushed my arm as I opened the door for her. I swore this place looked like a damn police station on the outside. However, the moment I walked inside, that thought left my head. The polished cement floors were clean enough to see a vivid reflection of myself, and the African art on the walls caught me totally off guard. Finally, there was a Black-owned realty office in the area, or at least I was hoping anyway.

You didn't run into white people in this area that displayed African art in their places of business. So, if someone white came out of the office, I would be surprised as hell.

I signed in and led Kiana to take a seat on the couch in the waiting area. I wasn't sure why Jamie was still seated in her car, but she needed to come on in. Getting this shit over with was all I could think about. After this, we would be heading to Kiana's parents' house to get her car so she could head to class. Although we hadn't talked to her dad, her mother had said for us to go by there and that the key would be in the garage. Kiana knew the code to unlock it, so she wouldn't need to go inside the house at all.

I grabbed her hand and asked, "You ready to be rolling on your own wheels again?"

"Absolutely. I miss my car. I wonder if anyone has been driving it. Do you have jumper cables in case it won't start?"

"Yeah, I do."

The door opened, and Jamie walked through it wearing shades and dressed like she was here to pick up her millions from a lotto win or something. I wanted to laugh, and I almost did, until my supervisor walked in behind her.

What in the fuck is he doing here?

When he rested his hand at the small of Jamie's back, I knew exactly why he was here. If they thought I was the least bit concerned with whatever they had going on, then they were delusional. However, I knew this could possibly present a conflict of interest.

It made me wonder if this was the reason why I was off this week. Before they could be seated, the realtor was calling us into a conference room. After offering coffee and donuts, the realtor began handing us papers to sign. Jamie and I didn't say a word to one another, and I was grateful for that. I believed that she wanted me to be upset about her new boyfriend. The only way I would be upset would be if I still wanted her. I didn't care who she fucked.

After signing the papers, the beautiful Black woman smiled at us and gave us each an envelope containing our cashier's checks. I opened it to see that it was a little over thirty-two thousand dollars and that the house key was in my envelope. I would have to have it back to the office by next Monday after getting what I wanted out of the house. I thanked her for handling the sale of our house, then stood from my seat and helped Kiana from hers. Floyd did the same with Jamie.

Once we left the office, I felt a hand on my shoulder. I turned to see Floyd standing right behind me.

"What's up, man?"

Without a word, he handed me an envelope. I wasn't sure what the hell it was. When Jamie appeared next to him with an evil smile on her face, I had a slight feeling that this wasn't good. My heart rate quickened and my hand trembled as I held what I knew was probably a termination letter.

I glanced over at Kiana, then proceeded to open it. Just as I figured. They were letting me go from the city. My lip began twitching when I saw that Jamie had filed assault charges on me for the night at the club when I grabbed her.

I had never called a woman out of her name until now. "You evil bitch!"

I frowned as Jamie stepped closer to me. Kiana's grip on my hand tightened as Jamie glanced at her.

"You actually thought I would let you get away with dismissing me like you did? That was your chance to admit everything your sorry excuse for a mother did to ruin my career. I saw her name listed as the reference on Tomorrow's paperwork. I can play tit for tat. Since I don't have a job, now neither do you. Let's see how long she'll stay with you now. You better use that money wisely, Lazarus, because they will probably fire you from the club too. Dre hates having negative attention on his spot. Take what you want out the house. I don't need any of that shit. Unfortunately, my mama passed away yesterday and left me a nice chunk of change. Good luck with everything, and hopefully Natalie and your woman can take care of you while you're in school."

Jamie tried to walk away with Floyd, but Kiana grabbed her by her hair and slapped the piss out of her. I quickly pulled her away from Jamie. I didn't want her getting in trouble on account of me. I felt like weak-ass Lazarus all over again. I was going to have to withdraw from school and find another job. I didn't know how I would if she'd pressed charges on me. I hadn't even been served yet. Just as I thought it, a constable walked through the door and handed me paperwork.

Jamie just stood there holding her face, clearly shocked that Kiana had smacked the shit out of her. Her lip was bleeding and everything. She never once lifted her hand to attempt to hit Kiana back either. She wasn't crazy.

When the constable left, Kiana lunged her way, trying to get another piece of her, but I was able to restrain her.

"You will not get away with this. Only miserable people go out of their way to make other people miserable. This man gave you everything! This is how you repay him? No matter what roadblocks you throw in his path, he's going to come out on top. And you? Bitch, you ain't seen the level you will sink to. I just hope you can recover from it."

Kiana jerked away from me and walked to the car. I unlocked the door, then turned my attention back to Jamie and Floyd. My heart felt like it had completely melted and drained out of every orifice of my body. I felt crippled by her hate for me, and I wasn't sure how I would get through it. However, I couldn't let her see my fear or weakness.

"I can't believe you're just going to allow this, Floyd. You heard what she said. This is about revenge. I didn't assault yo' ass, and you know it!" I yelled as I turned to Jamie.

She laughed, and I wanted to grab her by the neck. Floyd nudged her as a frown graced his face. Apparently, he hadn't known of her plot. She'd probably fed him a bunch of lies about me, and he showed his sympathy by falling off in her pussy.

He looked remorseful as hell now, but he said, "The charges are still there, Lazarus. As long as those charges are there, you can't work for the city. We've already listed your job as being available."

I turned and walked away before they would have had a real reason to file assault charges. When I got to the car, I felt drained, like I had no reason to go on. Maybe I wasn't supposed to go to school. Maybe I was just supposed to be a regular nigga with a regular-ass job. How was I even going to find a job with an assault case pending? I surely couldn't afford an attorney.

Once I got in the car, I rested my head on the steering wheel for a moment. Kiana rubbed circles on my back, but that didn't have the usual tenderness. She was angry, and so was I. But more than anything else, I was worried about my future.

"I'm sorry, Ki. How am I gon' take care of you and go to school without a job? This shit isn't fair. It's not. I don't know where to go from here."

"I know a few attorneys, and I can assure you, you'll have the best. One goes to my church, and she always does pro bono work, especially when someone is being wrongfully accused of something. She loves fighting for the underdog. Her name is Sidney Taylor. I'll get her information for you, and maybe for me too. If she files against me, I'm gonna be pissed that I didn't go all the way in on her ass.

"You don't owe me an apology, baby. We'll figure this out. At least you have money to make it through. That should hold us until I graduate next semester and start working. I got'chu. You don't have to worry about me abandoning you. That's what she wants, and I refuse to let her win. I love you. Now, lift your head, Black king. You got this."

I lifted my head from the steering wheel and nodded repeatedly. Turning to her, I grabbed her hand and said, "Thank you."

That was all I was able to verbalize as I backed out of the parking lot, catching a glimpse of Jamie and Floyd getting into their cars. Hopefully, he would do something about the information he'd heard today. He seemed blindsided by it and clearly upset about it. I was one of his best workers, and everyone in the department knew that. The hard part would be revealing what happened to my mama. She was going to want to find Jamie and kill her ass.

The moment I stopped at the traffic light, Kiana turned to me and pulled my face to hers, kissing me deeply.

Once she released me, I asked, "What was that for?"

"You needed it, baby." She paused for a moment as she looked forward, then mumbled, "To release the tension I had built up too. I could have easily went to work on her ass."

I chuckled, then shook my head. I had never had a woman ride for me like this besides my mama, and despite the situation, it was refreshing.

"Well, this chapter of my life will be done as soon as I get my stuff out of the house and this case falls apart. This money will help out so much. I'd originally planned to quit my job at the club. Now, I need it so I can have some money coming in, if they don't fire me."

She angled her body toward mine and her eyebrows lifted. "You were gonna quit?"

"Yeah. The whole point was to give me an extra cushion while I was in school. With this check, I would have had that."

"I know I've never said anything, but I hate you working there now that we're together. I don't like women ogling you and trying to touch your hair. That's only for me to do."

I chuckled as I listened to her. "Oh, really? It makes you jealous?"

"Not jealous, but I don't want women thinking they have a right to what belongs to me. You belong to me, every part of you. That club was a cesspool filled with ho activity. So many women flirted with you the night I was there, including me. Although my flirting was subtle."

Grateful for the reprieve from the main conversation, I entertained this one. "Yeah. It was so subtle I barely noticed. I just thought you were being friendly until I saw you at the school. I was interested that night too. There's no way I would have gone through that much trouble for anyone else. I was at work, though, so I couldn't really come at'chu like that."

"Hmm. That's good to know. I just took it as you were shy or reserved."

"What grown-ass man calls himself shy? I mean, I'll say I'm reserved or quiet until I get to know a person, but I'll never say that I'm shy."

She frowned as she stared at me. "Isn't that the same thing, though?"

"No. I'm reserved and observant. I like to have at least an inkling of who I'm talking to. I could tell immediately that you were a good girl, though. I realized later that you were a bad girl sometimes too," I said as I wriggled my eyebrows. "My kind of woman."

She chuckled and slowly shook her head and turned to look out of the window. I knew that her mind was switching gears. We were headed to her parents' house to get her car. She was preparing to face her father. Although he was supposed to be at work, apparently she thought it was a possibility that he would be at home.

"Baby, you good?"

"I'm okay. This is just surreal that I'm finally getting my car. I didn't think I would ever get it back."

"And if you didn't get it back, we would have made sure you got another one. I was already saving for it." I lowered my head slightly and swallowed hard, realizing that without a job, I wouldn't have been able to do a thing. I was grateful her mother had finally come around.

"I would have waited until I started working to get a car. I would rather not put unnecessary burdens on you. Things were going just fine with one vehicle. Mama Nat and I enjoy time together. We stop and get breakfast every Monday, Wednesday, and Friday, so it was working."

"I'm happy y'all get along. That was one of my biggest worries. My mama can be somewhat confrontational, so when she suggested that you move in with us, I was iffy about that. When I saw how well the two of you were getting along, I was relieved."

She nodded. "I love her. She didn't know me, but she was there for me when my own mother wasn't. I'll never forget that. She even told me that my mom would eventually come around. No good mother could stay away from her child for something that frivolous."

"Frivolous? She used that word?"

"No. I don't remember exactly how she said it, but it was along those lines."

"I didn't think so. Natalie don't say words like that. Don't be tryna make my mama sound bourgeois."

She laughed, and I did too. Within seconds, we were turning in her people's driveway. Once I killed my engine, their garage door went up, and her parents were standing there in front of a car with a bow on it. It wasn't her old car.

Her hand went to her mouth, and it was then that I knew this moment would be more than she thought it would be. It would be filled with love and forgiveness, and I was all for that. My baby needed to heal from this. With her dad on board, I knew there was a much better chance of that happening now.

I smiled at her as the tears streamed down her face, then I got out of the car to open her door. Before I could get to her, she had hopped out of the car and ran to their arms. Yeah, this would be just what she needed.

Now if only I could figure out what I would do about my situation. I was trying to keep that shit at the back of my mind so I could celebrate with her, but I was worried. Without a job, I felt like I was back at square one. Now that I'd gotten a taste of what it was like being back at school, making progress toward accomplishing my dreams, this time felt worse. To have to accept defeat again wouldn't sit well with my soul this time.

As I walked to the front of the car to watch Kiana's tearful reunion with her dad, I could only hope that her faith was strong enough for both of us, because right now, I couldn't see a way out. Even if I found a full-time job, it would be hard to find one that would work around my schedule at school. If they did, they probably wouldn't pay enough to cover my bills, including the loans I was still paying.

Jamie had snatched all the positivity out of me, and with camera footage of me somewhat snatching her at the club, I wasn't so sure how the assault charges would turn out. Going to school would be the least of my worries if I ended up with a criminal record.

Chapter 22

Kiana

When I saw my parents standing in that garage, I was in a state of shock. I had halfway expected one of them to be home, but I wasn't expecting to see them this way. They were standing in the garage with smiles on their faces in front of a new car. I couldn't contain myself. Before Lazarus could even get to my door, I hopped out of the car and ran to them, falling into my father's outstretched arms. The tears that rained down my cheeks couldn't be contained, and I wasn't trying to contain them either.

"I'm so sorry, Kiana," my dad said as I laid my head on his chest.

While he and I didn't have a bond like I had with my mother, it was still a father-daughter bond that I missed. Him treating me like a stranger off the streets had hurt me tremendously. There were nights that I lay awake while Lazarus slept and silently cried my eyes out. I was happy with Lazarus, but I'd missed my family. We'd never gotten into an argument like this before, had never been at odds in all my twenty-four years.

I'd never witnessed my dad's controlling ways until I wanted to do something he didn't agree with. We were usually in agreement with what I thought were *my* decisions. I had realized with this incident that they were his decisions, not mine.

As I lifted my head from his chest, I stared up at him. "I forgive you, Daddy. I love you."

"I love you too. Your mom talked some sense into me this weekend and made me really see myself. I can't believe I'd disowned my oldest daughter simply for her choice of who she wanted to love. You've always been mature for your age and had decent judgment and reasoning abilities. You're smart and wise beyond your years. I didn't trust you to make a sound decision, and I was wrong. You've more than proved yourself capable of that."

He looked up at Lazarus, who was standing at the front of his car, giving us our moment. No matter how heartfelt his apology was, our relationship wouldn't be any different than it was now if he didn't accept Lazarus. Laz was the love of my life, and anyone that couldn't respect him couldn't have a relationship me. I would be just as bad as they were if I allowed that. It would mean that I didn't respect him either. I had the utmost reverence for that man. He was right under God in my book. Despite his reservations, he'd come to my rescue and planned to take complete care of me. He was the type of man I had longed for.

However, I wouldn't dare tell my father of the shit that had just happened before we got here. That would only serve as ammunition for his reasons why he *didn't* like Lazarus. I wanted to kill that bitch. I'd never hated anyone in my life. Maybe I'd disliked a lot of people, but not hated. She was the first. The way she treated Lazarus was evil. I couldn't believe she would go to those lengths to cripple him when he had done nothing to her. She'd better be glad that after Lazarus had restrained me, I was able to calm down somewhat and not go apeshit on her ass. A busted lip would have been the least of her worries.

This situation with his mom that she spoke about, if it were true, needed to be chalked up to the game after what she'd done to Lazarus. Mama Nat didn't play about her son, and I didn't play about my man. What Jamie didn't realize was that Lazarus had a real one now. I wasn't with him to use him. Shit, my parents had more than he did. I was with him for him. I loved that man, and I refused to make him look bad in front of anyone, including my own family.

Just the fact that he was there for me in this moment proved how sincere he was in his feelings

for me. He had put his issues on the backburner to
assure I could have this moment with my parents.
That was love. Love makes sacrifices and rejoices
for others no matter how life is going on their end.
That alone proved to me that he was the man that I
would build a family with.

He was strong, and I refused to let that bitch
break him. She had come close. I could see the
defeat all over him. I couldn't allow that. I would
carry him on my back if I had to until he could walk
again on his own.

My dad walked away from me and headed toward Lazarus as I turned around to watch.

My mama put her arms around me as she said,
"I told you not to worry about him."

"What did you do?"

"I told him either he got on board and made this
right, or he would suffer the loss of not only his
girls, but his wife. I've never threatened to leave
him, so I suppose it scared him straight. Plus, I
knew he was fighting his feelings anyway. He
missed you just as much as I did."

I smiled slightly as I watched them shake hands.
My dad led Lazarus to the garage. When he reached
me, he grabbed my hand and placed it in Lazarus's.

"I apologized to Lazarus. I had no reason to
treat him the way I did. His age bothered me for a
moment, but I liked everything about him before
I knew his age. He clearly loves you. I respect you

completely, Lazarus. You manned up when I was behaving like an egotistical, chauvinistic jackass. You came to my daughter's rescue when I dropped the ball. I couldn't ask for a better man for her," he said, turning his attention back to Lazarus when he addressed him.

He looked back at me and said, "This was your graduation gift, but I decided to give it to you now. I traded your car in a month after you left and had evil intent when I did. I was going to use it to try to lure you back and away from Lazarus. That was a tired and played out way to get your attention. Your mother is a true woman of God, and I have a lot to learn from her."

He pulled the keys from his pocket and handed them to me. "I know you have to get to class, so I'll let you go. Lazarus, if you're free, maybe we can go to get a bite to eat."

I looked over at Lazarus to see a slow smile spreading across his lips. "Yes, sir, I have time."

Since Lazarus was no longer employed and didn't have class that day, I thought it was a perfect time for them to get to know one another. I hugged my mama and said, "Thank you so much."

"Of course, baby."

She kissed my head, then I released her and headed back to my daddy.

"Thank you, Daddy. I missed you."

"I missed you too."

After he kissed my head as well, I went to
Lazarus and hugged him tightly, then kissed his
lips. I pulled him to me by the back of his neck
and said in his ear, "I love you, Lazarus. Today has
been difficult, but we are victors, baby. God has a
reason for everything He does and everything He
allows. He allowed this for a reason. Stay strong,
enjoy the early lunch with my dad, and I'll see you
when class is over."

"I love you more, Ki. I'm happy that things are
getting back to normal for you."

"Better than normal, baby, because I have you."

He pulled away and smiled at me, then kissed
my lips again. I went and got my purse and bag
from Lazarus's car and got in my new Toyota
Camry and wiggled in the leather seat. This car was
extremely nice, and I was grateful for restoration.
Not only had God restored my relationship with
my parents, but I felt like it was on track to being
better than it was before.

I couldn't wait to see Kinisha at school to tell
her about our resolution and renewal. While I
wouldn't be moving back in, I would visit now, and
she didn't have to sneak around to see me either.
Hopefully because of Daddy seeing the error of his
ways, he would lighten up on her as well.

"You know, since I moved out, I haven't been
hoing around as much? Nigga just been chilling."

I stared at Braylon as we sat on the bench outside the library. Everybody knew where to find me when I wasn't in class—although I was probably going to have to take it elsewhere, because it was starting to get unbearably cold.

I was still in shock about my new car and had shown it to Braylon and his sister, Ramsey. She'd gone to class, but Braylon had a break before his last class. When he wasn't chasing ass, it was routine for him to come find me.

Our relationship had changed for the better, though, and I was happy about that. We'd gotten back to being friends, like we were as kids.

"Why you looking at me like that, Ki?"

"Because being a ho has been embedded in who you are. You think you were just relieving the stress of living at home through sex?"

"Embedded? Really? I just like having sex. That's it. There are no psychological issues. The apple don't fall far from the tree, right?"

"What if you aren't an apple? What if you are a flower and the wind took you a different direction?"

He side-eyed me as I did my best to hold in my laughter. "Ki, don't play with me. Ain't nothing soft or feminine about me, and that's what I think when I see a flower. This nigga is the furthest thing from being delicate," he said while pointing at himself.

I died laughing because I knew he would take it there. Braylon's name was the only thing about him that was somewhat soft. While he wasn't a hard gangsta thug type, he definitely wasn't soft. One time when we were kids, we were horse playing, and that fool forgot I wasn't a boy and knocked the wind out of me. The horrible part was that his ass just walked off like nothing had happened, didn't apologize or even acknowledge that he'd hurt me. Stupid me didn't even tell on him. I should have, though. It took me a couple of minutes to catch my breath.

"Shut up, fool!" I said through my laughter.

He joined me then shoulder bumped me, causing me to fall over. "You so damn extra sometimes. I didn't bump you that hard."

"You don't realize how strong you are, though! Ugh!" I said as he helped me up.

My phone began ringing. He said, "That's probably Lazarus and my cue to go on about my business. I'll holla at you Wednesday."

"Okay," I said to him then quickly answered the call. "Hey, baby. How was the outing with my parents?"

"It was good, Ki, but can you meet me at the hospital? Don't panic. I'm just getting mama checked out. She was having chest pains, but I just need you here with me if you can be."

"Absolutely. Nothing is more important than you. Let me go cancel my sessions for the day. Which hospital?"

"Baptist."

"Okay. I'll be there in a few minutes."

I quickly hopped up from the bench with my bag and purse and ran into the library, letting another tutor know that I had a family emergency. I quickly sent out a text to the students I was supposed to be meeting that day and practically ran to my car. I'd never been in this much of a hurry. Mama Nat was extremely important to me as well, and I needed to make sure she was okay. Lazarus could have just been saying that it was minor so I wouldn't panic. The woman was on her way to congestive heart failure. Chest pains were a serious issue.

She'd been doing well with her exercise routine, or so she'd said. She was supposed to be exercising on Monday, Wednesday, and Fridays whenever she dropped me off at school. Her meals were a lot healthier, and instead of using the TexJoy seasonings that were high in sodium, she'd bought Mrs. Dash and had even googled how to make her own seasoning. Surely all that had to be helping in conjunction with the medicine they'd prescribed her.

My heart was beating a mile a minute as I turned into the parking lot of the hospital. I knew the chances that her condition could be reversed were small, but it was possible. I refused to speak anything but life over her. She had to be okay. If she wasn't, it would kill Lazarus.

When it rained, it poured. I wondered if he'd told her about the job situation and the bogus charges Jamie had filed and it had affected her this way.

After parking, I ran inside but didn't see them, so I called Lazarus.

"We're in the back in room twelve, baby," he said as soon as he answered the call.

"Okay."

I ended the call then walked to the desk to get a visitor's pass. Once I stuck it to my shirt, they opened the doors for me, and I power-walked to her room. The friction of my thighs rubbing together was slowing me down, but I was doing my best. Shit, I needed to be exercising with her, not necessarily to lose weight but to increase my stamina. I was way too young to be tired already.

When I got to the room, Lazarus was in there alone, staring at the floor.

"Hey, baby. I got here as fast as I could. Everything okay?"

"They just took her down to x-ray. They seem to think it may be a muscle issue. If they don't find anything in the x-ray, they'll do an MRI. It's hurting on her right side, and the pain is piercing she told them. So, we're optimistic. She probably did too much when she was working out. I told her she can't be tryna lose weight to snatch her a young cub. Her body ain't used to all that action. She gotta take it easy."

I chuckled as I exhaled. *Thank God.*

"So, are *you* good?"

He put his hands at the back of my thighs and pulled me to him. "I'm trying to take your advice from earlier. Things have to work out. I thought my news about my job landed us here, but she assured me that it had been hurting since yesterday. So, I'm better than good now that you're here, wit'cho sexy ass."

He slapped then gripped my ass as I gushed in my panties. I loved when he did stuff like this. When we got home, it was going to be on. I would most likely be the aggressor. I always was when he warmed me up like this.

I slid my fingers through his hair and gripped it how I always did when I straddled him. It was never rough, just enough for him to know I had my hands in it. He brought his other hand to my ass and gripped both cheeks, his fingertips resting near my gold mine.

"This is a hospital, Lazarus. Don't be feeling up my daughter-in-law in public. Nasty ass," Mama Nat said as they wheeled her back inside the room and helped her to the bed.

I pulled away from him and went to her bedside as he chuckled. "Mama Nat, don't be scaring me like this. You think your heart is weak? You should've felt mine earlier."

"Girl, I thought I was having a heart attack, especially when Lazarus told me about today's events. The truth gon' come out, and they gon' be calling to get him back at work. Mark my words. Stupid bitch don't know who she fucking with." She mumbled that last sentence, then continued. "Turns out I probably just pulled a muscle when I was exercising yesterday. When I went to exercise today, it was really hurting. I'm not ready to leave here yet. I got plenty of things to do, especially since I have a new man."

"A new what?" Lazarus said from across the room.

I chuckled. I already knew about the man she was entertaining. We talked about everything. He was forty-nine, slightly younger than her. He owned his own business, and more importantly, he wasn't married. I was just happy that she was happy. She said he was good to her, and that was all that mattered. I couldn't wait to meet him, but I knew that Lazarus would be on one since the last man she was dating was married.

"You heard me. A new man."

"Come on, Mama. You ain't told me about a new man. Who is he?"

"Lazarus, last time I checked, I was grown as hell. I don't answer to you, boy."

As she was trying to get herself comfortable, another person showed up with a wheelchair. She huffed, and I giggled.

"Why didn't you come five minutes ago before I readjusted myself?"

"Sorry, Ms. Mitchell. I'm here to take you to have the MRI."

"I know," she responded as she sat up and swung her legs to the side.

"I ain't gon' forget about my question. I need to know who this dude is that you're seeing," Lazarus said.

"Boy, bye. Go find you something to do," she said as the transport helped her from the bed. "I'm a grown-ass woman. That fool wasn't getting away with anything the last time. I already knew who he was and who he was married to. So again, find you some business to mind."

They wheeled her out of the room, and Lazarus just stared at me for a moment. "You see the bullshit I have to deal with?" he asked.

I couldn't help but giggle. He gestured for me to go to his lap, so I walked over to him and did as he requested. As badly as I wanted to straddle him, I didn't. I sat on his leg as he wrapped his arms around me.

"I can't wait to taste this chocolate skin. You are so beautiful, Ki."

"Flattery will get you everywhere."

"Oh, yeah? Well, let me really turn on the charm."

I giggled as he nuzzled his face in my neck. Then I said, "You need to stop before we go too far in this hospital. Mama Nat ain't finna be talking about me."

"Whatever. You scared of her?"

"Hell yeah. And you should be too. I'm not trying to feel her wrath, and I know you aren't either."

"But tasting you will make it worth it. Let me touch it, Ki."

"Noooo. Quit playing," I said as I stood from his lap.

Lazarus was so damn nasty. I loved this side of him, though. It let me know that he was extremely comfortable. That was a good thing because I was extremely comfortable too. I leaned over and kissed his lips as he smacked my ass.

"Laz, that shit kind of stung!"

"My bad, baby. I got excited. Let me kiss it and make it better."

"You know what? You're something else. You didn't actually think I would fall for that, did you?"

"Well, I didn't know. It didn't hurt to try," he said with a chuckle.

I rolled my eyes playfully, then sat in the chair next to him. Mama Nat was going to be just fine.

I was sure of it. Then we would all go home, get her together for bed, and retreat to our bedroom for some extracurricular activities. His dick was hard and waiting, ready to tear down some strongholds, and I was going to let him. We couldn't get home fast enough.

Chapter 23

Lazarus

When I had gotten home and told Mama about my dilemma, then later found her lying in her bed clutching her chest, it scared me shitless. I seriously thought I was about to lose her. Congestive heart failure is nothing to play with. While she said she was doing better with her diet and exercise, I wasn't there every second of the day. I just had to trust that she was doing what she said she was doing. Most times, by the time I got home, she was home.

Since she had a pulled muscle in her chest, she was going to have to take it easy for a while. I'd briefly toyed with the idea of withdrawing from my classes for the spring semester. I was trying to have faith that everything would work out like Kiana had made me believe, but I was struggling big time.

The outing with her parents had gone well, and we didn't talk about anything too heavy. They were mainly concerned with Kiana and how she was really doing, things she probably wouldn't tell them. I only told them of how much I knew she missed them and how I knew that she lay in the bed awake at night, crying. She didn't know I knew, but my spirit was so in tune with hers until whenever she was restless, I was too. I would often roll over and put my arms around her and pull her close, trying to assure her that everything would be fine.

I was grateful that they didn't ask too much about me. I felt like I was putting on a front anyway, because I really wanted to be alone. It was probably best that I wasn't. I was extremely susceptible to depression, and being alone would have invited it in. The payment for my classes was due soon, and I was at war with what I would do. I only had to pay half and could make payments for the rest, but I had to be cautious with how I used that money from the sale of the house. I still had bills to pay, and I refused to put the responsibility of taking care of everything on my mama and Kiana. That was something I could never do, especially because they weren't in a financial position to be able to handle everything.

By the time I was about to call the automated system and withdraw, Kiana had shown up. My sunflower and ray of light. Just her presence gave me the courage to tough it out and pray for the best, just like she'd done the night she left her parents' home, not knowing what the next day would bring. Furthermore, I knew she wouldn't have stood there and allowed me to give up so soon, no matter how unsure I was about how everything would turn out.

We'd just gotten home, and Kiana was helping my mama get situated. I'd already taken a shower, and I was lying in bed, waiting for her with my dick in my hand. She had me so riled up at that hospital that I could have thrown her to the hospital bed and had my way with her while Mama was getting her MRI done. The moment she grabbed my hair, I knew that shit would get wild that night. I liked it when she took charge and did with me as she pleased.

One time, she didn't ask any questions, just brought her pussy to my face and took a seat. That shit had turned me on so much that I skeeted nut on her back. When she realized I'd nutted just from her aggressiveness, she went to my dick and sucked the hell out of it. She was on that demon time for real. The way she slurped my shit up, I was in heaven, and I was hoping that she would be on that same type of time tonight.

I knew she had to take a shower first. That waiting time was going to kill me. I thought about hopping right back in the shower with her.

When she entered the room and saw me, she licked her lips. "Getting him warmed up for me?"

"Mm-hmm. You got something against that?"

"Hell yeah. Let me warm him up. I love feeling him get hard in my mouth."

"Girl, go take your shower before you make me cum. You can't be talking to me like you don't value your life. I want to take my time, but shit, you making that feat harder and harder to accomplish. Go get your fine ass in that shower."

She bit her bottom lip as her slanted eyes lowered like she was imagining my taste. That shit was so sexy. She began undressing slowly as I watched and stroked my dick.

Making her way to me, she took off more articles of clothing, then said, "I thought I told you to stop." She grabbed my hand, pulling it away from my dick and threw it to the side, then bent over and sucked my shit up like it was the best popsicle she'd ever had.

I was squirming, trying to contain myself, but Kiana was gagging and spitting on my shit like she was Super Head. I grabbed her hair and pulled her off it, then lowered her back to it. Seeing all the saliva leave her mouth was better than any porn I'd ever watched. I sat up more and smacked her bare ass and watched it jiggle from the front. I couldn't wait to watch the ripples it would make when I fucked her from behind.

"Ki, fuck! What you tryna do, woman? I'm already stuck *on* you, but now you tryna make me a part *of* you. My dick gon' stay in your mouth, letting you digest all our kids. You ready for this load?"

She looked up at me as she sucked, and I swore I wanted to rip her head off her body so I could have her mouth with me always. Her hands rotated around the base of my dick as she bobbed on it, taking as much of me into her mouth as possible. She had me in here wanting to scream. The head of my dick was feeling the pressure of what was to come.

"I'm about to nut, Ki. Fuck!"

She sucked harder and increased her pace as I released my load at the back of her throat. She kept sucking, allowing what was in her mouth to cover my dick. Church girls were nasty as hell, and I was glad I had one. When she lifted her head, my nut was running down her chin to her chest.

"Damn," I voiced.

My dick was still hard. That greedy nigga was waiting on the main course. I couldn't wait to dive in her pussy and let my name be known. Just the way I planned to make love to her was heightening my senses, and I hadn't touched her yet. Lazarus means "God will help," and that was the only man that would be able to help her. I planned to fuck her in every position imaginable until she tapped out, begging for a break.

I watched her walk away from me and head to the bathroom. The view was amazing. Watching her ass bounce as she walked had quickly become one of my favorite pastimes. When she got to the bathroom, she started her music. I wanted to lay here like this, but I knew I needed to get cleaned up so I could put a condom on. I couldn't wait for the day when I would be falling asleep covered with her cream.

I could see a future with her, and if she allowed me to, I would make sure she saw it too. There wouldn't be much work to that, though, because I knew she already saw it.

As I lay there thinking about where our relationship was headed, I couldn't believe how the sequence of events had led to this. Like she had said so many times, I knew that God had brought us together. To be with someone that you got along with and loved being around was rare these days. It was like some people craved toxic individuals.

I was just happy that she decided to be with me, through the good and the bad.

After getting a towel and cleaning myself up, I went back to the bed to wait for her. It took a lot of willpower not to get in that shower with her. She was in there, humming to the sounds of Asiahn. I knew her music well. She had a distinct, light voice. It was powerful at the same time, though, because she'd been classically trained. She was perfect to keep the mood going. However, it was a different mood Kiana was creating. It was one of love and devotion, not one of back shots and fucking up the way she walked.

When she came out of the bathroom, she wore a sheer white dress that showcased her dark nipples. She came close to me, and I reached up and pulled the string on her dress to untie it. After it fell open, I stared at her nipples for a moment in admiration. They were hard and long, perfect for sucking. I brought my mouth to one of them and toyed with the other with my fingers. The heat coming from her middle was about to take me out, though.

I slid my hands up the backs of her legs and pulled her to the bed. Once she straddled me, I knew it was game over. I loved for her to ride me this way, but she was playing with fire. She was rubbing her slit over the head of my dick, and everything in me wanted to slide up in her hot, wet paradise.

"Ki, you playing, but I will lay my seed to rest right at your cervix."

"Do it then. I'm on the pill, Lazarus. I've been on it for the past two weeks. I just wanted to give it time to get in my system. So, fire away, baby."

"See, you gon' make me move faster than I wanted to. Come sit this pussy on my face."

As I lay back, she made her way up my body, stopping to kiss my lips first. "I want to remember these lips the way they are, before I fuck them up."

I swore she was getting nastier the longer we were together. In the beginning, I could barely pry two words out of her when I wanted her to talk dirty to me. Now she had sexual prowess and confidence in everything she did. I loved that shit.

She slid her pussy up my chest, leaving her juices in her wake like a damn snail. However, when she dropped it right on my lips, I indulged, eating it like the delicacy it was. I slurped up her juices, then slid my tongue between her folds to her clit. As I sucked it, she began rotating her hips on me. I took the opportunity to smack her ass, then grip it like I was holding on for dear life.

"Yeeeeessss, Laz. Right there, baby."

She started bucking harder, so I turned my head slightly to get some air, then went in like I was scuba diving, sucking her clit with everything I had. I wanted her to know that I would die for this shit. Kiana had me in every way, hook, line, and sinker. There was nothing she could do to push me away. I loved hard, and I had fallen for her completely.

"Laz, I'm about to cum! Oh God! Oh shit!"

When she began, I quickly sat up and slid her down to my dick. The way her walls gripped me, I wanted to stay there forever. I began bouncing her on it as she screamed out in passion. My mama was gon' be pissed, but she would get over it. I couldn't hold nothing back right now.

"Ahh, fuck!"

Her pussy felt so good without a condom. There was *no* way we would ever go back to that. Kiana wrapped her legs around me, sitting down completely, taking every inch I had to offer, and began gliding on it. My eyes closed as they rolled to the back of my head.

My grip on her ass got tighter, and my head dropped back. When she slid her hands in my hair like she'd done at the hospital, that did it.

"I'm about to shoot the club up, baby." My damn legs and feet were tingling, and that feeling was making its way through my entire body.

"Give it to me, Laz! Fuck!"

She began bucking harder, and my dick exploded within her walls. I fell backward to the bed, and she continued rolling her hips until I couldn't take that shit anymore. My dick was so sensitive after nutting so hard. That wasn't anything new, though. Kiana always had me giving her my best. My orgasms were the strongest they'd ever been.

She rolled off me and lay to my side, rubbing circles on my chest.

"Damn, baby. That was so damn good," I said as I panted.

"It's always good, Laz."

"You damn right."

As we lay there, gently caressing one another, I heard my mama outside the door.

"Nasty asses."

I chuckled as Kiana blushed. She would be calling us nasty again, because I wasn't done with Kiana's thick, fine ass.

I hadn't realized just how much I would love a BBW. I wasn't shallow or anything, but Jamie was the only woman I'd dated or been with. Sex with a big woman was where it was at. I swore Niagara Falls was between her legs. She got so wet for me. I was hooked from the first time I dived into her waters.

I kissed her head, then whispered, "Get on all fours so I can watch that ass twerk."

She didn't hesitate to do just what I asked of her. When I went to my knees behind her and saw just how juicy she was, I couldn't help but lick my lips. Slowly, I pushed inside of her and pulled out to see that she wasted no time covering my dick with her cream.

"Mm. Good shit, Ki."

I slid back inside her as I rested my hand on her hip. Starting a slow rhythm, I wound my dick inside of her, being sure to touch every crevice in her gold mine. I closed my eyes and knew that one day, she would be carrying my seed. I was already familiar with the thought of her being my wife and us having at least a couple of kids. I was just waiting for it to come to fruition.

I watched my dick slide in and out of her for a moment, then I quickened my pace as I watched her ass bounce on me. *Lord have mercy*. I slapped her ass cheek, then slapped the other as I said, "Work that shit out, baby."

Pushing her flat to the bed, I climbed on top of her and fucked her mercilessly. Her screams were muffled by the mattress, but my grunts were loud and uncontained. As the sweat rolled down my face, I blasted off as she gripped my dick like vice grips. We'd orgasmed together, and it seemed like we were both caught off guard by it.

"Fuck!" I yelled.

When I fell off her, she turned to look at me with love in her eyes. "I can't wait for you to marry me,

Lazarus. I'm a church girl at heart, and I want to be married . . . make all this right."

"Don't worry, baby. We gon' get that piece of paper as soon as the time is right. I love you, and I'm not letting you get away. So whatever you want, you get. No question."

Our court date was the following week for that stupid-ass assault charge, and I had an appointment tomorrow with the attorney Kiana had recommended. I knew I had better move the shit I wanted out of the house before Jamie showed her ass up. She said she didn't want anything out of the house, but I knew that was a damn lie. Just like I had things of sentimental value here, I was sure she did as well.

I'd come over to the house yesterday and saw that I still had so much shit here. I'd rented a small U-Haul truck to be able to take the things I wanted. There were pictures of my dad and grandparents still here. Things I wouldn't have been able to replace.

As I looked at pictures of them and pictures of me and Jamie, she appeared next to me, nearly scaring the shit out of me.

"I didn't know you were coming today. Sorry. I'll be on the other side of the house."

I wanted to reach up and strangle the shit out of her. However, I was able to restrain myself, knowing that it wouldn't make things any better. I discreetly grabbed my phone and hit the record button. She was going to drop these frivolous charges one way or the other. It probably wouldn't get me my jobs back, but I couldn't have this bullshit on my record. Dre, the club owner, had fired me by phone, just like Jamie said he would.

Now that she seemed to be vulnerable and acting like Monday had never happened, I knew this was the perfect time to get answers for all the questions that had been running through my mind in my moments alone. It meant I would have to be "weak-ass Lazarus" for a bit to get what I needed out of her. Why would anyone want to be alone around someone who had assaulted them anyway? That would be my whole defense if she didn't say what I needed her to say in the recording.

"Jamie, did you ever love me?"

She stared at me like she was in shock that I had even asked her that question, then she quickly turned away. I waited patiently for her to get her thoughts together to answer my question, although if she had, there wouldn't be any thoughts to get together. It was a yes or no question. Her taking so long to answer my question let me know that she hadn't.

I nodded repeatedly. "So, you used me, just like I thought. And now you wanna make me suffer by filing those frivolous charges because I don't want to be used by you any longer. I grabbed your arm to escort you out of the club. Nothing was rough about it. I can't believe they are even going on with this trial."

She exhaled slowly, and she seemed nervous for a moment. "It wasn't that simple, Laz. In the beginning, when we were in school, I liked you a lot. You were cute, funny, and caring. The problem came when you bought all my senior stuff. My mother saw that you would do anything for me. She was the one that pushed me to marry you. You are an amazing guy. The way you took care of me was something I don't think I'll ever feel again, just because of how I treated you. Floyd is a nice man, but he's not even close to the man you were to me. I fucked that up, though. He broke up with me anyway. I was only using him to get close to you."

I slid my hand down my face as I processed what she said. "So your mother forced you to use me. I mean, you were a grown woman, capable of making your own decisions. How did you continue to use me, knowing that you weren't in love with me? Some of that had to be you. Your conscience should have been eating you alive. But my guess is that you *wanted* to do what she suggested."

"At first, it was uncomfortable. But as time went on, it got easier to do. I did love you, Lazarus. I just wasn't *in* love with you. Then when our baby . . . Niko died, it was hard. I wasn't trying to get pregnant, but since I did, I was excited about bringing a life into this world.

"It's still not too late, Lazarus. We can have all that again. If you take me back, I'll drop the charges. I can fall in love with you. I know I can. I want to give you a family."

The tears streamed down her cheeks. Niko had always been a soft spot for us, which was why I never talked about him. Sometimes I just wanted to forget that he even existed so losing him wouldn't hurt as bad. However, I was able to accept it better through counseling. I also knew that she had a different bond with him. She was carrying him. She was his mother.

I looked away, trying to keep my composure. She was still hurting from that, and it made me sad. Just the fact that she was a psychologist and didn't take her mental health seriously bothered me. *How can you help others and not help yourself?*

Something was clearly wrong with Jamie to think I would even consider giving her another chance. She had to be delusional. It was like she was a different person than she had been Monday.

Ki was right. She was miserable, and she needed serious help.

"It was extremely hard when Niko died, but you completely shut me out. I was there for you. I'd always been there for you. Whether you were using me or not, that was my baby too. I was the father of our child. We were both hurting and should have been a source of comfort for each other. I feel like after that, you were just tired of me being around, after I'd paid thousands of dollars for your education.

"That shit wasn't fair to me, Jamie. I was in love with you and would have given my life for you, someone who didn't even respect me enough to treat me like I mattered. Even if you weren't in love with me, you didn't have to treat me the way you did.

"That shit messed me up and almost caused me to miss out on real love. I didn't want to give to her what I'd given to you, because I feared being used again. Thankfully, I was able to get past that. I just want to know why. Why and how could you do something like that to me? Especially with all I did for you. The way you kicked me out of our house . . . that shit was cold, Jamie.

"Not to mention this bullshit. You caused me to lose my jobs, my only sources of income, knowing that I'm in school trying to better myself. My chances of getting another job is bleak, pending the outcome of these crazy-ass charges you filed."

"I'm sorry, Lazarus," she said quietly.

She offered no further explanation, and I knew it was probably because she couldn't explain why she did what she did. There was no logical explanation to warrant her treating me like trash.

I turned away from her and continued boxing up my things, hoping she would just walk away and tend to her business so I could tend to mine. I only had plans to take one bedroom suite and the deep freezer, besides my personal belongings. I didn't want to take anything that would remind me of Jamie, not because I once loved her, but because being reminded of her put me in a bad mental space. I refused to take steps forward only to be knocked backward.

When I looked up, she was gone. To get my mind in a better place, I texted Kiana.

Hey, baby. I know you're probably tutoring, but I wanted to tell you that I love you. I can't wait to see you this evening.

Once me and my trusty dolly got everything loaded, I would be out of here and wouldn't take a look back. I stopped recording on my phone and would let the attorney hear it tomorrow. I was sure this case would be thrown out. My past was officially done, and I could fully concentrate on my present and my future with Kiana by my side.

When I got home, I was worn the hell out. I didn't know what I had been thinking by doing all that shit by myself. Plus, my mind was going crazy about how Jamie should have given me her share from the sale of the house to pay me back for all the schooling I had put her through and the bullshit she had put me through. Had I wanted to really fight her, I would have gotten my money back when we divorced. However, I knew that God would bless me for what I endured, and He had. Karma had come around, although it came swiftly, thanks to Natalie. Everything Jamie tried to do to me showed how miserable she was.

After my shower, I put on some sweats and a t-shirt. Kiana and I had planned to study this evening because I had my chemistry final tomorrow. We'd been studying all week because my anxiety had me stressing. She had finals on Friday, Monday, and Tuesday. I had another on Tuesday as well, but chemistry was the one I was worried about.

When I opened the door, I could smell food and hear soft jazz playing. I frowned slightly. My mama didn't listen to jazz. She said it made her sleepy.

As I walked down the hallway, my stomach growled, reminding me that I hadn't eaten a thing all day. I'd been fully committed to getting everything moved so I didn't have to worry about it anymore.

When I got to the kitchen, Kiana was setting a plate of food on the table wearing only heels and an apron. My dick hardened immediately. I didn't know how she expected me to concentrate on the meal she'd placed on the table when she had my favorite meal on display.

"Damn, Ki. What you did with Mama?"

She giggled. "When I told her that I wanted to cook dinner for you, she said she'd be a fool to stay here and get an earful."

"Smart woman," I said as I walked closer to her. I slid my arms around her waist and pressed my dick against her ass. "You know this shit is spreading. All this sexing we doing."

"I know. I need to start working out."

"Like hell. I love this shit, baby. All this shit for me to grab ahold to, it's sexy as hell."

I kissed her neck as she giggled. "You have to eat first. I slaved over these fried ribs, macaroni and cheese, mustard greens, and cornbread."

"Damn, baby. What'chu know about fried ribs?"

"Your mama showed me how to cook them. She said they were your favorite. So, you eat this meal, and you can get dessert."

She slid her fingers over my lips, and they smelled like the essence of her. She was fucking with me.

"Ki, you been playing with yourself?"

She didn't answer me verbally. Instead, she slid her fingers in my mouth, causing me to close my eyes and savor her flavor. There was no way my mind would be on anything else but getting in her insides.

She bent over and picked up a fried rib from my plate and put it to my lips. I took a bite and immediately knew that my previous thought was wrong. I would definitely be eating dinner. It was so good. My stomach started growling as she stepped aside so I could sit at the table.

The food looked so good. When she got to the table with her plate, I took a moment to actually look her over. Her thick ass was gon' get fucked right on this table just as soon as I finished this meal.

"Thank you, baby."

"Thank *you*, Laz. I just want you to know how much I appreciate you. We aren't studying tonight. You're ready, and I need you to be confident in that. I want you to relax, and there's no better way to do that than through good food and good pussy."

"What the hell you said? Ki, I don't know why you wanna keep fucking with me," I said as I yanked her chair to me.

"Baby, I'm just grateful for you. That's what this dinner is for."

"Mm-hmm. Keep playing with me."

We said our grace and indulged in our meal. I couldn't wait until I could get to dessert, though. That would be the part of the meal that was the most filling. Every time we made love, I found myself hoping she forgot to take her pill. However, it was on my mind more today since I had the conversation with Jamie. Our son would have been about six years old, probably getting his feet wet in little league sports. It was probably divine intervention that he didn't make it. That would have tied me to a woman who was never in love with me. Either she would have been pretending like she had been all those years, or we would have been divorced as we are now and having to coparent.

But this woman, Kiana Solé Jordan, I wouldn't mind being tied to her for the rest of my life, and as soon as I could, I would make that a reality. She was my lifeline, my confidant, and the love of my life. There was nothing more to consider.

Epilogue

Kiana

Five months later...

"Kiana Solé Jordan, summa cum laude."

I proudly strutted across the stage, accepting my Pharm D degree. I'd already accepted my master's degree in chemistry. I could hear the cheers from my family and colleagues. I was so happy that I was finally done. I'd already been offered a job at the university, starting this summer, teaching chemistry. Chemistry was my bread and butter. I loved learning it and teaching it. My students loved me, and it just made sense to go where my heart was leading me.

As I made my way to my seat, I waved at my family. Lazarus was standing there with a bouquet of sunflowers in his hand. I was so happy that he was able to share this moment with me. We'd only grown closer over the past five months, and I was grateful for his love and devotion.

We were still living with Mama Nat. When we even talked about finding a place, she would adamantly refuse to hear of it. She'd told us that as long as we were in school, we shouldn't have to worry about unnecessary bills. Having our own place was unnecessary. She gave us all the privacy in the world. On the weekends, we rarely saw her because she was always with her boo, Mr. Sonny.

We'd met him a few months back, and he was a kind, gentle soul. He'd just turned fifty, a few years younger than Mama Nat. He treated her like royalty, and he wasn't married. Lazarus was sure to do some digging on that front, unbeknownst to her. He said he refused to condone that type of relationship, especially being that Mama Nat had known that Mr. Greer was married.

He and Mrs. Greer legally separated and were going through a nasty divorce. He'd even had the audacity to pop up at the house, talking about he wanted to take Mama Nat out and that he really cared for her. I almost laughed in his face.

Braylon and Ramsey had told me all the details about their pending divorce and what had led to the decision. Their mom was sick of him screwing around on her, but when he started mistreating her by being rude and verbally disrespectful to her, she was done. I didn't understand that philosophy. It was like she could deal with him being with other women as long as he "treated her right." Whatever floated her boat. If she liked it, I loved it.

Braylon was graduating as well. He was receiving his master's degree in engineering. He even had a girlfriend. She was new to the area. She almost had to be, because everybody around here knew that he was a ho and didn't take him seriously. She was from a small town in South Carolina and had moved to Beaumont for a job. They met at some kind of gala put on by ExxonMobil. He said when he noticed she was alone, he made a move, and it proved to be the right one. They'd been inseparable ever since, and everyone was having a difficult time processing it. The new Braylon was likeable, funny, and somewhat caring. I'd gotten to see his caring side firsthand.

I glanced at my parents and Kinisha as I sat there wishing the time would pass and reflecting on how far we'd come. We were on great terms. Lazarus and Daddy had become best friends almost. It seemed like Lazarus spent as much time with Daddy as he did with me.

Only God and my mama could have softened my dad's heart because he wasn't hearing me or Kinisha. I was so grateful for that. I loved the change in him and loved that he was trying to be a better person all around. Judgment was for the Lord to execute, not us.

Sometimes we tried to do God's job, and that was where we missed the mark. A lot of church people found themselves trying to be God, knowing that we couldn't be as perfect as He on our best day.

As I tuned in to the speaker, I was just in time to hear him tell all the graduates to stand. He was making the point that we all finished on different levels and at different times, making the point that age didn't matter, but getting the degree did. When he called out how many years it took from high school graduation to get the degree, we were told to sit. He got as far as thirty years, and some people were still standing, which had the crowd on their feet applauding. When he reached fifty years, there was still one woman standing. Everyone congratulated her as she sat. She was receiving a Pharm D degree like me. I had never realized she was that old. I always thought she was in her late forties or early fifties.

When it was time to file out of the building, I was extremely excited to go be with my family. There was a graduation party planned at one of the parks in Beaumont. Lots of people from church would be in attendance, along with my extended family.

There was one person I was dying to see, though. Lazarus had finished both the fall and spring semesters on the president's list, which earned him an academic scholarship for the upcoming semester. It would take care of more than half his tuition. I was extremely proud of him. He took his grades seriously, and he wasn't afraid to ask for help when he needed it. That made all the difference.

The case pending was thrown out when the recording was shared, and just as Jamie began mentioning filing charges against me, her lawyer shut her up. My eyebrows had lifted, and it took quite a bit of restraint for me to keep my smile hidden. They, in turn, filed against Jamie for filing false claims. She was on probation, doing community service. Lazarus's attorney had recommended he file a civil suit against her for his loss of wages and tarnished reputation, but he refused. He just wanted to be done with it all.

He was now working part time at the railroad with my dad, earning just as much as he had been earning as a full-time worker with the City of Beaumont. My dad had helped get him on about three months ago when he popped up at Mama Nat's house when Lazarus was supposed to be at work. He practically scolded us like kids for not coming to him about helping Lazarus and trying to handle things on our own.

When I got outside the Montagne Center, I searched the crowd for my family. There were flowers and balloons in every direction I turned, so I couldn't gauge their location by that. However,

I soon spotted them waving and jumping up and down. Kinisha was the main one.

Before I could reach them, Braylon stopped me for a hug. "Congratulations, Ki. I'm so proud of you."

"Thanks, Bray. I'm proud of you too. We did it! Nothing stopped us from reaching our goals. ExxonMobil is waiting for you, and Lamar University is waiting for me."

"Yep. They are definitely gaining assets to their company and campus. Go meet your family. I'm going to meet mine. I'll see you later at the party."

"Okay."

We hugged again, then I quickly made my way to Lazarus's arms.

"I'm proud of you, baby. Congratulations!"

"Thank you, baby. Before long, it will be your turn."

He handed me the flowers, and I admired their beauty. Once I sniffed them, I asked, "Can you hold them while I hug everyone else?"

"Absolutely."

Kinisha was standing there, impatiently waiting. I giggled when she rolled her eyes as I kissed Lazarus's lips. They always teased us, saying that we were inseparable. When we weren't together, we were constantly calling or messaging one another.

The minute I left my Lazarus-induced haze, Kinisha pulled me into her arms. "Congratulations, Ki! You did it and on your terms! I'm so happy for you. Even when I couldn't see your vision including Lazarus, it all worked out for your good. I applaud you for standing up for yourself, what you believe in, and for who you love."

She'd brought tears to my eyes as she applauded my efforts. Before the first tear could roll down my cheek, my mama was right there to hug me next. I hugged her back, along with my dad, and thanked them for the amazing qualities and work ethic they instilled in me. Without the foundation they built, I wouldn't have been able to accomplish half the things I did. They taught me how to persevere, to have determination, how to go after my dreams, to be patient, and not to give up on myself. My mother instilled self-love in me, and I believed that made all the difference. Despite our hiccup with Lazarus, they were amazing parents to me, and I would be forever grateful to them for that.

Mama Nat was next on the hug list. She'd also played an important role in my success. I appreciated her support at the beginning of my relationship with Lazarus. We'd been a couple for nearly nine months now. She nurtured our relationship and helped it grow with her advice. We flourished, and it was partly because of her.

After greeting other family members, we loaded up to head to the hall. Once Lazarus helped me inside and got in the driver's seat, he turned to me and laid the juiciest kiss on my lips. I was ready to straddle him right there in the car. My tiger was purring, ready to pounce. It didn't help that he was looking delicious in his black slacks and white shirt, with his hair pulled up into a man bun. The dark shades added the sexual mystery that I liked.

We role played often, so I asked, "Where are you taking me, chauffer?"

"Mm. To ecstasy if you let me. You down for a daytime quickie?"

"I'm always down for piece of you."

He chuckled as he made a U-turn in the street and headed to the house. There was nothing this man wouldn't do for me, and I loved every minute of that. He got the same treatment from me as well. There was nothing he could ask of me that I didn't break my neck to provide.

When we got to the house, Lazarus didn't waste any time getting me out of my clothes and touching my cervix with his love. I nearly needed a shower by the time he got done with me. I'd creamed on him so much, and that only fueled his fire, turning our quickie into a nearly thirty-minute session.

Once we were heading to the park, my phone started ringing. It was Mama Nat.

"Hello?"

"Get y'all nasty asses to the hall. Everybody is looking for y'all. I never knew my son was this nasty until you came along."

I giggled and said, We're on our way, Mama Nat."

When we got to Alice Keith Park, the parking area near the building was full.

"The people really showed up to celebrate you, baby."

"I know. This is amazing."

I wiggled in excitement as Lazarus found a parking spot. I was so excited. My mama had gotten some of my favorite foods catered, but I was looking forward to the shrimp fried rice.

Lazarus opened my door and grabbed my hand, helping me from my seat and leading me to the entrance. When he opened the door, "Share My World" by Mary J. Blige was playing, and everyone was standing on their feet, applauding. I had a huge smile on my face as I looked around at all the happy faces.

Half the people in attendance were from church and had seen me grow up right before their eyes. It was probably the deaconesses who had helped my mama and Kinisha decorate. There were red, black, and white balloons scattered throughout the place, and red and black tablecloths, which were Lamar University's school colors. I noticed the two-tier cake, and I couldn't help but smile.

After taking in my surroundings, I turned back to see where Lazarus had gone only to see him right behind me . . . down on one knee. My hands instantly flew to my mouth, and the tears fell from my eyes.

After the screams and applause died down, he said, "Baby, you are the one, my game changer. As you've said time and time again, it was destined for us to meet. It was God's plan for us to meet just the way we did. It was also His plan to put us to the test. I say we passed with flying colors. I want the rest of my life to be this way. I want to love you for the rest of my life, but as my wife. Kiana Solé Jordan, will you marry me?"

I stared into his tear-filled eyes and nodded. "Absolutely."

I held out my hand for him to slide the diamond ring on my finger. After staring at it for a second, I hopped in his arms. He lifted me in his arms as he chuckled.

When he released me, he said, "I love you so much."

"I love you too, baby."

I kissed his lips as everyone cheered. That was why he didn't hesitate to kill time. He knew what he'd planned and that it made more sense to be late.

I had to be the happiest woman alive. I had a new degree, a new job, and a new man that was now my fiancé. While it felt great to be with him, marrying him would be the icing on the cake. I was too happy to continue to see where our relationship would progress to.

Being stuck on Lazarus Mitchell was almost like being addicted to Jesus. Nothing was wrong with it, and it didn't harm my body. Being with him nurtured my soul, and I was more than ready for the journey and where it would lead.

The End

From the Author . . .

This book was so emotional! I absolutely loved Lazarus and Kiana, and I loved them for each other. The moments they were apart nearly killed me, especially the last time. When she fell in Lazarus's arms at school, practically begging him to be with her, I was crying like I was Kiana. The love they had for one another leapt from the pages, and I felt it in my heart. I can only hope that you felt it too.

It was Jamie and Kiana's parents that rubbed my nerves raw.

Jamie had the world. She had something most women would give their right lung for, and she used and mistreated him. Lazarus was an amazing man, and Jamie never deserved him. It's sad, but this sort of thing happens all the time.

I wanted to paint the picture of a Black man that knew how to love and take care of his woman, and Lazarus didn't disappoint. The way he loved Jamie only prepared him for Kiana. While the transition was hard, it made him even better than he already was.

Kiana had a great upbringing in her eyes, so when the shit hit the fan, it floored her. She'd placed her parents on a pedestal and had practically painted them as being perfect only to discover they weren't. They were just fine with Lazarus, until they learned of his age. Their overprotectiveness went too far, and it became toxic, controlling behavior, especially since they knew they'd raised their daughter right and that she was exhibiting all the qualities they'd instilled in her.

The other supporting characters were cool. Kinisha was a little on the fence toward the end, but she came around. Braylon was an entire mess. Even with all his toxicity, I liked him. I was glad that he reverted to being the friend he once was to Kiana when she needed him most.

Whether you enjoyed the book or not, I would appreciate your honest review. Please be sure to leave one on your outlet of choice for this title, including Goodreads and Amazon.

There's also an amazing playlist on Apple Music and Spotify for this book, under the same title, that includes some great R&B tracks to tickle your fancy.

Please keep up with me on Facebook, Instagram, and TikTok (@authormonicawalters), Twitter (@monlwalters), and Clubhouse (@monicawalters). You can also visit my Amazon author page at www.amazon.com/author/monica.walters to view my releases.

Please subscribe to my webpage for updates and sneak peeks of upcoming releases! https://authormonicawalters.com.

For live discussions, giveaways, and inside information on upcoming releases, join my Facebook group, Monica's Romantic Sweet Spot, at https://bit.ly/2P2lo6X.

Other Titles by Monica Walters

When's the Last Time?
Best You Ever Had
Deep As It Goes (A KeyWalt Crossover Novel with
Perfect Timing by T. Key)
*The Shorts: A BLP Anthology with the Authors of
BLP* (*Made to Love You*- Collab with Kay Shanee)
All I Need is You (A KeyWalt Crossover Novel with
Divine Love by T. Key)
This Love Hit Different (A KeyWalt Crossover
Novel with *Something New* by T. Key)
Until I Met You
Marry Me Twice
Last First Kiss
Nobody Else Gon' Get My Love (A KeyWalt
Crossover Novel with *Better Than Before* by T.
Key)
Love Long Overdue (A KeyWalt Crossover Novel
with *Distant Lover* by T. Key)
Next Lifetime
Fall Knee-Deep In It
Unwrapping Your Love: The Gift
Who Can I Run To
You're Always on My Mind

Behind Closed Doors Series

Be Careful What You Wish For

Other Titles by Monica Walters

You Just Might Get It
Show Me You Still Want It

Sweet Series

Bitter Sweet
Sweet and Sour
Sweeter Than Before
Sweet Revenge
Sweet Surrender
Sweet Temptation
Sweet Misery
Sweet Exhale
Never Enough (A Sweet Series Update)

Sweet Series: Next Generation

Can't Run From Love
Access Denied: Luxury Love
Still: Your Best

Sweet Series: Kai's Reemergence

Beautiful Mistake
Favorite Mistake

Other Titles by Monica Walters

Motives and Betrayal Series

Ulterior Motives
Ultimate Betrayal
Ultimatum: #lovemeorleaveme, Part 1
Ultimatum: #lovemeorleaveme, Part 2

Written Between the Pages Series

The Devil Goes to Church Too
The Book of Noah (A KeyWalt Crossover Novel
with *The Flow of Jah's Heart* by T. Key)
The Revelations of Ryan, Jr. (A KeyWalt
Crossover Novel with *All That Jazz* by T. Key)

The Country Hood Love Stories

8 Seconds to Love
Breaking Barriers to Your Heart
Training My Heart to Love You

The Country Hood Love Stories: The Hendersons

Blindsided by Love
Ignite My Soul

Other Titles by Monica Walters

Come and Get Me
In Way Too Deep
You Belong to Me
Found Love in a Rider
Damaged Intentions: The Soul of a Thug
Let Me Ride
Better the Second Time Around
I Wish I Could Be The One
I Wish I Could Be The One 2
Put That on Everything: A Henderson Family Novella
What's It Gonna Be?
Someone Like You

The Berotte Family Series

Love On Replay
Deeper Than Love
Something You Won't Forget
I'm The Remedy
Love Me Senseless